PRAISE FOR EDMUNDO PAZ-SOLDÁN AND *NORTE*

"Edmundo Paz Soldán is one of the most creative voices in current Hispano-American literature."—Mario Vargas Llosa

"The issues addressed in [*Norte*] are . . . crucial to current debates about the border and immigration . . . compelling. . . . A thriller."—Professor Ignacio M. Sánchez Prado

"*Norte* is Paz Soldan's best novel."—Lluis Satorras, *El Pais* (Spain)

"Edmundo Paz Soldán (Bolivia, 1967) has lived in the United States for nearly twenty years and knows a lot about the difficulty many of his countrymen face making their way in a society in which the coveted 'dream' is becoming less and less attainable. 'There are many who lose themselves following this big dream,' points out the writer. That is precisely the subject of his new novel, *Norte*, three stories linked by the theme of displacement."—Emma Rodriguez, *El Mundo* (Madrid)

"[*Norte* is] a rigorous and intelligent narrative that focuses more on the inner complexity of its characters than on simplifications and stereotypes. . . . Paz Soldán's writing is compact, fluid, and totally absorbing. . . . The shifting between characters and times is accomplished with ease and agility, keeping the reader, from beginning to end, engrossed in the twists of the plot."—Pedro Gandolfo, *El Mercurio*

NORTE

A NOVEL

EDMUNDO PAZ SOLDÁN

Translated by Valerie Miles

University of Chicago Press
Chicago and London

Paz Soldan

EDMUNDO PAZ SOLDÁN is the author of ten novels including *Norte* (2011), *Los vivos y los muertos* (2009), *La materia del deseo* (*The Matter of Desire*, 2001), and *El Delirio de Turing* (*Turing's Delirium*, 2003), as well as four books of short stories. He has won the Bolivian National Book award twice (1992 and 2003), as well as the Juan Rulfo Short Story Award (1997). In 2006 he was awarded a Guggenheim fellowship; he has also been a finalist for the Hammett award for best noir novel in Spanish (2012) and the Celsius award for best science fiction novel in Spanish (2015). His works have been translated into ten languages. His most recent novel is *Iris* (2014). He is professor of Latin American literature at Cornell University.

VALERIE MILES is a translator, editor, writer, and professor. She is currently the director of *Granta en español* and the *New York Review of Books* in its Spanish translation. She is also a professor for literary translation at the Pompeu Fabra University in Barcelona. Her recent works include *A Thousand Forests in One Acorn: An Anthology of Spanish-Language Fiction* (2014), *Because She Never Asked* (2015), a translation of Enrique Vila-Matas's work *Porque ella no lo pidió*, and *This Too Shall Pass*, a translation of Milena Busquet's novel *También esto pasará* (2016).

The University of Chicago Press, Chicago 60637
The University of Chicago Press, Ltd., London

Printed in the United States of America

25 24 23 22 21 20 19 18 17 16   1 2 3 4 5

ISBN-13: 978-0-226-20720-9 (paper)
ISBN-13: 978-0-226-20734-6 (e-book)
DOI: 10.7208/chicago/9780226207346.001.0001

Library of Congress Cataloging-in-Publication Data

Names: Paz Soldán, Edmundo, 1967– author. | Miles, Valerie, 1963– translator.
Title: Norte : a novel / Edmundo Paz Soldán ; translated by Valerie Miles.
Description: Chicago ; London : University of Chicago Press, 2016. | Includes bibliographical references.
Identifiers: LCCN 2016018244 | ISBN 9780226207209 (pbk. : alk. paper) | ISBN 9780226207346 (e-book)
Classification: LCC PQ7820.P39 N6713 2016 | DDC 863/.64—dc23
LC record available at https://lccn.loc.gov/2016018244

♾ This paper meets the requirements of ANSI/NISO Z39.48–1992 (Permanence of Paper).

TO LILY

And you, why do you have to be on this side?

YURI HERRERA,
Kingdom Cons

As to the majority of murderers, they are very incorrect characters.

THOMAS DE QUINCEY,
On Murder Considered as One of the Fine Arts

Evil does not exist; once you have crossed the threshold, all is good. Once in another world, you must hold your tongue.

FRANZ KAFKA,
Diaries 1914–1923, January 19, 1922

CONTENTS

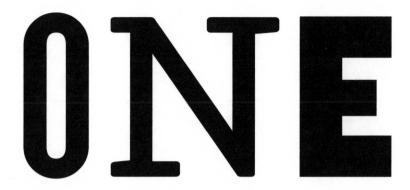

1

Villa Ahumada, Northern Mexico, 1984

He dropped out of school to hang out more with his cousins. He liked to watch them working the crowds at the market and train station, picking pockets or snatching bags, though he didn't take part himself. His cousins tried to avoid confrontation whenever possible but didn't shy away from a little violence if it came down to it. In darker alleys they'd flash their knives, which was usually enough to persuade their victims to give in without a fight. The police knew about them but left them alone as long as they stuck to petty theft, no bloodshed.

Around midnight they'd head over to the California, the only strip club whose bouncer would let Jesús in as long as they greased his palm a little bit. Jesús had a baby face and was slightly built, so he looked even younger than his fifteen years. The California served a cheap, nasty signature shot made of sotol and strawberry Nesquik in milk, called a "Pink Panther." They'd throw a few back and order some beers, ogle the strippers shimmying under the neon lights. They were known as troublemakers and, even worse, as bad tippers, so most of the women kept their distance. Only Quica, one of the older whores, was ever happy to see them; she hated sleeping alone in her rented room down by the river. Quica would cruise from table to table and lower her rates to steal clients from the Guatemalan girl named Suzy, a peroxide blonde with a bob and pneumatic tits, or from Patricia, the bimbo from Guadalajara who planned on ditching out as soon as she had enough cash to pay the coyote to cross the border. There wasn't much else for Quica, she was twice their age. She tried not to let it get to her, though. She might have loved the girls like daughters, though she swore no daughter of hers would ever turn into lowlife *putas* like them.

At three in the morning Quica finally told them it was time to go, but Medardo said, "Let's wait till the song's over, I love Chavela." Justino seized the opportunity to cop a feel and said, "You got a great ass, lady!" Sometimes she'd sleep with Medardo, other times with Justino. She figured Jesús was the type that got off by watching; she'd call him over, tell him to join in, but he always stayed on the couch and beat off.

One Thursday Jesús's mother asked if he would stay in and babysit his younger sister over the weekend, she had work in Júarez and would be back on Monday. He said fine, for a little cash.

That Friday night Jesús lay sprawled on his mattress with its broken springs and piss stains, at the foot of the bed his mother and María Luisa shared. The room stank of kerosene, and the stale kitchen odors seeped into everything.

María Luisa was asleep. Jesús killed time staring at the posters of Mil Máscaras on the wall. One of them showed the wrestler soaring high above Canek in a magnificent jump while El Halcón eyeballed him menacingly. Another was a movie print of *Misterio en las Bermudas* starring El Santo and Blue Demon.

Jesús liked *lucha libre* for being a rough sport with spectacular maneuvers like the slingshot crossbody or the suicide dive. He had four masks of his own and a wrestling action figure, a parting gift from his father before he crossed the border into thin air.

That's what he was doing when he dozed off.

A sudden noise roused him from sleep. He opened his eyes to a half squint and pawed at his face, trying to remove the mask he had been wearing in his dream. It irritated him not to find it. Slippery raindrops clung to the window.

Jesús straightened and sat up on the mattress; he felt edgy, as if he were afraid he might turn into a monster like he'd done in a repeating dream so many times. Dawn was breaking and the first light of morning filtered into the room. His eyes tried to focus, to sharpen the contours of things, until they fixed on the bed where María Luisa lay. There she was, Jesús thought, all alone.

He moved in a little closer, watching her, noticing how her black hair framed her face, how her eyes were closed, her breathing measured. A pang of fear mixed with titillation gripped his stomach like an electric current. María Luisa was eleven now, her breasts were developing, you could see them pressing against her clothes, getting the neighborhood boys all riled up. She'd always been a pretty girl, with pouty lips held in a gesture of wonder before the world, and wide, almond-shaped eyes whose deep green contrasted with the cinnamon tone of her skin. She was filling out, swelling, growing restless.

Several hushed minutes passed.

Jesús climbed onto the bed.

"Wh-what you doing?"

"I just . . . I wanted to visit with you."

"Mom's gonna have a fit, Jesús."

"She don't have to find out. You want me to stay or not?"

"Mom's gonna have a fit."

It aggravated him to see how difficult she was to figure out anymore, and it'd been this way for a few years now. She used to be so easy, so see-through, like she was made of glass. Mamá had had a hard time keeping things together after Papá left, so Jesús and María Luisa had stuck together a lot. They shared a bed, and at night he would let her keep the light on since she was scared of the dark. Then when Mamá got home from the cantina, she'd stretch out in the middle of them. Most of their afternoons were spent playing in a hollow tree in a field near their home. He'd make up stories inspired in the radio serials he liked to listen to so much, about grave robbers, killer mummies and the undead. Things had gone on that way for a few years until Mamá made him start sleeping by himself on the old mattress he and Luisa had shared before Papá left. He slept there on the floor now, while Luisa spent all her time with her school friends. She was slipping through his fingers and he couldn't do anything about it. He asked her to sleep with him like they used to one day when he was feeling depressed, but she answered with a curt "We can't," and he said, "We can wait till Mom's asleep," and again she said decisively "We can't."

Jesús rolled on top of her now and tried to kiss her, but she slapped him in the face and jumped off the bed. "Are you *loco*?" she said, trying to keep cool, self-assured. "You're not allowed to do that."

He recovered from the slap. How easy it would be for him just to corner her and take what he wanted. But that wasn't how it was supposed to go.

"You gonna be sorry you did that, *hermanita*," he said.

She turned around and strode out of the room, into the kitchen.

Jesús lay back down on his mattress and plunged his face into the pillow.

When the sun finally came up, he was still awake.

He found his cousins sitting near the river, on the far side of an iron archway by the soccer field. They were sitting quietly, watching a game. Justino followed the ball closely; the metal buckles of his black boots flashing in the sunlight. Medardo's mustache looked like a theater prop.

Medardo and Justino were a few years older than Jesús. Medardo had done a three-month stint in prison for running stolen cars across the border, and Justino had had to skip town for a few years, until the rumors of his having raped a neighbor girl died down ("she's a hot piece of ass for sure, but it wasn't me, all I did was stick my fingers up her pussy a little bit").

They stood up to leave and Jesús followed behind. They strode down a hill to the riverbank and followed a pathway that led through piles of debris at a dumpsite. Jesús had the creepy feeling that someone was watching him from the mountain of garbage: he finally spotted the blue eyes of a doll that were staring, wide-eyed, straight at him. The boys stopped under a low bridge where bats were slumbering along the ceiling, hanging, waiting for twilight to fall.

The bridge groaned with the weight of the trucks passing overhead. Would the structure hold? What if it collapsed and crushed them?

Medardo pulled a plastic bag from one of his socks and inhaled deeply. He passed it over to Justino, who did the same.

Justino handed it to Jesús, who wedged his nose into the bag and breathed in the fumes that smelled like fresh wood.

They pulled out the bottle of sotol. Jesús took a swig and it burned his throat. He started giggling hysterically and had to make an effort to control himself.

There was more glue and more sotol, until Jesús finally stretched out on the ground. His mind wandered back to a time he was with Papá and María Luisa strolling the streets of Villa Ahumada; whenever the circus came to Juárez or Chihuahua they'd go see it together. Papá would spoil them buying all kinds of candy and toys. He had taken some accounting classes and was good with numbers, but work was scarce back then. He did odd jobs to make ends meet, from managing a boxing club to running a pawnshop called La Infalible. Papá developed a little side business while he was working at La Infalible, keeping part of people's payments and then lending it to others at bargain rates. The last few months before he left were like a bonanza: they got a black-and-white television set, there was meat and fruit on the table, they even bought some new clothes. It didn't last long, though. One night he gathered the family into the kitchen and told them he had to go look for work across the border. The sweat beaded on his forehead and he wiped it away, looking around anxiously. He promised us he'd be back soon. María Luisa bawled, but Jesús was optimistic: Papá had never let them down before. He left the next morning at the crack of dawn, before Jesús got up. Eventually Jesús would come to understand that it wouldn't be easy for him to come back. The owner of La Infalible had detected the missing funds and had threatened to kill him if he didn't pay the money back.

Jesús cackled anxiously. Then he bawled. He laughed again. Finally he fell asleep.

On Monday morning, Jesús cruised over to María Luisa's school, Padre Pro. He waited for gym class to start, then stood at the fence to check out how the girls were filling out. María Luisa pretended not to see him there, but Jesús knew she could feel his presence, watching her. A nun came over to scold him and she called security, a man with a beer gut who promised to crush his skull if he ever saw him in the vicinity again.

Jesús found his cousins in the market this time. They were sharing a plate of meat and beans and drinking horchatas. A stench of stale piss seeped from the nearby urinals.

Medardo was all worked up because Suzy had rejected his advances the night before. "All I did was touch her waist and she slapped me."

"I saw her," Jesús said, "but I didn't know it got you so pissed off."

"I wish it didn't, but I'm still bent about it *wey*. Fucking bitch said you look but you don't touch. So I yelled cunt, what you dress that way for then. You pay me, she said, we'll understand each other, so I go baby I never pay cause the ladies just love to play with my bazooka. And she told me to grow up before I talk back again. And we're the same fucking age, the *puta*!"

Jesús tried to calm Justino down but only made things worse: "Who does the bitch think she is, so full of herself, thinks we're a waste of time or something."

"Yeah, well I know where the bitch lives," Justino said. "We could wait for her to get home."

"And beat the shit out of her?" Jesús asked.

"First things first," Medardo said. "Give her a little of my good stuff, *wey.*"

Jesús liked the idea. Suzy had been nice enough to him in the California, but she had a way of looking down her nose, acting all superior when she talked to him that irked him, like she was his mother or something. As if her peroxide hair and diamond belly-button stud were too good for him, like those tights stretched hard over long sexy legs, the thigh-high stiletto boots, were out of his league, only for truck drivers and *polleros*. But Jesús had graduated from being a mere bystander to his primos; he'd robbed his first couple as they left the station the other day, and he'd done a good job. He swiped the woman's pearl necklace right from her throat and, when the man ran after him, pulled a knife on him, stopping him cold in his tracks. The pearls were fake but no matter, he proved he could do it and that's what counted.

"I got some *lucha libre* masks at home," he said. "We could use them for protection. Just in case someone sees us."

"You learn fast little cousin," Medardo said.

They finished working the market and went back to the bridge. There was enough sotol and glue for the party to last through the night.

It was 4 a.m. when Suzy got out of the cab and made her way to her apartment building, the heels of her boots clacking in the night air.

She opened the door to her building with a flick of her wrist, holding the key like a blade in her hand. She felt a little woozy. Not a day went by that she didn't imagine herself free of the stinking puddles of the California's floors, the smoke that stung her eyes all night, the ear-splitting Van Halen and Prince, the *rancheras*, the drunk men constantly groping her.

Suzy was closing the door when she heard a familiar voice.

"What's the rush, bitch?"

"Who's that?"

"How quickly we forget."

"Oh, it's you . . . You scared me."

"Don't move," Medardo said flashing his knife.

She took a few steps backwards, clutching at her purse, until she felt the cold tile of the wall behind her. There were bags of trash heaped up in the corner.

Medardo, Justino and Jesús entered the building and closed the door behind them.

"What you *chamacos* want? It's late and I'm tired. Please just let me be. Don't make me have to call Patotas."

Medardo grabbed her and threw her into the stairwell. Suzy felt a sharp pain in her back when she fell against the edge of one of the steps: she wanted to scream but a hand covered her mouth. She tried to squeeze out of Medardo's grip and crawl up the stairs; they struggled until he finally turned her over to immobilize her. Where was her purse?

"Please, please don't."

Medardo pulled down her tights and ripped her thong off. Suzy continued to struggle, though her strength was quickly draining. She felt him penetrate her and tried to scream. Maybe the couple who lived in the room next door would hear the noise?

Justino tore open her red blouse and sucked at her tits, licking and smearing his saliva all over her. By now she was letting them do what they wanted without putting up a fight; the knives terrified her. She conjured up images of her daughter Yandira, who was with her mother in Tlaquepaque—imagined her running around the courtyard at home with her blue skirt and black hair, the only good thing she'd inherited from her prick of a father. Her baby's hair was gathered in a splash of colorful barrettes. She'd get out of this alive and report them all to Patotas.

Now it was the last one's turn, the one who hardly ever spoke.

Jesús climbed on top of her. She had curled up into a ball and couldn't stop crying. Her clothes were ruined and she covered her face with her hands.

Now was his chance to show his cousins a thing or two.

He grabbed her by her wrists, forcing her arms open wide, and had each of his cousins hold one arm while he unbuckled his pants and told her to blow him. He struck her on the cheek so hard it made her bleed. He could see Medardo's and Justino's shocked expressions just out of the corner of his eye. They never thought he had it in him. Fucking bastards.

Suzy opened her mouth and started sucking Jesús's dick. She was trembling and had the hiccups. "Careful she don't bite you," Medardo sniggered.

Jesús watched her face transform into María Luisa's.

He closed his eyes and opened them again.

Still María Luisa. "So you didn't want to sleep with me, huh?"

He forced the handle of his knife up Suzy's ass. She squealed like a scared pig and Justino covered her mouth again, cursing her mother and telling her she don't deserve to be alive, she'd better shut the fuck up or things were going to get really ugly.

Jesús penetrated her with his fist and Suzy shrieked. He moved it around inside of her more and more viciously, as if he were feeding off her growing desperation. He opened his fingers as wide as he could and plunged them into the soft, gummy inner walls. Then he punched her in the face with the same fist.

"You didn't want to sleep with me, huh?"

The pain in his knuckles made him stop.

Suzy's cheekbones were black and blue and her nose was shattered. Nearly unconscious by now, she slumped against the stairs. She was lucky though: she hardly felt the blade puncture her heart.

"What the fuck you do that for?" Medardo asked Jesús.

"She was gonna rat on us."

"Primo, you shouldn't'a done that."

"Better safe than sorry, *wey*."

"I never thought you . . . ," Justino stammered.

"Me neither."

2

Landslide, Texas, 2008

Last night I went to Wünderbar with Sam and La Jodida. We
hung out for a while on Sixth Street, getting drunk and arguing over whether Joy Division or Nirvana had been the most
influential band of our generation. They said Nirvana, I said
Joy Division. There's a before and after Cobain's death, La
Jodida said, flirting with a redhead at the table next to us. It's
not about a single defining moment, I said, it's about the long
haul, being influential. Ian Curtis carved a space for himself
over time. Sam looked at me with a twinkle in his eye, putting
on his telltale satyr's face, insinuating that he might just come
back to my studio and who knows, stay the night, see what
happens.

We took off and headed for the Underground. Fergie's voice
belted out a techno arrangement. The air was so humid my
glasses fogged up, and I took them off as I walked toward the
bathroom down a dark hallway where there were couples making out. I bought a few hits of ecstasy from a kid who had just
finished vomiting, and then locked myself into one of the stalls.
Sitting there, I was overcome by a shining vision of Fabián in
his better days. I shut my eyes hard, until the ache let up a little.

Sam was standing there, waiting for me at the bathroom door when I walked out. An Oasis song played over the loudspeakers. He hugged me and I suddenly felt tenderness toward him.

"Knock it off, Michelle."

"Why does your gaucho accent always come out after you've had a few drinks?" I quipped.

"What can I say? Time in Paradise never comes without strings.

Sam had spent a semester in Buenos Aires researching his thesis. He was surprised to find it the most anti-American city on the continent, yet it didn't stop him from falling in love with the cafés, the women, and the chaotic university scene. He came back with an Alan Pauls autograph, Sarlo's email address, and a colossal stash of books in boxes he hadn't yet had a chance to open.

He kissed me. I didn't want to be alone, so I figured what's the harm in fooling myself for a few more hours.

I liked the softness of Sam's kisses, the frisky look in his eye, his clever conversation, and the way he giggled when he came. He was four years older than me, just twenty-nine, but in many ways he was less mature. We were too close as friends to make it work as a couple; I had come to terms with that by now, but he hadn't, though he tried. He made an effort not to take me seriously, and La Jodida warned me not to fuck him if I didn't want anything to come out of the relationship. I would nod in complete agreement, then do whatever I pleased.

We scanned the place trying to locate La Jodida, but she showed up again when a Killers song came on, grabbed my hand, and pulled me out onto the dance floor. She took a swig from a pocket flask of cane rum. Her eyes were glassy, she'd had a fight with her girlfriend Megan the night before and had taken off clubbing, snorting coke with a pleasant but ugly waitress she'd picked up to avoid having to go back to her apartment. They partied in the girl's Nissan until La Jodida passed out around six in the morning, but the waitress woke her up when she had to leave for class. La Jodida killed time traipsing around the streets of Landslide, waiting until she was sure Megan had gone. But when she was finally home she couldn't get to sleep, so she went back out and caught up with her hardcore party buddies like Tennessee, who had tried to kill herself last winter with rat poison. They kept the bender going in her room with shots of tequila and more lines. Now I regretted having invited her out. The last thing I felt like doing was looking after her.

She hugged me in the middle of the dance floor and said, "I love you, you're like my little sistah."

"I love you too, *hermanita*."

"I know you don't like partying with me anymore, getting shitfaced. It's all my fault, I admit it. As of New Year's I'm done with all my vices, I promise. I'm gonna throw a *macrofiesta* to say goodbye to the life and never smoke another bong again."

"You know it's not that, it's that nobody can keep up with you. Don't forget it was me who called you to go out in the first place."

"Please don't leave me alone, pretty please?"

"Nobody's leaving you. What's up, *niña*? What's going on?"

She hugged me. I wanted to make her feel better but didn't know how, what to say. I patted her on the back a few times, as if she were a child.

"We're in this together, *tu sabes*. You got me into it in the first place."

"I didn't get you into anything. Nobody forced you."

"You're so much more rational than me. You cut out in time."

"There's a point when it takes you over, you lose control . . ."

"I can still control it," she countered immediately. "It's just that I don't want to yet."

I didn't answer. What for? Nothing I said would make her stop kidding herself.

She turned around and ran back to the table with Sam. I just stood there on the dance floor a little while. I met La Jodida at a party in one of the university dorms our first semester in Landslide. She's Puerto Rican and was studying biology; we hit it off from the get-go and ended up getting drunk and going back to my dorm room. I gave her a joint, it was her first time.

By the time I walked back to the table, she'd gone.

"She told me to tell you she's taking off," Sam said, "she didn't feel well."

"Good. She should never have come out in her condition."

"She left her purse, but it doesn't really go with my outfit. Can you get it back to her?"

I nodded. It wasn't the first time I heard La Jodida say she was in control when obviously she wasn't, going on about how I shouldn't feel guilty. Regardless, I couldn't help feeling responsible.

The whole situation with La Jodida depressed me. Sam could tell and tried to make things better by telling bad jokes. He made me smile and in a way it did cheer me up.

I called Mamá after Sam left that Saturday morning, and she told me Papá was bent on going back to Bolivia. He was tired of repairing televisions for Best Buy. I told her not to pay attention to his ranting, that he'd been saying the same thing since we first set foot in Texas. Papá was incurably homesick, but he was also a practical man and knew what was best for them. He blew off steam by insisting on returning to Santa Cruz, especially when times got tough there; it helped take the edge off his guilt and made it easier to stay put. "There's nothing easy about it," Mamá said. "He's home now, but it's as if he weren't here at all. His head is always somewhere else." "So what else is new?" I asked. "Don't make fun." "*Tranquila, mamá*, if he were really serious, he wouldn't be talking about it, he'd just buy the tickets and that'd be the end of it."

I was eager to finally sit down and draw out the story that had been on my mind for a while. I had to take advantage of my day off from Taco Hut, not having to deal with sticky-fingered kids asking for crayons all day, or fat ladies complaining that their chicken fajitas were cold, or rowdy fratboys spilling beer on the tables and asking for my phone number behind their girlfriends' backs. The working title isn't very original: *The Living Dead*. It's a zombie story: adults turn into dead people when they lose their will to rebel, they adapt to the system, marry, have kids, hold down a nine-to-five job. A world full of the living dead: only a few would be able to survive. My heroine, Samantha, fights the zombies. She infiltrates their nests and destroys them with a silver dagger. The problem is that the zombies always come back to life; that's why they're called zombies.

I'm looking for the way to end the story, the narrative that will allow Samantha to kill the zombies once and for all, and forevermore.

I read a chapter of Laurell Hamilton's novel for inspiration.

Her books about Anita Blake and *True Blood* helped give me a structure to follow. They're vampire and zombie stories, or paranormal episodes set in the ordinary, everyday places of middle America like Walmart and Denny's, instead of gothic cities like New Orleans. Her novel *Guilty Pleasures* is pure kitsch—there's even a striptease in a vampire club—but I could salvage a few things from it, like how her vampires behave like mundane fixtures in the routine life of the city.

A zombie devours Samantha's boyfriend, so she goes on a crusade to avenge him. That's the point where the two of us diverged: I wasn't on a crusade and didn't have anyone to avenge. We shared some of the rage, true, and maybe a touch of helplessness.

By noon I had eight pages completed. I drew my zombies with fangs, like vampires. Now I had to color them in. Samantha's dress will be blood red and she's wearing boots. My brother Toño would want me to give her Hispanic features—he discovered his Latino identity in his last year of high school and hasn't stopped criticizing my illustrations since then, saying they don't deal with "the struggle of a minority against the oppression of the Anglo majority." And I won't pay any attention.

Samantha is an unassuming superheroine, thanks to her job as a librarian in the state university. But what sort of powers should I give her? And what will they call her?

All superheroes have a mythical origin. Tony Colt became "The Spirit" after he was buried alive. So there you have another case of the living dead. All roads lead to Will Eisner.

A mythical origin. The first chapter will have to tell that story.

I was catnapping when my cell phone rang and pulled me out of my afternoon dream. I grabbed my cell phone from the night table without opening my eyes, and heard Sam's voice say:

"About last night . . ."

Silence.

"You know how I feel about us," I said. "Let's not complicate our lives."

"Why do you have to be so difficult? Look, we could just . . ."

"We could just what?"

"You're going to miss me when I'm gone."

"I never said I wouldn't."

"Fine. Let's change the subject then."

"That's what I always say."

Sam's voice brought me back to our first week of school, when I sat down next to him in Professor Camacho-Stokes's class on Transculturation. I had already noticed him around campus. He let weeks go by before getting up the nerve to make a first move, but by then I was completely absorbed into Fabián's world. And that was that. We might have spared ourselves all this suffering if only I had got up the courage to approach him myself, or Sam had acted on his instincts.

Sam went on and on about his thesis. I was so thankful to have gotten out of there in time, before the tyranny of critical thinking completely took over my way of approaching things, narrowed my vision. My ex-colleagues only read to analyze, while I preferred to enjoy reading, to leave room for the whimsical. "But I really enjoy it," Sam said as justification when I accused him of allowing the study of literature to get in the way of feeling the joy of it. "It's just a another way of enjoying it. So get off your moral high horse, already. Remember what Blanchot wrote about Heidegger in that article."

"Aha."

"Oh come on, who says you can't have it both ways?"

Sam was proud of *Tabloid*, a university radio program he anchored on Monday nights at midnight, about sensationalist crimes and the "pure pulp" of serial killers, the violence of the Mexican cartel wars, or legendary stories like Bonnie and Clyde. He had built himself a respectable audience for the program, and it was his escape valve for the pressures of academia.

I told him I was delighted that I'd quit; by shunning a cushy scholarship, I could now explore my own "inner voice."

"Oh don't give me the inner voice crap," he said, "and drop the new age vocabulary. You left because you were afraid of running into Fabián in the hallway, or having to take his tests or his classes."

I didn't respond, and Sam realized how rude he'd been and tried to apologize. He needled me into agreeing to meet him at a café near my studio. I was in my autistic mode and really wanted to spend my time alone, drawing, but I gave in and said yes.

Sam and I met up in Chip & Dip, which was just next door to Comics for Dummies (Chuck, the owner, talked me into buying *Fun Home*, about a lesbian girl who discovers that her father is gay, "very Proustian"). The weekend micro-story was already posted on the café windows: Nortec musicians at the Palladium, a Julieta Venegas lookalike contest was taking place at the bar Bring Me The Head of Joseph Wales, and a professor from Nuevo Laredo was giving a talk on violence along the border.

Sam went back to talking about his thesis on figurations of the intellectual and the writer in contemporary Latin American literature. He commented on *Respiración Artificial* by Ricardo Piglia (the intellectual as an exile), *Our Lady of the*

Assassins by Fernando Vallejo (the intellectual as a deracinated figure), *The Savage Detectives* by Roberto Bolaño (the poet as a vitalist, an antiestablishmentarian, capable of choosing not to write to avoid being co-opted by the institution), and *La fiesta vigilada* by Antonio José Ponte Mirabal (the intellectual as the last survivor of a postapocalyptic world). His early conclusion centered on how the traditional role of the intellectual was being discarded by a reconfigured cultural system.

I listened halfheartedly and then tried to aggravate him by bringing up *The Eternonaut* by Héctor Oesterheld. "Are you going to include it or not? The intellectual as a man of action in spite of himself. Someone who is critical of any genuine encounter with people."

"I'll mention it. But I can't give it a full chapter or the thesis would be too long."

"Or because it's just a comic."

"You know that's not why, Michelle. Cut the bullshit."

He could be such a pain in the ass. Finally I just made him skip to another subject. We were alike in that way, so self-absorbed, fascinated at hearing ourselves speak, like everyone else in our little world.

We paid and were getting ready to leave when I told him I needed some downtime that night, I wanted to draw. He looked hurt and annoyed. He had taken for granted that we would spend the night together again, as if sex was the prize for how well his dissertation was coming along. I was being inconsiderate. Last night's fuck hadn't been one of our best, but I had to admit it lulled me into a sound sleep.

Walking back to the studio I had another flash of Fabián's face in my mind's eye. I had to stop for a second to catch my breath.

3

Stockton, California, 1931

Martín counts his fingers: one, two, three, four, five, six, seven, eight, nine, ten. Now the even ones: two, four, six, eight, ten. Now the odd: one, three, five, seven. Nine. And start all over again.

His head is aching. He can't stop coughing.

Sitting on a bench in the train station, he thinks it isn't bad to do what his mother taught him. When you get angry, it's best to count and keep on counting. It takes the upset away. Shouldn't lash out of a sudden. When he was a boy, Martín vented his anger on the toads that would croak on rainy nights and wake him up. He'd go out on the patio or the street, find a colossal stone, and drop it on the toad and squish it. His mother followed him once though and said how can you do such a thing you disgraceful child, and he begged her forgiveness, eyes staring hard at the ground, ears burning like when he felt shameful. And he felt shameful a lot. His life was one long *shame on you* for all the things that happened to him.

He was sitting next to a newsstand. Men stopped for newspapers, women for magazines. What happens to all those newspapers and magazines in the dark quiet of the night, when the agent goes home, he wondered. Bet they get to yakkety-yakking, or up to no good, arguing about this and that. Come morning the centerfold of a magazine's on the front page of a newspaper.

He wished he could get in on the commotion in the news-stand. The ruckus, the troublemaking. He picked up a magazine once when he had one of those breaks at work, SaTurdAY evening pOst. He stretched out on the ground to read it but couldn't make sense of nothing. Peculiar language. The cover read:

An Illustrated Weekly Founded. May 31, 1930.

Booth Tarkington. David Laurence. F. Scott Fitzgerald.

The effort drained him. The world carried on. Words ran into each other and piled up. People spoke as if they had a hot potato in their throat. Every word the foreman barked those scorching afternoons spent out laying tracks sounded like an insult. He never could make sense of it, had to wait for the other men to start moving, then he'd follow their lead. What's he saying? Made his blood boil!

The foreman was like a cashbox full of peculiar words. He lived to keep them all safe inside. But they'd haul a getaway right through his open his mouth.

He hacked again. His head exploded with each coughing spell.

Martín imagined himself asleep in a big bed where words hovered overhead, then scattered into letters that fell down like a hard rain. They weighed heavy and beat hard on his skin. His bed turned into a bog, and the quicksand sucked him down, down. He tried to save himself by clutching at the ends of the longest words, or ones with a *th* since he liked that sound, but the words shunned him and he sank lower and lower till he woke up startled and covered in sweat.

But words aren't what he cares for most in the magazines. It's the pictures. NoRman RoCKwell was the best of them all. There's one of a little girl wearing glasses and a pretty red sweater and a green skirt. She is running off to paint with her brushes and pad. Or drawings about drawing, those are slickest. Now there's an actor on the cover. Gary Cooper in some movie. *The Texan*. Noooo, they'd correct him: two vowels side by side like owl-eyes are pronounced as a single letter, and not even the same one. Cúper.

He wanted to draw. Such a fine thing to do, made stuff so easy. Why use words when you can just draw?

He should have learned English. Specially if he was coming here. It had been some hard times when he was laying the tracks, though work got easier for a spell. No need to speak while picking strawberries or oranges. He'd done all right in the mines, too. Lots of folk like him gathered there, same age and some older ones and even a few kids, from all sorts of towns. Some wore hats and others didn't. Some wore belts with big buckles shaped like pistols, others didn't. Some wore boots and others wore sandals with soles made out of tires.

Now he's counting his fingers in the train station.

Yeah, it had gone all right for a spell. No work today though. No work for Mexicans, that is. They told him to watch himself. They like to go after the ones like him, loitering, they like to send them back.

So if María Santa Ana were a toad, what would he do? Would he squish her with a gigantic stone? No. Teófila and Agustina and Juana and Candelario would be left motherless. Bad enough their father has been away for so long. Now their mother's running with the Federales, betraying her people. He knew it for truth. His brother Atanacio wrote and told him that *el señor gobierno* was defacing the churches. The Federales had already got as far as San José de Gracia, confiscated their houses, and ransacked the churches and was using them for stables. The Federales burned the ranch to the ground and killed the animals, Atanacio said, and María Santa Ana had straddled her blood bay horse to wreak havoc on the peasants who had armed themselves with rifles and sabers, shouting "Long live Cristo Rey" and "Long live Santa María de Guadalupe."

Martín grasped most of what Atanacio wrote. He answered that if María Santa Ana is collaborating with the Federales, then her children should be taken away from her. Anyone who goes around burning churches is an enemy. That includes María Santa Ana.

It had happened the minute he'd left. *El señor gobierno* had been waiting for him to go before defiling the churches. The peasants had waited till he was gone to take up arms. María Santa Ana waited till he was gone to join the struggle and get up to her other things, too. The ranch that he'd gone into debt for is nothing but ashes now. The house built of stone and adobe, all gone. The cows, the pigs, the sheep. His horse was the most painful loss of all. He used to love riding out to hunt rabbits in El Picacho, or into town to sell eggs and peppers.

It was all his fault. He left. That one single act had called down a catastrophe. María Santa Ana had told him not to go, it wasn't right to leave on San Bartolomé, there's a high wind and the devil's walking loose today, she said. But he went ahead and put on his hat, his overcoat, and paid her no mind. He had said goodbye to each of his daughters and headed for the other side with four of his friends. What else was there to do? The ranch was yielding a little, but even so, it wasn't enough to pay off the debt.

Martín wondered if things would return to the way they were if he went back. Would his beloved Mexico be restored to law and order?

He coughs. His head feels like it's about to explode. One, four, seven, ten. Two, five, eight . . . eleven?

Martín's famished but completely broke. That's what he deserves for being so open-handed. He sent everything back home and kept too little for himself. They don't even appreciate his sacrifice. They don't know what it's like to live alone. Not even a dog to bark at you. They think the only thing you're good for is sending money back. That's why you were born. Why you exist.

But there's no more work, so what's he supposed to do? His old boarding house is too far away now, it was like a barracks out in the middle of nowhere that he shared with other men who came from places like Jalisco, Zacatecas, Chihuahua, Guanajuato, or Michoacán. Anyway, no cash. He used to get free eggs and beans in the mess hall, he could fix himself something to eat, but the place had been cockroach-infested and it disgusted him, the sink always overflowing with filthy dishes and rank, grease-smeared pans.

He's missing out on seeing his daughters and Candelario grow up. Martín keeps photos of his girls in his pocket. And one of himself with María Santa Ana. Such a long time ago. A long time and a place that now seems so far away. When the struggle broke out, Atanacio told him he better not even think of going back. Men were coming with news of *el señor gobierno*'s cruel ways. Processions were canceled. Statues of the Virgin were hidden in mountain caves for safekeeping. Masses were celebrated in secret rituals and under pain of death.

Martín hadn't planned on staying for very long. Now there was no way back.

Then the rumors started. They took her down to the river. He'd imagined as much. But Martín had no way to share what was on his mind, he was tired of being tongue-tied all the time, constantly misunderstood, and figured it was better to just hush up. Not that he used his mind all that much, a little bit here or there, he had little pieces of ideas that never really settled into a coherent whole.

His brain: a desert landscape with an occasional prickly pear or acacia bush. Something's growing in there. Something.

He could jump a train. Pick any one of the city names from that shifting announcement board, then head to the platform. It'd be a snap.

All these towns had developed thanks to him. So many afternoons spent under the blazing sun laying tracks, and then he'd see them pop right up where there had been nothing. The tracks were all they needed; so he'd come around and lay them. Then overnight, pop! There they were, ready for the train to come. The train created them. The railroad workers brought the trains, and the trains brought the cities. So it was partly his own doing that they were there in the first place.

It was so hard to follow directions in this strange language.

It took so much out of him just to find the barracks. He had memorized how to get to work and back, every single step of the way, so as not to get lost. And he was always worried they might change his routine. What would he do then?

He can't stop coughing.

He was easygoing but not stupid. Mornin,' mornin' he'd say. Write to me, he had begged her, please write to me, don't force me to live in despair like this, like some idiot drunkard, or as if I were feeble-minded.

At first she wrote, but then nothing. Goddamn her.

Just tell me it's all a lie so I don't have to live in this heartache. I'm afflicted by memories of you, the time I spent by your side. Ana, Ana, Ana. Santa. María. Tasan. Ríama. Tttt. Rrrr. Uuuu. Eeee.

He felt pain like a jackhammer boring a hole into his skull.

He should eat something. But he couldn't pay for it. Maybe he could trade something for food. A drawing? He always had a notebook and pencil on him, at times it was his only form of communication. Cat got your tongue, boy? Someone cut it out? Too bad the others weren't more like him. Don't speak, just draw.

Martín had come to the station to simmer down a little. No work, anyway, what else was he going to do? He sat there on a bench near the newsstand and studied the suited, suspender-wearing men walking by. He listened to the announcements, scanned the posters on the wall, they were so colorful. He let his mind wander untethered. Counted the light fixtures hanging from the ceiling, the windows that let in the light. He stood on the platform and watched the trains come and go. The cars were shiny-new, the metal was freshly painted and they purred down the tracks, whistling as they approached the station, but they didn't blow smoke. Nothing like the old, graffiti-riddled trains he remembered from childhood, boxcar walls covered in graffiti. As a boy, he'd wait till sundown, sneak in with a few cans of paint, and devote hours to painting murals from memory—talk about determination.

María Santa Ana, oh she was a cutie, and so much fun to be

around. A real doll. How's he supposed to get over something like her? She was the center of everything. A hot number. Her ass drooped a little maybe, but no matter: her big titties made up for everything else. She had the kind of curves a man could hold on to. Others used to gawp at her. Most women get fat and ugly when they get old, and that's when you have to say oh, she's so nice, she's so good. But his María Santa Ana was both at the same time: a good-looker and a good woman.

They weren't together but a year before she got pregnant. They took that tiny next step and got married. Some people recited that old proverb "Get married, Johnny, and stones will turn to bread." Others said, "Get married, Johnny, and bread will turn to stone." She listened to the first group.

A daughter was born. Then another. And another. And then the boy, but by that time Martín wasn't around anymore.

As a couple they got used to keeping hushed around the house. First man who said something out loud to María after he left probably startled her to death. No doubt it made her go sweet, though. And lightning can strike the same place twice.

He had been a whole man when she found him, but now he was broken, alone.

How could he stand it?

He drifted over to the wall and remained standing there between the men's and women's toilets. He took his pencil out and wrote "It's going to rain today" in big letters on the white wall.

And again he wrote: "It's going to rain today." And again. And again.

He wrote it seven times before the officer stopped him and asked him for his papers. Martín just looked at him and kept quiet. The officer asked him for his name. He didn't say a word.

Another officer showed up.

They took him to a room in the station where another officer started screaming at him, tried to get him to answer, in any language. The man looked like he was about to snap and warned him as much with a cocked fist. "Now what? Yeah, that's right, now what?" Martín took out his pencil and paper. He drew a winged horse. Then he drew a steam engine with the smoke coming out in rings that escaped the frame of the page. A few tunnels and empty town squares. He drew the cobblestone and colored in some of the mosaic pattern in black.

"Fuckin' retard," one of the cops said. He enunciated his words so that Martín would understand. He had wits enough to know that there was nothing good in those words. No matter, he was accustomed to it by now. People always lost their patience with him.

They called in an officer who spoke Spanish. He was a burly, square-backed man with a salt-and-pepper mustache. He kept calm and repeated the word *carnal* several times. He asked what Martín was drawing. Martín acknowledged his presence but didn't offer an explanation. It wasn't such a bad place after all. They could holler all they wanted, long as they didn't touch him.

"Nice drawings," the policeman said. "But what the fuck do they mean?"

If only he could tell them about María Santa Ana. See if they agreed. Surely they would, but then who really knows? They're cops, they might just take her side. Didn't his brother say that María took up with the Federales? Didn't he? Maybe one of them forced himself on her. He should never have left her alone. He should have brought her with him.

The policeman jotted some words in his notebook. Martín couldn't decipher them.

He smoothed his mustache, left, right, left, right. Better not release him. It wasn't half bad in there. Would they feed him? How long since he'd eaten a decent meal?

They took him to a cell. They tried to confiscate his notebook but he didn't let them. He held his palms together as if begging forgiveness or a blessing. One of them said something and they all left.

He remained vigilant, sketching on the blank pages late into the night.

He was given a metal tray with a bowl of meat and lentils. The meat was salty and hard, but he devoured it so quickly he nearly choked. There was a glass of water, a piece of bread, and half an apple. Now he needed to see a doctor. His headache wouldn't let him rest.

The police and the Federales must have struck a deal. María Santa Ana gave them his whereabouts and he was being arrested as a prisoner of war. After all, he was behind enemy lines.

He covered himself with the blanket and lay down on the rickety old cot, which sagged with his weight. He had nightmares of trains bursting into flames, and drowning girls.

A nice gentleman came to see him the following day. He sat down beside him in a well-lighted room, shook his hand, and smiled.

I'm Mr. Walker, he said. I'm pleased to meet you.

Mr. Walker disappeared whenever Martín closed his eyes. When he opened them back up, there he was again, just in front of him. He had brought Mr. Walker into being in a single movement, created him from scratch. Same way he had created his cot and the floor, the walls and the ceiling and the building and the officers and the train station and the city where he had helped lay the tracks and the country where he and four friends had gotten lost while looking for work and the border where they got separated and the town of San José de Gracia where María Santa Ana and Atanacio and his children were living and el Picacho, where he went to hunt astride his blood bay horse.

But it didn't matter, he could close his eyes again and his horse appeared and it was the same one yet it was another one, and the town appeared and it was the same one and another one and the sky appeared and it was the Mexican sky and another one.

Mr. Walker spoke to Martín in Spanish. He said he would defend his rights. He needed to know where he came from so he could call his consulate. They would expel him if he didn't give his name and nationality.

Martín wrote in his notebook: M a r t I n. He had learned to spell his name when he was little in the classes his father taught for the hacienda workers where he and his mother labored. Something inside told him it was better that he didn't say what country he was from. Mr. Walker was just making nice, acting like he was a friend, but what he really wanted to do was to extract information. Maybe even arrest Atanacio. These folks are double-crossers.

Mr. Walker asked him for his last name. Martín didn't know it, he'd never had a birth certificate, and he signed his marriage license with an X. He scribbled an X on the sheet of paper. Mr. Walker looked at him as if he didn't understand. Another

X. Mr. Walker signaled him to stop. Martín made another X. And another. And another. Just to prove that he was able to make things appear whenever he felt like it.

Martín closed his eyes. Mr. Walker disappeared. Let him know his power.

Mr. Walker picked up Martín's wallet from a tray. The police had confiscated it, but there wasn't anything there to steal. He pulled out the photo of María Santa Ana and his girls. Martín's manner softened. Just look at that woman, so good and so beautiful.

Teófila. Agustina, the middle one. And Juana. No Candelario.

Mr. Walker asked the name of his hometown. Martín stared at his shoes.

Mr. Walker got up and left. Martín stayed in his cell. The rest of the day he drew toads and stone showers in his notebook.

A few days later they moved him to a building with shiny walls painted white and landscaped gardens. He could tell it was a hospital.

He closed his eyes to see if the hospital would disappear. It did.

He opened them. Better not take any risks.

Maybe it's his head what should disappear, not the hospital. Damn *coco*.

He spent the whole day being shuffled from one room to another. Men and women in white robes and plastic gloves and canvas shoes told him to open his mouth. Close your mouth. Undress. Lie down. Get dressed.

They hammered his knees. They poked his chest. They checked his back. They pointed their machines at his ribcage.

He was ashamed. One of these x-rays might show why it was so hard for him to speak.

They sent him back to his cell.

Two days later, Mr. Walker came to clarify things for him. Martín understood they were moving him to another building. They would take better care of him there. It would only be for a little while, until they were able to resolve his case. They never asked for his opinion, they just did what they saw fit.

Must be a hospital for prisoners of war, Martín concluded.

He'll have to put up a fight then. Make the place disappear. Like that time when he was a boy and went to the circus with his father. The clowns scared him so badly that he shut his eyes for a long time. But he got to feeling sorry for the people in the stands, so he opened them again. But only the clown, a trapeze artist, and a scrawny tiger came back again. He cried and cried because everyone else was gone, the elephant, the sword swallower, all gone, and he didn't know where they had gone. That's how he learned the lesson to be more careful with what the good Lord had given him. He'd learn better, perfect the technique, figure out how to bring everything back, or nothing at all. Things shouldn't be separated like that, some here and others there.

Mr. Walker extended his hand, Martín smiled and shook it firmly.

4

Villa Ahumada, 1984

Justino and Medardo were hiding out at an uncle's house in a neighboring town. At first Jesús had drifted around the streets of Villa Ahumada sleeping in the plaza, at the foot of a statue of Fray Servando. Then he snuck into Father Joe's church to hide and spent a few nights there sleeping in the pews. The nave was broad, out of proportion for the size of the town. The plaster-cast saints, decked in gold leaf, looked down at him from alcoves along the walls. Santa Engracia's cracked face trembled in the heat of the forest of candles placed before her, always ready to help the lovesick. San Alonso looked skyward, his chest covered in wounds, feet chained, pleading for divine intervention against mortal illness.

Jesús only went out to eat. When he did, he saw the photos of Suzy in the newspaper, her face smashed in by his own fists ("Murderers Brutally Assault Working Girl"; "They Drank Her Blood!"; "Police Haven't Ruled Out Satanic Ritual"); he ripped out the article and photos and shoved them in his pocket. He got a kick out of reliving the scene. No more voices, though, just an overwhelming silence: Justino and Medardo's mouths moved, but he couldn't hear them; the woman screamed, but he couldn't hear her. All that existed within the silence was a blinding sense of power, and the woman's body sprawled on the stairs. The knife became an extension of his arm, and he used it sadistically, as if this is exactly what was expected of him. Every blow, every thrust of his knife puncturing her flesh with astonishing ease, turned him into the instrument of an avenging angel prepared to wield justice on earth.

One day Jesús saw Father Joe enter the confessional and he decided it was high time he said something.

Two women dressed in black were on their knees reciting prayers in the front pew. Jesús walked by, nodded in greeting, and continued to the confessional. He knelt down. Someone cleared his throat from inside the narrow confessor's cubicle. He tried to discern the face through the jalousie. It was Father Joe all right. Originally from California, Father Joe measured well over six feet. His nose and cheeks carried the characteristic red tinge and patterning of a rampant case of rosacea. He had worked in an oil refinery in Texas when he was young and did stints in Monterrey every fifteen days. Partial as he was to alcohol and cheap whores, he just loved it when the time came to cross the border. But he screwed up and got sweet on one of the girls, and asked to be transferred out to Villa Ahumada to keep her close. When her boyfriend found out, he shot her dead. Overcome with sorrow and guilt, Joe looked for redemption by offering his life up to the Lord's work.

"Father," Jesús said. "I have . . . something to confess."

"Same as usual?" the priest asked in his intimidating boom of a voice. He spoke decent Spanish after spending decades there, though his gringo accent was still thick.

"Partly, yeah."

"Spit it out then, you know I have to hear you say it."

"I felt desire for my sister."

"I know. But have you done it again?"

"Done what?"

"What we already know. How many times has it happened since the last time you were here?"

"Four. Maybe five."

"No way, so it's getting worse?"

"Have you seen my sister lately, Father?"

"Don't say it like that. You want me to congratulate you or something? Tell you it's OK?"

"But that's not what I'm here to confess, Father. I want to talk about something else."

"The monsters again?"

Jesús remained quiet. The nightmares had begun a few years ago. Monsters with green heads and nine fingers haunted his dreams. Jesús would fight them relentlessly, wearing a mask and carrying a sword. The monsters' bloody, pock-marked cheeks didn't intimidate him, instead they made him feel heroic, confident. Every time he was on the verge of death, some sudden noise would startle him awake, and he'd slowly come back to consciousness scrutinizing the objects littered around the bedroom he shared with Mamá and María Luisa—scribbled notebooks, dresses with broken elastic, photos and posters of masked wrestlers along the walls, cobwebs stuck to the cracked ceilings, the closet where he hid his collection of porn magazines.

"Go on, son. Speak your mind."

He answered by taking the newspaper clipping from his pocket and sliding it to the priest, who read it and understood instantaneously.

"You have twenty-four hours to get out of town. If not, if you . . . Son of a bitch!"

The priest left the confessionary and disappeared through the doorway.

He waited for María Luisa to get out of school. He sat guard near a cedar tree, riveted by the bustle and chaos of so many white uniforms when the bell rang; parents picked their children up by car, on bikes, daughters bought candies and snow cones at the entrance, they waved goodbye to each other, kissed one another on the cheek.

María Luisa left together with a couple of friends; Jesús stalked them, keeping out of sight behind trees and in the shadows of the houses as they passed by, careful not to be seen in case one of them might turn around unexpectedly. Jesús considered how hard it would be to live in any city without his sister.

When María Luisa said goodbye to her friends, Jesús put on his Mil Máscaras disguise and continued to follow her.

As she reached the front door, María Luisa spun around and walked straight toward him. Jesús froze in midstep.

Keeping a safe margin of a few feet, she said, "Will you take that mask off, please?"

Jesús panted like a cornered wolf.

"Please," she insisted once more.

She took the mask off his face with a single fluid movement of her right arm. She registered his bloodshot eyes, the tremble in his lips, and could hardly recognize the face and features of her onetime playmate, her brother. Jesús played back a scene from his memory of when they were in a pasture near the river frolicking one late afternoon a few years earlier, just before dusk. María Luisa had tripped and fallen, and he acted as though he meant to help her up but instead jumped on top of her, and took advantage to feel up her scrawny tits. He fumbled at her pants, trying to pull them down, and she screeched at him between sobs, "You're not allowed to do that, please Jesús, don't, you're not allowed, not like that, not that." Jesús came back to the present in a flash.

"When are you coming back home?" she asked. "Mom's worried about you."

Jesús wanted to say something, but his tongue couldn't formulate the words. He stood frozen in the middle of the street, staring at her. María Luisa went up to him and hugged him. He laid his head on her chest that heaved under the effort to restrain her breathing, betraying how desperately she was trying to appear calm.

"It's me, María Luisa, I'm still the same person I've always been," she said.

Better she didn't try to lie to him.

He grabbed the mask back from her and took off running. He didn't have the nerve to look her in the eye.

Jesús left town that same afternoon, in a truck heading for Juárez.

5

Ciudad Juárez, Mexico, 1985

Jesús woke up with a start, drenched in sweat: his sister had appeared in his nightmare holding a meat cleaver in her hands.

"You going to stab me with that thing?" he shrieked, and she nodded in assent and continued walking toward him one slow step at a time. Finally María Luisa stood over him, arms raised, ready to bring the cleaver down. He jolted awake, eyes open wide as dinner plates.

He leaped out of bed and shuffled around in the dark room, trying to locate his underwear. He found the window shade and pulled it open. A pickup truck was parked crooked on Calle Guerrero, one of its wheels was up on the sidewalk. Posters with the slogan "We'll Never Forget October 2" were glued all over town, announcing a Grupera band's upcoming show.

He didn't feel like going to work today, waste his time patching tires and getting his hands filthy with engine grease.

Braulio, one of his bosses at La Curva's machine shop, had offered him the chance to run stolen cars over the border. "Piece a cake," Braulio had said, "everything's all set up." He'd cross over to Texas and make his way to El Paso or Landslide, where the cars were waiting for him. All he has to do is drive back across the border, *ningún problema*.

"But how do I get over there?"

"A mule. It's all arranged. If you end up in Landslide, you can jump a freight train to El Paso."

"And the border check?"

"No worries, *hermano*. We have our arrangements."

"With the gringos?"

"Everyone's got a price, *güey*. You just drive the *stolo* across like nothing was up. The *puercos* never check anything traveling to this side."

It seemed easy. He'd already considered crossing, but not to come back.

He didn't trust Braulio, something about him was shifty and fly-by-night. Jesús's gut told him to keep his distance. He'd be better off going to the town square where people hook up with coyotes to cross over, he thought; see how much it'd cost. Problem was the lack of cash. Though he couldn't complain: not a year in Juárez and he'd already landed a job.

He grabbed the plastic Mil Máscaras action figure from its spot on top of the television set. Mil Máscaras, there's a smooth operator, Jesús thought. He'd sneak up on his adversaries without them ever noticing, then pin them down in a cross-body block and deal the final blow for victory. Why weren't he more like Mil Máscaras, able to cross the border on his own? Have the right moves to bring those haters down who stand guard and don't let anyone else access the country— think they're such badasses.

His neighbor was listening to the radio full blast, some program with news of the people who had dared to cross by themselves. He thought about it but always chickened out in the end. Would Papá have come this way to cross? How'd he do it? By himself or with *polleros* and coyotes? Was he still alive? If so, where?

Every once in a while, he'd hang around the vicinity of Juárez Bridge and watch the bustling lines of people on their way over to El Paso; he wished he was one of them but didn't have the papers. Graffiti sprayed on the wall said, "No human is illegal" and "Death to the Empire," and he agreed with the slogans. A line of buildings cut a silhouette against the sky in the distance. Signs of the promises offered on the other side hung there in full view: "Wells Fargo" and "Chase."

Something might happen to that radio, Jesús thought. It could fall over the balcony. Or the neighbor lady too, nobody'd even notice.

Some people crossed at the narrow segment of the river, near El Paso, then got sucked into the city streets and disappeared. They'd hide and wait till the Migra's jeeps finished making their rounds. There were sections of the barbed-wire fence on the other side that were either broken or down altogether. Braulio suggested that he take that route: it's risky, but if you make it through, everything else was in his favor.

He combed his hair back in front of the mirror, which was cracked into two parts. He put on his pants, a shirt, and a University of San Diego baseball cap, then walked down the hallway on the second floor of the boarding house and out onto the street. A sudden blast of hot, merciless wind nearly took his breath away.

He liked to pass by the train station on his way to work. Curiosity got the better of him, and he decided to duck into the building with its stucco walls and rusty iron braces that clutched the oblong ceiling. A deaf-mute held out his hand asking for money, but he ignored him.

The arrivals and departures sign announced trains coming from and going to cities on the other side of the river. A policeman eyeballed him uneasily. The ticket seller, a plump woman with robust braids, attended a long line of passengers. A family stood together by the tracks next to a pile of suitcases; the children played atop one of them, made of black polyethylene.

He wondered how much a ticket would cost.

Doesn't matter if he doesn't have papers.

Exiting the station, he caught sight of a freight train in the distance, a red-and-yellow-striped locomotive with rusty, ochre-colored boxcars. He drew closer and read Burlington Northern on the side.

The train seemed to go on forever. It moved him to watch how sluggishly it rolled along the tracks.

The rest of the afternoon was spent quietly doing oil changes, repairing radiators, and fixing worn-out brakes. He kept his mouth shut when his coworkers teased him, even when they called him a retard. If they only knew, he thought to himself, who they were messing with.

But it was better for him—for them—that he keep a low profile and just ignore them.

When his shift ended, he headed over to the cantina where Rocío worked. He sat down and asked for a *chela*. The place was empty. Flies scurried across tabletops and windows. The waiter stood at the end of the bar, lazily working a crossword puzzle. The cook watched him, leaning against the kitchen door with his arms folded. A singer's grainy voice crooned a *narcocorrido* over the speakers, pledging allegiance to the "court of el Señor de los Cielos," the drug lord who had taken over the Juárez cartel and used his fleet of jets to traffic across the border.

As soon as the song was over, Jesús sauntered to the jukebox and selected a few tracks by Juan Gabriel and ABBA.

Rocío finally showed up, wearing a blue skirt and shell-pink top. Jesús loved her big balloon tits and meaty thighs. She had an ex-lover's name tattooed on her right forearm, and promised to have it removed as soon as she had enough guts, it hurt so bad when she got it done in the first place. Jesús gave her a peck on the cheek.

"What's up? Didn't expect you here so soon."

"Slow day. Boss let us off early."

"Nobody around here ever lets me go early. You good?"

"Good as can be."

"I can't talk now, you know."

"Ain't no one here but me."

"And my boss is a *cabrón*. Pick me up in two hours?"

"Let me finish my beer first."

Rocío grinned at him flirtingly before vanishing into the kitchen.

Jesús was waiting for her by the exit. He grabbed her hand and they went to a neighborhood on the outskirts of the city, where she rented a room with its own bathroom in an elderly couple's home.

They greeted the owners politely as they walked by on their way to Rocío's room. The man had been a cop and remembered the days when the only people who needed arresting were the trafficking crooks who precharged people to cross the border, then left them stranded. His wife was addicted to soap operas. At times she'd look at the man snoring on the couch next to her as if he were some trespasser who came only to aggravate her by hiding the remote whenever she needed it.

Rocío switched the radio on and tuned it to a station that played Madonna, Elvis Presley, and José Alfredo Jiménez. She turned the volume up so the old folks wouldn't hear them, locked the door, and lowered the shades. She threw her plastic clown doll on the floor, jumped onto the bed, and perched against the wall, offering herself up lustily to their evening ritual.

Jesús kissed her lips and tore at her clothes, fondling her breasts clumsily, drawing their contours with his fingers and tongue. He turned her over and held her by the throat as if she were the clown doll, penetrating her hungrily, aggressively. She sucked on a silver crucifix she wore dangling from a chain around her neck, and bit down, eyes closed, as if holding her breath underwater. He finally found a rhythm that worked for both of them, and marked it with sharp, stinging spanks on her ass that left little reddish-pink welts on her skin. When he could feel she was about to come, he squeezed her neck tightly and grunted obscenities. For a second she thought he might strangle her, and was about to tell him to ease up but didn't. They came at the same time.

As soon as she could speak again, Rocío told him she loved him. Jesús muttered "It's a little early for that," and Rocío was sorry to have let her feelings show. She loved how they did it, the violence with which he possessed her, but afterward she often felt dirty, as if he had stained something of hers that was sacred. And she told herself that any man who took her like that, or adolescent in his case because he wasn't even a man yet—despite the hurt, the bitter rage in his eyes—no man with that inside of him could ever love her. One thing she knew for sure was that true love expresses itself through tenderness, and there wasn't a single drop of the tender or gentle about Jesús.

Jesús put his pants and sneakers back on and said he was starving.

"Want me to cook you something?"

"Nah, I'll catch a bite outside."

She covered herself with a blanket and didn't say anything. It annoyed her that he always left so soon after having sex.

Jesús adjusted his belt and said, "I have the afternoon off tomorrow. Wanna go see a movie? There's a new Jackie Chan flick playing." Roció answered, "Who knows, tomorrow's another day."

"Turn the lights off when you leave," she said from under the covers.

"You're just going to sleep like that, with all your clothes on?"

"For a while."

Jesús kissed her on the forehead, switched off the light, and left. On his way out he walked through the living room, where the elderly couple was snoozing, blanketed in the television's flickering light. He went to the kitchen, opened the refrigerator, and pinched a can of Tecate.

The following afternoon he went to the movies alone. He sat in one of the front rows to avoid other people, and sprawled out across the dirty seats. Popcorn and plastic cups littered the sticky floor. Jesús laughed at Jackie Chan's antics, and it thrilled him to watch how Jackie fought against four intimidating karate thugs. He was so agile and moved so effortlessly, he made it seem as though landing smack on his feet after a backflip or jumping from an eight-story building onto the roof of a moving truck was everyday stuff. No sweat.

Papá had seriously wanted to turn him into a boxer. They used to throw jabs, practice parries, and spar on the patio. Jesús was a natural, it was only a matter of time before he'd grown accustomed to the gloves and learned all the moves. But how much better to be Jackie Chan. Everyone else has to stick to using a blade or a knife.

By the time he left the movie theater it was dark out; the wind snapped him in the face and threw dust into his eyes. Pages of newspapers curled around street lamps. He drifted through the center-city streets searching peevishly for some sign of salvation, a church where he could find a friendly face like Father Joe's, a marketplace where he could hang out with his cousins, a strip joint with an old whore, a playground where his sister was jumping rope with her friends. He surveyed the posters that were stuck to windows and walls advertising a wrestling match in the Municipal Gym, or the concert of a popular singer of corrido ballads. His lips trembled and he bit down with his molars, setting his jaw hard. His sense of unease was getting the better of him.

The sodium streetlights switched on. He used up his last coins at a curbside vendor and devoured eight tacos *al pastor*.

Jesús picked up his pace when he noticed a van with tinted windows that seemed to be following him. Most likely a false alarm, but why take chances.

He went back to his room and slipped into bed. It didn't take long to fall asleep. He woke up at three a.m. in a daze, not knowing where he was, what time it was. He couldn't get back to sleep.

Thinking of María Luisa, he consoled himself with the adage that everything happens for a reason, even if you can't figure out what it is.

He finally roused himself from bed and went in to work. His boss repeated the offer to send him to Texas to run stolen cars.

"But the Migra . . ."

"You go with a mule, güey, you ain't gonna see no Migra. You gotta jump a freight train. *No hay problema*; like I said, we take care of everything."

It was Friday, "let me think about it over the weekend," Jesús answered, he'd let him know on Monday. Braulio touched his hat and winked. A hint? Would he lose his job if he didn't agree to do it? Maybe it was more than just a suggestion.

He called Rocío later that afternoon; she would swing by his place at nine and they'd go dancing.

A pounding on the door pulled him out of his dream again. Fragments lingered in his mind as he stood up: the war had come, and he couldn't find a knife anywhere.

It was Rocío. He opened the door for her. Sorry, *chamaca*, I fell asleep. She had a leather jacket on over a spandex top, and tight pants that didn't really go with her high-heeled white sandals. She was wearing too much makeup, green shadow smudged into blue on her lids and below her eyes, and her lipstick was smeared.

Jesús lay back down, lit a joint, and took a few quick puffs.

"Aren't you going to change? We're supposed to go dancing."

"You really want to go out? I kinda like being here."

"And do what?"

"Don't matter."

Rocío held the joint to her lips.

"I don't like *mota*. I don't like how it makes me feel."

Jesús cracked the seal of a bottle of tequila on the night table and poured two shots.

They smoked and drank for about an hour, then Jesús got up to go to the bathroom. Rocío lay on the bed, her back to the door.

She slowly sensed a presence, something moving in the doorway, and when she turned she saw a strange man hovering between the door and the bed; he was wearing a white wrestling mask with black lines. He stared at her from holes cut like snake eyes.

Rocío panicked and her breath caught in her throat.

Is that you, Jesús? Don't mess with me like that.

She saw the flash of a blade in the man's hands and wanted to scream but kept her cool. She perceived something ominous in the denseness of the room's air, a sickly sweet smell under the stench of stale food and dirty clothes strewn across the floor. Best to remain still, avoid unnecessary provocation.

Jesús?

The man drew closer and brought the knife to her throat.

Please . . .

He hit her so hard she flew back onto the bed. He ripped her top off and pulled her pants down. She tried not to lose control, not to panic. The pressure on her neck was suffocating her, and he smashed her face down into the tangled bedspread. All she wanted was to think of herself far away, distance herself from that room.

The man charged her viciously, like an animal. She held onto the pillow and thought how little a woman can do to protect herself from shadows. How is this going to end? Would it ever end?

He came hard and finally eased off her. When his panting slowed, he burst out laughing, hysterically. She recognized his laughter.

A moan welled up from somewhere deep inside of her, from a place she hadn't frequented in a very long time. She began punching him, sobbing, and he let her, making fun of her and laughing at her the whole time. You're a piece of shit, she screamed, *desgraciado*. She dressed quickly as best she could, concealing her ripped top under her jacket. She had the hiccups from crying so hard.

Don't you ever dare come looking for me again. If you do, I'll call the cops.

Jesús stopped laughing the minute he heard the word cops. He pulled the mask off and said in a sweet tone that was full of menace: better be careful what you say, *puta*.

Rocío slammed the door behind her. Jesús lay back on the bed and cackled till his jaw hurt.

The next morning Jesús called his boss and told him he was ready. Braulio grinned and quickly gave him instructions: he would cross the next day, before dawn, and hop a freight train to El Paso.

After work he went straight to the train station. It looked empty, so he jumped from the platform and walked between the tracks out to where a freight train was stationed, carrying a load of aluminum pipes.

He walked around it, observing the train's features till it lurched into motion about half an hour later.

6

Landslide, 1985

Braulio dropped Jesús off with a mule who carried him across the river on his broad shoulders. It was early morning and the water reached his knees. Jesús thought back to the stories Mamá used to tell him of how she'd made the crossing several times over the years. She would journey across to find work as a maid or a waitress in El Paso whenever they'd needed money. As soon as they reached dry land on the other side, Jesús bolted for the train station on Calle Santa Fe. He relaxed when he saw the Freight House sign hanging above the door-way of a tiny building. He stole down to the tracks and hid inside one of the boxcars.

Jesús arrived in Landslide at the stipulated time. He caught a glimpse of the city's tall buildings from the train—he remembered the skyline from some postcards Mamá had kept at home—and he could distinguish the silhouettes of the nearby houses as the train approached the station. He read the advertisements and billboards announcing "KFC Texas-size buckets!" and "New Coke: The Best Just Got Better!" His muscles ached from lying on the hard floor.

The whistle announced their arrival. "The train slows but it don't stop," Braulio had warned him. When he felt the train slowing down, he got up and moved closer to the door: there were the tracks, then dirt, then bushes, then trashcans. And finally, a barbed-wire fence with holes in it.

He couldn't think about it too much or he'd miss his chance, the train would just continue on past Landslide.

Jesús jumped impulsively. He banged his shoulder on the ground and did a few somersaults on impact before finally coming to a stop. He stood up gingerly.

He hid in the bushes until he was sure the coast was clear, then hopped out into the street. An obese woman was pushing an old man in a wheelchair; a white woman passed by lugging a heavy suitcase. His presence hadn't drawn any notice, not even from the cop who was sitting in his car on the corner in front of a hamburger joint. Jesús couldn't believe he was actually standing in the country he'd considered out of his reach his entire life.

Braulio's contacts would be waiting in a cafeteria nearby. Jesús asked a gas station manager for directions in English. The manager answered him in Spanish.

It didn't take long to find El Dorado. There were only two clients sitting at the bar, both wearing ten-gallon hats. He approached, and they acknowledged him with a smile.

"What's up yo, who the fuck are you?"

"Don Braulio . . ."

"Goddamned partner's a reckless sombitch. Why he send us a boy to do a man's job? Y'ain't a day over fourteen. What's up with that?"

"Damn right," the other said.

They both burst out laughing. They shook his hand. "Don't pay us no mind, boy. How's about we get you a shot of tequila?" Jesús couldn't say no.

An hour later they left the bar feeling tight. The Toyota he was supposed to deliver to Juárez was parked along the sidewalk on the opposite side of the street; the plates were false and the back doors and trunk were mud-splattered. Overall, the car was in good condition, though—a few scratches on the back fender on the right side, a crack in the front left headlight.

The car was parked in front of a store whose neon sign read V NT GE CLOT NG. There was a gray blazer in the window that caught his eye. The price tag sticking out of the pocket read $19.99.

Jesús walked in, and a blond woman approached with a clean, wide-toothed smile. She had a fake tan and wore her belt tight, showing off her wasplike waist.

"How may I help you today, sir?"

He pointed to the blazer; the blond brought it to him. Jesús read the tag on the inside of the neck: "J. Crew, broken in, medium." He walked up to a full-length mirror in a back corner of the store and had a good look at himself. The blazer was a little big for him—the arms hung over his hands just a tad too far—but he liked the color. He went up to the register and paid for it.

The motel Braulio had recommended near the station was called the Cleveland. He paid in cash and settled into his room. There were cigarette burns on the rug, and the tub had some rust stains. The Latter-day Saints had provided a New Testament Bible.

He grabbed a pen from the night table and drew a picture on the last blank page of the New Testament, a solitary figure in the middle of a flat landscape beside a lonely nopal cactus. The sole survivor of a nuclear war.

He took a nap and woke up famished, so he went out to
look for a place to eat, switchblade tucked in his pocket. As
he walked along, he noticed the names of the streets; Spruce,
Austin, Benson. It was dark and he didn't know the neighborhood, so he figured he might as well go back to El Dorado. He
ordered chicken wings at the bar and sucked on them for a
while, nibbling at the meat and drinking. There was a football
game on the television, Packers versus the Broncos. Just his
fucking luck, the 49ers, his favorite team, wasn't playing. Joe
Montana was fucking God. Son of a bitch had an arm.

He left the bar all boozed up and took a pedestrian-only
street that bordered the station. As he made his way back,
he heard footsteps.

There was a woman walking ahead of him, about a hundred meters away.

He started following her.

In the distance he could hear a couple shouting, locked in
a bitter argument. Better hurry.

He moved in closer to the woman. He wanted her to feel
his presence, to be afraid. He touched the switchblade in
his pocket. She was white and was wearing high heels with
a knee-length skirt. She glanced over her shoulder uneasily
and saw how his shadow grew along the cobblestone street.
She grabbed her bag tighter. Her steps accelerated.

It would have been better if she hadn't tried to run or scream,
but she did both. He caught up with her and shoved her into
the bushes and off the sidewalk in a single tackle. He covered
her mouth and pulled out his knife. Her eyes expressed dis-
tress, round as plates and open wide, and her skin was covered
in little goosebumps. He could see she was just a *chamaca*. She

had looked older from a distance, but close up he could tell she was barely eighteen, if that.

He dug around in her purse, took out her lipstick, the photos from her wallet, stared at her driver's license for a while as if trying to memorize her information; Jannsen, Victoria. She had a passport. He examined the seal and the words below, written in some strange language. He couldn't figure what country she was from. He opened it and inspected the girl's radiant picture on the first page, her green eyes. She had changed her hairstyle: it was curly then, now it was straight.

OK Victoria, *deja de moverte.*

He stroked her hair. He'll be quick with her. He raised her skirt and pulled down her panties. She started to cry, saying no, no, please, between sobs, please no. *Callate, puta.*

She tried to wriggle out from under his body. Jesús told her again to shut the fuck up and stop moving but she kept it up. So you don't want to play, huh? Almost without thinking, Jesús plunged the knife into her chest. A single sharp thrust was all it took.

She froze with her mouth half-open. The air exited her lungs: going, going, gone.

Now what?

He had never fucked a white chick before.

He pulled his pants down and entered her, counting by fives in his head.

He came fast. It would have been more fun if she were wiggling a little.

Don't worry bitch, you'll be in a better place soon, he said as he closed her eyes. Then he threw her passport into the shrubs, stuffed his pocket with her credit cards, and took off running.

By midmorning Jesús was on his way back to Juárez, listening to rancheras on the radio. The harsh desert light reflected off the shiny hood and glared through the Toyota's windshield.

He had stopped at a Seven Eleven for supplies, bought M&Ms, Snickers, and a Three Musketeers bar. He sipped at a Dr. Pepper's from the six-pack he had bought to help him stay awake as he drove.

The road was straight, and every once in a while he couldn't help nodding off for a few seconds. Truth was he hadn't been able to rest much. He couldn't sleep, and when he did, nightmares kept waking him up, like the one of María Luisa and the butcher knife. The night had been unpredictable, as if his life had morphed into some sort of drug-induced hallucination.

He could do it again, though, *sin problema*. The thrill of the hunt, the turn-on of being ruthless, the risk.

1

Landslide, 2008

I stopped by the university before my shift started at Taco Hut to check my box at the department, since I still received some random mail there.

I took a shortcut through the campus. Doric columns lined the entrances of stately buildings; nineteenth-century shields and Latin phrases decorated the arcades. The carefree students played Frisbee or napped, or argued over *Gossip Girl* or read *Paradise Lost* on perfectly manicured lawns. Though Texan women may put on a casual look, their outfits are all but spontaneous: they preen and redo their makeup endlessly, even shorts and flip-flops are fastidiously color-coordinated.

A huge American flag swayed in the wind high above the rotunda at the center of campus. I was like a spy sussing out suspicious faces in a neighborhood I had once belonged to, homing in on any expression of annoyance at being required to get out of bed and go to class. But no, not here. You'd be hard-pressed to find any sign of skepticism in this place. They all had the same hopeful air. No dazed passengers in this boat. Same as me back in the day, until crisis struck and I decided to jump off the deep end.

But that wasn't the only reason, and I knew it. It wasn't only because classes at the university had seemed like a long parenthesis in my life, as though I wasn't really living in the "real world." The only good thing to come of the two years working on my master's degree was being forced to reconsider the doctorate. I was racked with doubts and felt compelled to create something of my own. Always talking about other people's creativity bored me. It came down to one basic truth: this wasn't my world, I didn't belong.

I yawned. I hadn't slept well. My cell phone had startled me awake at five a.m. It was my dad, sloshed, telling me how much he loved me, asking when was I going to visit, maybe I'd never see him again, he wanted to join the struggle for Santa Cruz's independence from Bolivia. From the fog of my dreams, I asked him what on earth he would do there. Who is going to hire you at your age? You only have a few friends left there anyway. I poked fun, calling him Pedro and saying he was like that little shepherd boy who cried wolf so many times nobody believed him anymore. He hung up on me.

I took the elevator to the fourth floor of Gwain Hall. I knew Sam would be in class, I'd calculated the time of my visit to avoid running into him; he would have asked me what I was doing, and I would have said that I'd come to pick up my mail, then he would ask why I hadn't just asked him to pick it up for me, why go to so much hassle? With Sam, everything was complicated.

The secretary, Martina, stood up to greet me. "Our missing person!" She gave me a kiss: "So are you reconsidering? We're holding out for you to change your mind."

The chair, a medievalist who had dedicated his life to drawing a topographic map of the books he taught—*Amadís de Gaula*, *The Poem of the Cid*—had told me the door was still open if I wanted to return. All I had to do was let him know a semester in advance. That was eight months ago. My renunciation of the program had been registered as a "temporary absence." Their attention made me feel appreciated, even important, but I knew I was never going to take them up on the offer.

I said goodbye to Martina and grabbed the mail from the box: subscription renewals for MLA, book offers from the Instituto Internacional de Literatura Iberoamericana. As I contemplated the mug shots of the new doctoral students in the hallway, arranged beside their standard-issue descriptions— "she discovered Latin American literature as an adolescent while reading *Cien años de soledad* during a trip to Mexico," and "reading the classics allows her to better understand the present; *Don Quixote* is the first 'postmo' novel ever written"— it occurred to me that Samantha had run away from her own world and come to earth, where a family of gravediggers living beside a cemetery adopted her. She had enjoyed a quiet and uneventful childhood until she realized that people from her own planet had begun infiltrating Earth, taking the forms of its ghastly myths: vampires, zombies, and the bogeyman.

That will be my character's mythical origin. Neil Gaiman by way of the Transformers. It's a meta-comic, in fact. Just the type of comic strip an ex-doctoral candidate would come up with.

The doors to the professors' offices were closed. Mina Swanson, the Renaissance expert who attracted students to her classes through audacious titles ("Sex, Lies and No Videotapes Whatsoever: *La Celestina*"); Joan Barral, the fervent

Catalanist who used his articles to crusade against Catalan writers who expressed themselves in Castilian; Tadeo Konwicki, the Pole who analyzed Elmer Mendoza according to Žižek and Jean-Luc Nancy; or Ruth Camacho-Stokes, the expert in Latin American literature who was preparing a study about how Chicano art influences contemporary narrative. Taped to her door was a poster advertising next year's exhibit centered on the work of Martín Ramírez, the recently canonized self-taught midcentury artist. The poster was a reproduction of one of his images: a train coming out of a tunnel through hills formed by wavy lines. I didn't find it particularly interesting. I wasn't into the naive style.

I stopped at the door just beside the elevator. *Calvin & Hobbes* comic strips were taped to the frosted window. It seemed as if nothing had changed.

The light was on. I knocked at the door. Footsteps. The door opened and a bald man's pate poked out. His eyes were devoid of emotion when he saw me.

"Hey, what a surprise. Come in, come on in."

He left the door open a sliver and invited me to have a seat. His white shirt was wrinkled, and the seat of his corduroy pants drooped a little—the typical absent-minded professor look. I asked how he was doing.

"Having authority issues, as usual. I was the type of kid who bit his teachers. And the deans are full of shit. You can't imagine how much they're fucking things over."

"Is something wrong?"

"I prefer not to talk about it; it puts me in a bad mood. I'll let you know some other time."

There was a calendar on his desk showing Vasto, the Abruzzo town where the Colamarino family came from. Fabián used to spend summers in Vasto; he said it was the perfect spot for writing since it was isolated, had an incredible beach and great ice cream and pizza ("an oasis of peace amidst a hell of boredom"). He had promised to take me with him sometime, and I'd believed him. That was before I learned how short-lived his promises were.

The table was crammed with books and manuscripts.

"They write more than what we can read, you know. How are you going to get by?"

"Honestly, I read fewer and fewer novels. I read less in general. They publish so much crap these days!" He waved his hand at a pile of books with a gesture of contempt. "Go ahead, take anything you'd like, take it all."

I remembered the staggering clarity of his ideas. I took his seminar during my second semester and experienced those flashes of epiphany in his class. I took furious notes and wanted to be just like Fabián Colamarino: a literature professor who could dazzle students using Ángel Rama's ideas to renovate nineteenth-century literature. What was his secret? He tackled cutting-edge ideas without reading from notes, took off on the craziest, most imaginative flights of fancy, and always managed to land safely, a little worse for the wear maybe, but safely nonetheless. This seduction of the mind landed me in his bed by the third semester. For three months I fell prey to his competitive angst, his ability to work into the wee hours, the traumas and fears that cut him to the quick, the escape valve of alcohol and drug abuse to cope with being hailed as one of his generation's most brilliant scholars. There were fabulous days, but I still haven't gotten over my sudden change of heart.

I picked up the novel of an Ecuadoran writer and asked myself where Fabián's bitterness was coming from. He often complained about "the lack of poetry in life," but his enthusiasm for books, music, film, ideas usually overcame the muck he saw everywhere, threatening to suck us all in.

"I haven't been reading much lately either," I said. "Novels, I mean."

"But you left the department for a reason, didn't you? How's the drawing coming along?"

"The ideas are there. But it's not enough. You need discipline and patience, and I don't know if I have that."

"The learning curve is long. You'll do fine."

I smiled: that's how he won me over. My dad had laughed at me when I told him I wanted to study to become a video-game designer. When I was fourteen, a high school teacher in Santa Cruz found one of my illustrated notebooks and communicated her concern over seeing me squandering my talent. My brother Toño's favorite sport was making fun of my superhero stories. Everyone told me how ridiculous I was to take my calling seriously. It was barely even a hobby.

When I thought we were familiar enough, I showed Fabián some of my short stories and a notebook with storyboards. He criticized them ruthlessly, told me they were rehashes of Borges and Philip K. Dick, but he also encouraged me: there was talent here, the drawings were good and I didn't lack imagination; it was a matter of perseverance, hard work. They were my first words of encouragement; he made me take myself seriously. Believe in myself. For a while I thought they would forever bind me to Fabián. For someone whose family background wasn't conducive to becoming an artist, getting that kind of approval was intoxicating.

"The important thing is that I'm drawing," I said. "Honestly, I think the days for literature as we know it are numbered.

It's the century of the graphic novel, the vooks, digital novels hooked up to Wikipedia and YouTube."

"Yet another voice trying to kill off literature. Get in line."

"It's scholars like you who kill it off a little bit every day: theory as an end in itself, books that can only be read by other academics."

There was a pregnant pause. I hadn't gone there to reveal how angry I was, but it slipped out. I tried to change the subject.

"How's your never-ending project coming along?"

"More and more like Macedonio's narrating machine. The stories proliferate, but without a common thread tying them together."

"Maybe you should respect that chaos."

"You should respect it in life, not in literature."

The framed cover of Fabián's book on Modernism hung on the wall. It had recently been translated into English. What must it have felt like to be published so quickly, I wondered, not even three years into assistant professorship; his work was now required reading, praised by everyone. At first I had admired the book, but now it almost seemed like a shameless confession. It was hardly coincidental that Fabián chose that period of time in which the turn-of-the-century poets rejected the new society of the "bourgeois king" (to use Rubén Darío's expression) and instead locked themselves away in what the Uruguayan poet Herrera y Reissig called the Torre de los Panoramas. It was hardly a coincidence that this ivory tower had become the ideal metaphor for Fabián to develop his own argument: Latin American literature seemed to make social and political themes central, but in truth the writer, the artist, was alienated from that world and far more concerned with trying to build a refuge from the bustle and vulgarity of modern life. That was Fabián to me.

"You should let me read something."

"I'm the only one who can understand what I have so far."

"Well, at least you're writing."

"I write and I write. And dream that I write that I'm writing."

He brushed one of his manuscripts with his fingers. Is that what he's working on now? *A Unified Theory Capable of Explaining the Totality of Latin American Literature.* A wild, feverish, neurotic project that had consumed him over a number of years: he stopped publishing, stopped going to meetings. When I met him he had just gotten tenure, but the irony was that in his quest for some rigorous order in literature, his life had fallen into complete chaos. Mayra, his wife—a Dominican woman who worked in the university library—had disappeared one day, leaving a note that announced her return to Santo Domingo and warned that he'd better not come looking for her. He started canceling more classes than he gave, and his addictions were getting the best of him.

He coughed. I looked at the books on the shelves. Bhabha, Derrida, Sarlo, García Canclini, Culler, Spivak. I gathered up my nerve.

"This isn't what I came here for. You can read and write whatever you damn well please. Like you always have. It's just that—I don't know, I guess I'd just like to understand what happened."

The muscles in his face tensed up immediately, he opened his eyes wider, his jaw stiffened, he became more alert.

"I was straight with you from the get-go, *niña*, and you agreed. Everything was just fine, until . . . Don't get me wrong, I don't blame you. I suppose it's inevitable. One thing always leads to another, and suddenly what began as a roll in the hay ends up at the altar."

"What if we gave it another try? I'm willing to accept the conditions."

"I don't know, honestly, I just don't. I mean, what's done is done, right?"

He turned around and went back to his computer and started writing again, as if I didn't exist. That was his way of dismissing me.

He told me one time that I'd never be able to understand his despair after Mayra left him. I'd never met her myself; she left a year before I came into the picture. He said he finally resigned himself to the fact that she was gone, and could almost empathize with her. He's so edgy, and his heart is autistic; he lost his way somewhere in the confines of his own closed world and had forgotten about her. It had clearly been a traumatic experience: Mayra was always on his mind, and he wasn't truly over her yet. I figured the reason he avoided becoming involved in another stable relationship was for fear that I might take off one night, just as she had. He couldn't face losing someone else that way again. He preferred to anticipate the risk, control any possible futures that could get out of hand. But now there I was, the one who really didn't know how to live with losing someone. In spite of myself, I had become just like him, someone who couldn't suffer a broken heart.

Yes, I fully understood his despair. But he didn't understand mine.

I could hear voices and footsteps in the hallway. I stood up, turning my back to the door to hide my face. I grabbed a book by an Ecuadoran writer from his desk.

"How is this one?"

"They say he's the best thing to emerge from Ecuador. I wouldn't expect a whole lot, though. It's like saying a soccer player is great because he has the most goals in the Albanian league."

I walked out of his office without saying goodbye.

2

Stockton, 1931–1948

The ward where Martín had been assigned a bed was over-crowded. There were cots arranged in row after and row like soldiers' barracks in times of war. Could this place be set up for prisoners of war? People doubled up in spaces usually allotted for a single person, or took the floor, and if they were lucky they got a blanket, maybe a pillow. Some fancied sleeping underneath the beds. Men and women in white uniforms came and went at all hours, and some of the old folks spent all night just staring at the wall. Others urinated wherever and when-ever they felt the need. The violent patients were the worst, they attacked their companions for any reason at all. Martín learned from the start not to look others straight in the eye.

The windows near the beds were protected by mesh screens that allowed glimpses of the trees and shrubs in the yard out-side, the stone archway where carriages came in, the waves of golden hills in the distance, the train that passed by regularly at noon and again at sundown. The tracks skirted a side of the building where the yard ended, separated by a row of trees and a brick wall.

The sign atop the main entrance read STOCKTON STATE HOSPITAL.

His ward mates' heads were shaved just like his. Their cheeks were pale and they had a vacant, muddled look in their eyes. Several were missing teeth; others had a flattened skull or swollen lips or a neck that was a little too long. Their bodies made a constant racket: they hiccupped or belched or squealed or hollered or bawled. At night he would hear moans that sounded like those of a dying dog, wails that made his soul shudder, kept him alert.

What kind of fuss did he make? Aaaaaahhh. Aaahhhh. Eeeeeaaaaa.

Nothing too alarming, he reckoned.

All sorts of things came out those bodies. First were all the noises, but then there were liquids and solids too. Puke and mucus at the tables. Piss and shit in the hallways. Diarrhea and pus in the beds. Blood and tears in the bathrooms. The smell was hard to take at the beginning. The stench of ammonia hit him hard in the nostrils the first time he got there, and overpowered everything. But the ammonia blended with other odors too, like feces. Eventually he grew accustomed, though.

What sorts of things came out of him? Germs, lots of germs every time he had a coughing spell. Saliva would coat his lips and a trickle of drool would hang from the edge of his mouth.

They bathed him and shaved him nice and smooth. Most people were kind enough to him, though there was one orderly who never smiled, who was always cross and called him a "filthy Mexican." He recognized the second word but not the first. *Filti? Filti?* The bathroom was chock-full of bottles and towels and bandages and rubber tubes, and there was a metal shelf with trays and little balls of cotton. He knew how to shower by himself, but he let them do it since they offered to, why not? He liked when the water was so hot his skin turned red and even hurt a little, as if a thousand needles were poking his body.

He closed his eyes in the bathtub and the nurses disappeared. Once in a while one of them figured out a way to sneak in there behind his pupils. Eh, what do you think you're doing there? He felt like shoving them out, making them leave that place. Why can't they just let him be, leave him to enjoy the black night and twinkling stars of that dark world behind his eyes? But he always ended up feeling like a wretch, so he opened his eyes and brought them back again. There they were, smiling at him, so happy, happy. *Pobres idiotas*. They're lucky he decided to let them stay for now. But if they make any trouble, there will be consequences. It was easy to get irritated. To want payback for the awful things they put him through. How proud María Santa Ana would be if she saw him now. A prisoner who endured, who didn't surrender. A prisoner capable of bringing his enemies to their knees. They thought they had him under arrest, but they were sadly mistaken, it was the other way around, he had arrested them. The war was raging, but here he was way up north keeping the enemy from going off to fight in his country. He kept them distracted taking care of him. All of this was buying time for María Santa Ana. He knew for sure she was no turncoat. She was putting on an act just like he was doing here, pretending to be a prisoner, preparing the way for liberation. The churches will be reborn. What was destroyed will be undestroyed. What was burned will be unburned. *Viva Cristo Rey!*

He was partial to the injections. He heard a doctor say: morphine. Then a nurse said: scoplomine. Another doctor said: bromium. The pills came in assorted colors and the only reason he didn't collect them was because he had to swallow them with a glass of water. He let the pills float. The water seemed to hold them up. But shouldn't it be the other way around? Shouldn't the pills be holding the water inside? He shuffled across the building's mosaic floors, and it felt as if the entire building was floating and about to explode in space. It didn't explode because of him, though. It was one of his missions: hold the building together. The gardens. The earth.

He developed a chronic cough. His head ached constantly. Drawing was the only thing that calmed him. The nurses and doctors were considerate and brought him notebooks and colored pencils. Every now and then he'd write to María Santa Ana and his children, though you couldn't really call it writing: he narrated his daily life in colorful images instead of words, there was a man wearing a hat who entered and exited buildings under a bright yellow sun.

The orderlies asked Martín to draw things for them. One day he found one of his drawings framed and hanging on the wall in a doctor's office. He didn't like his drawings as much as the other engravings he saw around, though. In one, there was a man sitting on a chair in the middle of a meadow and beside him there was a man with pliers in one hand and a stone in the other, taken from the open skull of the man seated next to him. There was another of a man lying on a table with a bat fluttering around him. There were drawings of instruments that looked like they were for torture. Patients like him, their faces expressing despair, tongues lolling and eyes bulging in stupefied smiles.

Dates: 1583. 1623. Such a long time ago, and here these poor folks are still living in states of utter disgrace.

Martín was assigned manual chores outside, around the grounds. Some days he mowed the lawn and pruned the plants in the garden; other times he was taken to a farm to milk the cows or clean their stables, wash hogs or shear the sheep. He started drawing animals. After a while they stopped monitoring him so closely, and he was able to come and go more freely.

Once in a while the man who had brought him there would visit. He asked Martín all sorts of questions, some in English and others in Spanish. Martín understood some things he said but could never fully respond. One question came up every time: what year is it? He understood that much. He would plunge his hands deep into his overall pockets, as if the answer could be found in there somewhere. Then he'd pull his hands out, his fist closed around whatever he'd fished out to show Mr. Walker. Then he'd write "August 24, 1925."

Mr. Walker corrected him once: "June 16, 1931." And once more, "October 9, 1931." And yet again, "January 20, 1932." Martín kept searching around in his pockets.

The man projected drawings on a screen and asked him to choose the biggest one, the thinnest one, and the roundest one. Sometimes he'd show him stains on a paper. Martín didn't know what they were, but he had fun trying to figure out if it was a fish or a flower or a house. The visits weren't always pleasant, though; sometimes they'd take him to an empty room and make him sit on a gurney. They'd put cables to his temples, and an electric current shook him violently and left him aching for days.

Eeeeeehhhh.

Once Mr. Walker made Martín stare at a swinging pendulum for a while, until he lost consciousness. They had better not be toying around with him. He'll just go ahead and blink and that's that. And no way those disappeared doctors could come back whole. They'd be sliced in half, or left just feet and arms, or a head with nothing to hold it up or a man floating in the nothing. It had happened that way once, in his village.

They. Better. Not. Mess. Around. With. Martín.

The man brought him magazines with illustrations and photographs. He stared at the letters, touched them: Sa tur d ayEv en ing P ost. Lif e. Ti Me. Headlines in large type, photos and text that described what was happening in the world. He was partial to the advertisements more than anything else. A woman wearing a shower cap held out long, white arms that offered soap. They seemed to break through the surface and continue extending outside of the page. Martín noticed how much she looked like María Santa Ana. She was fair skinned, with a ski-slope nose, but the outline of her face was the same as that of his good-hearted and pretty wife. At night he dreamed about the soap woman, somehow she escaped from the magazine's pages and came to lie in his bed, and the pain, the noise, and the smell of ammonia mixed with shit, it all went away.

There was the picture of a train on one of the pages. It was all shiny and new, and there was a joyful family ready to jump aboard, all wearing bright smiles. He had never seen a train like that, so fresh from the factory, with aerodynamic lines and bright names painted on the sides; he liked Aztec Eagle the best. The rickety trains that passed by his white building were all rust-covered and mold-infested. He never saw trains like that when he was laying track either, how could he see them if he and the crew were fixing the crossties and anchor spikes? For the trains to come, they had to set the switchmen and build the level crossings to prevent accidents and the stations for passengers to get off. They board the trains from the stations too, you know. You can't only get off. Same as you can't only get on, either. There's a happy family who wants to board the train as soon as possible, get lost in a whirlwind cross-country adventure and who knows, maybe even a shopping spree in Mexico before the journey back home. Wouldn't that be splendid? But just for a second, imagine it wasn't Martín or his fellow Mexicans who had been forced to leave their country and survive somehow in the North, struggling to earn a few pesos so their families could live with dignity, spending so many nights alone, so far from their wives and children, so homesick. Imagine it was the other way around and now the happy gringo family was migrating, heading due south to find work and food because they weren't so happy after all, in fact they wanted for many things, were strangled by debt, *pobres cabrones*. So now Mexicans stayed in Mexico, and it was the white folks who were being forced across the border. Wouldn't that be better?

Or what if nobody was forced to migrate anymore? Leaving one's place on earth is a cruel experience. People should be allowed to stay at home. Martín should be allowed to stay in the place where he was born. The street where he was born. The ranch where he was born. The village where he was born. The region. The country.

Where. He. Was. Born.

But if that's the case, then how come trains exist? Or borders. Or countries. Aha, Martín, you haven't thought it through enough. If you had to choose, would you prefer a world with or without trains?

He couldn't say. But one thing was for sure: he preferred a world where there were magazines. With pages of drawings and photographs of trains. At night the trains would jump straight off the pages of the magazines and through his pupils. He traveled in the trains beside a white lady who was the spitting image of María Santa Ana, and she smiled at him and offered soap with her arms stretched out wide.

The soap was very fancy. He could always use a little washing up in that white building.

For a time he was overwhelmed by panic attacks and nothing would calm him down, so they started tying him to his bed. He bellowed so long and loud that within minutes the room emptied of people. An orderly slapped him once to get him under control, but Martín just went on bellowing. They enclosed him in a windowless room with an obese man who had a dimpled scar that cut straight across his right temple. He knew they were trying to scare him: you keep misbehaving like that and you'll see, we're going to cut a hole in your head like we did to the fat man, and stick our fingers in it and steal your brain.

He wasn't allowed to walk the grounds or work in the farm during those weeks. They took his magazines and notebooks away so he couldn't draw. Spending so many hours a day in the main building with nothing to do made him even unhappier. He was going to turn into one of those old people who don't do anything but stare at the ceiling. I wonder how long you have to stare at a wall before stains appear.

When the spell passed, he finally went out into the garden. And one evening when he was there by himself, watering the plants, it occurred to him to sneak off and run. He made it to the nearby city but didn't know what to do when he got there. He just stood at a corner and stared at the passersby. A woman who saw him was concerned and asked if something was wrong. Martín's answer was incoherent. When two adolescents tried to help him, he stuck his tongue out at them and had a coughing fit. Then he lowered his pants and masturbated in front of them. Someone called the police.

They finally brought him back to his bed, in his room, in the building. His building?

They brought him back to that room with the cables and shook his body with electricity.

A storm was unleashed. Lightning lit up the sky, and it was inside of him.

Aaaaahhhh.

Weeks later, Mr. Walker delivered a verdict before a board of doctors and Martín: dementia praecox, catatonic form. Martín didn't understand anything.

More cables. More storms. More lightning.

He escaped four more times. One time he made it far away and spent several nights in jail listening to the deafening sound of a passing train.

The other times he only lasted three or four days before he returned to the white building on his own. He must have slept in an alley or a park, and the nights were freezing; nobody fed him, and there was no place for him to draw.

What about María Santa Ana? She must be in the custody of the Federales. They were probably still fighting their common enemy who had stolen the animals and taken their children and burned the churches to the ground.

He would go back to his ranch and undestroy it. He would

return to his town and un-burn the images of the Virgin. They'll see. In the blink of his eye.

He wouldn't say a word. He wouldn't betray her.

He started drawing trains. Then came the winged horses, their riders dressed in hats. Naked women on horseback. When he was homesick, he drew the houses in San José, the farms, the churches, the trees, his family, his animals, the *fiestas*—men and women dancing and playing musical instruments, mostly the *guitarrón*—the bullfights. His blood bay mare. El Picacho. Sometimes he tried to fit everything into a single drawing, taping several sheets of notebook paper together.

He cut pictures and illustrations from his magazines, things like women's faces, airplanes, and cars. His favorite ones were taken from soap and train advertisements. He would spend hours at a time sitting on the ground, gluing cutouts to his drawings. Mr. Walker liked what he did. "What day is today?" he'd ask. And Martín wouldn't answer. February 21, 1936, he wrote. December 2, 1937. July 13, 1939. January 5, 1942.

That's how they got to 1948.

3

Ciudad Juárez–Smithsville, Texas, 1985

Jesús took on a few more gigs in Texas. He liked easy riding in the freight trains; he'd sprawl out on the floor, getting up every once in a while to stretch his legs and poke his head out the half-open door, let the rush of wind blow across his face. He still got jittery when the train slowed down to approach a station. He'd get low to the ground if he wasn't already, lie back with his hands over his chest, and shut his eyes. Jesús could always sense when the Migra was closing in, and soon he'd hear the dogs. One morning an agent's head popped through the doorway, his eyes scrutinizing the dark space inside. The dogs made a racket outside, tugging hard at their leashes, eager to pull loose and attack. But they closed the door again, and he could hear their steps slowly fade into the distance together with the growling animals.

He ran into agents a second time in El Paso, but the train hadn't left the station yet, and he was hiding among the metal containers in one of the cars. He couldn't believe they just left him alone, like he was invisible. That must have taken some serious cash. Fucking gringos don't come cheap. Someone told

Jesús an embassy employee in DF charged as much as thirty grand a month to green-light visas for cartel members.

Braulio rustled him some odd jobs in the city, like driving cars for special guests; he'd pick them up at the airport and take them to their hotel. He did Braulio's grocery shopping for him. He felt very fine driving Braulio's black Ford Explorer with its tinted windows. *Qué padre.* He could watch everyone without them seeing him.

Jesús slowly picked up on the fact that despite looking like a two-bit hustler, Braulio was actually a big shot. He had a wife but enough cash to keep a mistress too. Her name was Paloma, just a young thing about Jesús's age. Braulio paid for her apartment near the Instituto Latinoamericano, even splurged on fancy gifts: ermine coats that weren't climate appropriate, a huge-screen television, diamond-studded belts. Paloma was a tiny thing—at times Jesús imagined what they looked like having sex, imagined her body squished under Braulio's beer gut—but she had a twinkle in her eye when she smiled, and men paid attention to her. She wasn't Jesús's type, but he could see why Braulio was sweet on her.

Jesús was seeing a bleached-blond whore named Coquis, who lived in Colonia Anapro. She got off on rough sex, no frills, no foreplay or the games Jesús liked. Just changing positions wasn't enough for him; he liked to tie her up, spank her ass, slap her in the face. Once, when he had gotten drunk and stoned, he bit her in the neck until she bled. That frightened her. He tried to explain that when he was totally into it the limits simply disappeared. Didn't she want him to be fully hers? Complete surrender leads to cannibalistic urges: the need to scratch, to hear her cry out in pain that was also pleasure. But Coquis couldn't be persuaded.

María Luisa wasn't on his mind much these days, these weeks. Sometimes he wondered what Father Joe was up to. One of these days he'd figure out a way to get a message to him, let him know that things were fine.

He didn't bother showing up at the body shop anymore now that he was working as Braulio's personal assistant. He was his driver, his bodyguard, and his errand boy. He watched sports on television during his spare time: wrestling, baseball, American football.

He liked to stand in front of the living-room window, above the patio, and gaze out at the dusty trees lining the sidewalk. He could feel a kind of energy building up inside, fighting for a way out, some sort of a release.

One night when Coquis slept over, he snuck out of bed and rummaged around in his closet looking for his Mil Máscaras mask. He located it and put it on, then climbed back into bed and pounced on her, tearing at her clothes in a sudden rage. Dazed and still half-asleep, she screamed at him: What did he think he was doing? What the hell was going on? Nothing, *puta*. He struck her hard and grabbed her ass, penetrating her with force. Coquis wasn't aroused and it burned. She reacted by biting him in the hand. He brought his hand to his mouth.

"What the fuck is wrong with you? It's me, Jesús, for Christ's sake."

Maybe he should pull his knife on her. The Landslide incident was still fresh in his mind, how he got rid of that Victoria bitch feeling power-drunk, his blood hot and racing hard throughout his body. And that other puta from The California, what the fuck was her name? Lucy, Suzy . . . Yeah, Suzy! He needed that high again. *Las mujeres.* All just a bunch of bitches, like his sister. They'll see, he'll put them all in their place.

Coquis caught her breath while Jesús rustled through his drawers looking for something to alleviate the pain. She gathered her clothes and ran out of the room as fast as she could. On her way out she shouted, "Don't you ever come looking for me you fucking piece of shit."

Braulio wanted to send him on another job. A Ford Explorer was waiting to be picked up in Smithsville. The Explorers were brand-new and in high demand now; Broncos were yesterday's lunch.

He agreed to do it. At least it would get him out of Juárez for a few days.

Back on the train, in a boxcar carrying metal containers that stank of piss, he felt that high again, the dizzy freedom that comes from being on the move. He realized he was rolling toward a bright future. He had his lucky gray blazer on, hadn't changed a thing about it from the time he bought it, not even the little cardboard price tag, which still hung from one of the pockets.

The train passed through tiny, two-bit towns without even a station, and broad, dry fields with tractors and little white and yellow dots scurrying behind cows, leaning over and bending toward the ground to pick up—what? At sunset he started to get excited. The darkness was embracing him, stroking him. Soon the train would slow down as it approached the next station and he'd use his power again. Because now he was convinced that someone or something was protecting him and nothing bad was ever going to happen to him.

There was a wagon check in El Paso again, though he wasn't concerned yet that this recurring scene had turned into a routine. The agent didn't bring dogs with him this time, but Jesús still felt the thrill of having the Migra approach to within a meter of where he was lying on the boxcar floor. The agent mumbled something in English when his eyes detected Jesús, probably cursed at him, and the dirty guard continued on his rounds.

He wished he'd brought something to eat. All he had in his pocket was a pack of M&Ms and two Snickers bars. There were still a few more hours to go before he got to his destination, and he was famished.

The train slowed down a little just about forty-five minutes on, as it passed through the next town. What if he jumped off here? His stomach was growling.

He'd have to wait twelve more hours for the next freight train to come through. Which means he'd show up a little late, but Jesús knew that Braulio's contacts wouldn't go anywhere until he got there. They might call his boss, ask what happened, but that's all. Braulio would tell them to just hold on. Jesús was dependable, he'd never fucked up before, must've been a hitch.

There were rows of prefabricated houses along the tracks, with yellow light streaming through rectangular windows. Shadows conspired with each other along the rooftops. It all seemed so peaceful, so quiet, so worth a visit.

He jumped from the train without somersaulting but jolted his knee hard enough that it made him limp slightly.

One of the houses had a window still ajar. The lights on the first floor were off, but there were signs of life on the second floor, judging from the lively reflection of a television's lights in one of the upstairs windows.

Jesús jumped the fence with ease, crossed the yard, and approached the window. He opened it wider and found himself in a living room with old easy chairs and a piano covered in a plastic sheath. He thumbed through the magazines on the coffee table near the sofa—*People, AARP*—and for a second he could imagine what it would be like to live in this country that wasn't his: cut the lawn on Saturday mornings, watch television with his wife and children on Sunday evenings, a dog or a cat asleep on his lap.

The fantasy of that life nauseated him.

Jesús switched the light on in the kitchen and opened the fridge. There were turkey slices in a plastic bag. He ate all of them. Then he polished off an apple and some cheese. He poured himself a glass of milk, grabbed a box of cookies from the cupboard. There was a calendar stuck to the upper part of the fridge with a Ronald Reagan magnet, and another of the Taco Bell chihuahua, photographs of a white-haired older lady next to three women—her daughters? They looked happy. Where was the old man? Was he dead already?

He could leave the house now, just wander around the town until the next train came by. But instead he stayed and continued rummaging through the cupboards. What was he looking for?

His movements were growing brusquer, he felt his heart accelerating, pounding, beginning to race.

He slammed one of the cupboard doors shut. He heard footsteps on the second floor, a voice called down from the top of the stairs.

"Is that you, Joyce?"

He knew what he was craving.

"Honey, would you please say something? You're scaring me."

He rifled through a few drawers, found a knife.

Would he wait for her to come down? Or go find her himself?

4

Smithsville, 1985

Ranger Rafael Fernandez walked into the house, which had been cordoned off with yellow tape. The front door was ajar, and police were coming and going. As he entered he greeted Captain Smits, who was communicating with one of his subordinates by walkie-talkie. Smits pointed at the stairway and continued talking. There were chalk marks on the floor and on the last few stairs, marking where they had discovered the elderly woman's lifeless body. The corpse had already been taken to the morgue.

The captain finished his conversation and approached Fernandez. He put his hand on one of Fernandez's shoulders in his typical easygoing, chummy way. The Ranger stepped back. He didn't like it when people got too close to him.

"Anything new?"

"Olivia Havisham, seventy-five years old, widow, retired schoolteacher."

The captain handed him a folder with Polaroid pictures of the crime scene, together with reports by the coroner and forensic pathologist. The photos upset him: the murderer had been particularly vicious.

"He cut her throat with a knife, then stabbed her in the chest with it," the Captain explained. "According to the coroner's report, death was not instantaneous. Poor lady had time to realize what was going on."

"What's not going on anymore, you mean."

"Yup. Motive appears to be robbery. He sorted through the drawers where she kept her jewelry. A daughter says there are some earrings missing, a few bracelets and chains. That's Joyce over there, the only one who lives in the vicinity; the other two have been notified and should be getting in this afternoon."

Fernandez remembered something an FBI agent once said, a specialist in criminal profiles: the killer always leaves something behind and always takes something away from the scene of the crime.

"We know what he took," he said, giving him back the folder. "But what did he leave behind?"

"Fingerprints, all over the goddamned place. Wasn't premeditated. Didn't seem to worry at all about getting caught."

Fernandez asked permission to go upstairs. "Fine, long as you don't touch anything," Smits said. "Coroner says we aren't supposed to be walking around in here. We mess up his crime scene, ain't that a hoot? Leave footprints everywhere. Hooey. You'll find the daughter in her mother's bedroom. She doesn't want to move, she's still in shock."

"I can imagine."

But the truth was he couldn't imagine it. His own mother was in a hospice in Abilene, down to skin and bones and no longer able to recognize him when he visited. She was mostly bedridden, and whenever she wasn't sleeping she was watching television. She'd had a stroke and lost her ability to speak;

every once in a while she opened her mouth enough for him to see where half of her tongue had been burned off, as if struck by a bolt of lightning. Which is more or less what had happened: the stroke had decimated her brain cells, and along with them the ability to communicate, to articulate words.

In all, he preferred having his *vieja* in that condition rather than lying on a steel autopsy table in the morgue.

"Any suspects?"

"The window had been left open. I don't think the killer knew her. He saw the open window, came in to rob, found the lady there and killed her. All very clean."

"Opportunity makes the thief."

"Maybe the thief was already made. A damn clumsy one at that. We'll know in a little while if he has a record."

Fernandez cleared his throat as he scrutinized framed pictures of the woman and her daughters. Here they stood at the door of a restaurant. Here on a ski slope. There was one of them in a town square that could have been in Mexico. Now just another broken family. Though death seemed to have been the final blow to what had already been broken: the father was nowhere to be seen. Death merely accelerated the slow process of decay we're all subject to from the moment we're born. Fernandez considered his own family. It shocked him to think how much he hated Cherise, someone he had truly loved once. He'd spent so much time with his children when they were young, but now, as adolescents, they looked at him as if he were a complete stranger, just some spic who spoke English with a heavy accent (they constantly corrected his pronunciation of "comfortable" and "vegetable," saying "it's *evaki-ueizion* and not *evacueizion*," or "the 'l' in 'salmon' is mute," they scolded him for using articles or pronouns wrong, "pass me the Tabasco, please" or "I like the ice cream"). He didn't know how to listen to them and couldn't offer the advice they needed.

He climbed the stairs to the second floor with Smits. It had been a quiet day, and he was off the clock, but the boss called on volunteers to check in and report on what had happened. He'd left what he was doing the second he received news of the murder. The town was less than an hour from Landslide.

Before entering the elderly woman's bedroom, Fernandez inspected the window in the hallway, just between the stairs and the bedroom. The curtains were open and tiny specks of dust were floating in the sunlight. From this vantage point he could discern how the house just opened itself up like a big fat temptation to anyone walking along the train tracks. The home of a single elderly woman, just begging to be robbed or even raped and killed. There were savages in all parts, but it seemed as though people had gone a little bonkers these days. As if something in the air was making folks act more bizarre than ever. Even those of sound mind can feel the allure of the switchblade to finish a conversation gone awry, or a pistol to shoot dead that asshole who just dared raise his voice a little too loud.

Joyce, the woman's daughter, was slumped across a rattan chair in a corner of the room; a policewoman or nurse, or both, was kneeling beside her, taking her pulse. Fernandez approached and murmured a soft "My sympathies." He nodded and walked away without expecting a response. He felt uncomfortable encroaching on the private space of the bereaved. His job required it from time to time, part of the profession that he least liked. The dead were dead; but the living were the ones who had to bear the pain, deal with the problems, the debts, the specifics, the half-truths, not knowing how to fill the immense—or maybe not so immense—void left by their loss, the result of some thief's whim or an accident, there were so many ways to leave this world, it was so easy.

He walked over to examine the walls, look closer at a collection of wooden landscape paintings, obviously souvenirs from a trip to Guatemala. They narrated creation myths. The nurse stood up and left.

The victim had lain down on her bed to watch television, covering herself with a coffee-colored blanket decorated with southwestern motifs. Now it lay thrown over the pillow. There was a pile of books and magazines on the night table. Fernandez bent over to thumb through the books. He didn't feel curiosity for the lives of his coworkers or his neighbors in life, but when death came calling, even the slightest details took on enormous significance. What did they read, what cereal did they eat for breakfast, what time did they go to the gym, what were their favorite television shows? These details allow the dead, rendered speechless, to still have a say. People are generally nosy, they like to pry into the lives of other people who share the same space as they do; but somebody has to concern themselves with those who are no longer among us.

So what did the books tell him? That Mrs. Havisham was worried about her savings. She dreamed of taking a trip to the Mayan Riviera. She read detective novels that she checked out of the municipal library: Elmore Leonard, Ruth Rendell, P. D. James.

Wouldn't that have been interesting: the elderly woman was reading a detective novel about a murderer of elderly women who broke into his victims' homes through the window, when a murderer of elderly women broke into her home through an open window and killed her.

But no, it wasn't the case. She had been watching television. He would ask what channel she had tuned in to. Did the program she was watching tell him anything about her death? Doubtful. Yet these were the types of minor details, the specifics that mattered to Fernandez.

He stepped over to where the daughter was seated. She started talking before he even opened his mouth.

"It's all my fault," she said. "Mom complained about being alone, she wanted to go to an assisted living facility. I couldn't bear the idea, said it wasn't necessary, and promised to visit more often. But everything always seemed more important than coming to see her. I abandoned her."

"Right now you need to try to keep calm," Fernandez told her in a hurry: he didn't want to see her cry.

He would have told her the same thing he told one of his relatives in a similar situation: "When it comes down to it, we're all alone." But he had learned the lesson, these words didn't offer consolation, so he kept his mouth shut.

"If what you're asking is whether anything of particular value is missing, the answer is no. There are a few pieces of jewelry gone, but whoever took them wasn't being picky about it. He grabbed whatever he could stick in his pocket. There are a few library books missing, but I suppose that doesn't count. She was absent-minded, tended to leave them all over the place; you can't imagine the late fees. I don't know if *absent-minded* is the right word, she was forgetful."

Joyce had a noble, dignified face, despite the contrast between the taut skin of her cheeks and the crow's feet fanning around her eyes. She was a young-looking not-so-young woman.

Her mother hadn't been very cautious. She left her necklaces and rings in plain sight; nothing was kept under lock and key.

"You bet, that was her all right. We begged her to have her jewelry appraised and then store it in a safe deposit box. The housecleaners stole things from her. And I would say, 'Mom, when are you going to learn?' And she would say, 'What do you expect, they're poor, we should be helping them out.' As if her calling in life was to be there for them to rob her."

Rafael Fernandez thought briefly about the period of his life when he had gotten into petty theft. He was only twelve years old and was trying to help his parents, who were undocumented workers in a maquiladora in Calexico, California. His shoplifting career hadn't lasted long, though. In fact, as a boy in Mexicali he had dreamed of becoming a police officer. Rafael was crestfallen when he found out that these agents of the public good were the same racketeers who visited his father's liquor store every last Friday of the month and threatened to close him down if he didn't pay extortion money. The situation eventually spiraled out of control and an "accidental" fire stripped his parents of everything they owned. That was why they had decided to cross the border. A few months later, in the United States, Rafael knew there was no going back for him, this was his new and his only country.

Before leaving the room, Fernandez asked Joyce if she'd seen anyone suspicious lurking around her mother's house: a gardener, a housekeeper, someone capable of murder?

Joyce looked up at him reluctantly, as if all she wanted from him was the promise that he'd find his mother's killer. But she seemed to think twice and realized it wasn't worth making such an obvious request.

"Please let me know if you think of anything else," Fernandez said.

Smits was waiting for him on the landing of the stairs.

"The press is outside," he said. "We have to give a statement. They need some sort of feed."

Fernandez thought it might be best if the case were assigned to someone else. He'd have one less reason to feel guilty if he didn't find the killer. He was haunted by the ghosts of so many people whose murders were left unresolved. The architect who was stabbed to death by one of his partners, who ended up walking for lack of evidence to prove the crime; the young Norwegian girl whose cadaver was found near the train tracks in Landslide. They didn't even have a suspect!

"Tell them the investigation is ongoing, there are a number of leads, same old thing."

"I can do better," Smits said. "How about we tell them the truth. No suspects. The killer disappeared as if the goddamn earth had swallowed him whole. He's invisible."

"That would only pique their morbid curiosity."

"Well ain't that the idea?"

Maybe the captain was right. It wasn't the police's mission to calm the frenzied populace, assure them that order would be restored. These were troubled times, and to keep ahead of the game, the police needed to put pressure on public opinion, make people feel unsafe, encourage them to report prowlers in their neighborhood, awaken the fervor of the mob that would lynch a stranger for being an outsider.

He said goodbye to Smits, told him he'd check in at the morgue before going back to Landslide, and asked to be kept informed.

5

Ciudad Juárez; various US cities, 1985–1988

Jesús kept taking jobs on the other side of the border. At first they waited for him to cross and had the cars ready for him to drive back over. Eventually he was expected to steal them himself. Braulio trusted his ability, he'd seen him work in the body shop taking cars apart, opening the doors, and starting them up without needing keys.

Before long he became the consummate thief. Pickups and SUVs were trickier for him at first, but after a while they were a piece of cake too.

Jesús took advantage of his work to explore the country. He roamed around jumping freight trains, a blue canvas bag in tow, the kind tennis players use to carry their rackets, wearing his lucky gray blazer, no matter how soiled.

One of his favorite routes went to central California. Often he'd pass through Dening, Tucson, Yuma, Palm Springs, and Los Angeles before heading north by Bakersfield through Stockton. Other times he'd go from Bakersfield to Albuquerque and on to Gallup, Flagstaff, and Barstow. He also liked to travel toward the Great Lakes. To do that, he first went to Landslide and continued north to Dallas, Texarkana, and Little Rock to St. Louis, a sort of home base from where he would head over to Chicago and Detroit. At first he wasn't very interested in the names of the places he visited, but he started memorizing the itineraries because everything was easier when he knew where he wanted to go and the times the trains came and went.

If he got to a town or a city by night, he would jump off the train and look for empty homes to burgle, pinching jewelry and objects that he could carry easily in his pockets. He sold them in pawnshops and kept a few things that he particularly liked for himself.

At times he was tempted to break in when he noticed students at home, or an old lady by herself. He'd break in to burgle, but the robbery was a mere excuse for what really attracted him: the women who ignored him when they saw him loitering in a train station or a supermarket. Gringas who couldn't stand the fact that he was alive. How easy it would be to get rid of them. It was a powerful temptation, but he kept it in check. He didn't want to get into any trouble.

He looked for places to eat for free, churches, soup kitchens, and Salvation Army stores. He practiced his rudimentary English with the priests and volunteers who aided him or with the hobos and beggars who sat with him at the table. He followed as much of the 49ers season as he could.

Migra agents arrested him one time when his train stopped in Brownsville. They opened the boxcar doors and pointed their guns at him; Jesús was asleep on the floor and woke up startled and shaken. They cuffed him and dragged him into the office. They asked his name, entered the false information he gave them into a computer, and announced that they were deporting him back to Mexico.

"What's your real name, son?"

Jesús María José González Reyes. But he would never tell them that, not ever.

"Jesús González Riele."

That's a good name. He also went by Reyle, Reyles.

They told him he was lucky, he was just a kid. "But don't be stupid and go trying it again, boy. Better not push your luck."

One of the agents wrote in his incident report: "Arrested teenager illegally hopping freight train in the US. Deported him to Mexico through Brownsville."

The experience didn't intimidate him at all; by the time he was back in Juárez, all Jesús could think about was going back. Now he knew there was very little risk of being sent to prison, even if they arrested him again. The worse thing that could happen was that he'd be escorted to the border and deported. But they'd feed him and give him a place to sleep. Not so bad.

It wasn't long before the police caught him again, riding a freight train in Sterling Heights, Michigan. Three drunks had jumped the boxcar he was traveling in, and they drew attention. Jesús gave them another false name: José Reisel González: since there was no register for that name, the police sent him to McAllen. The Migra in McAllen deported him to Mexico a few weeks later.

Jesús was enthusiastic about both encounters because it allowed him to speak to the police in English. He had a long conversation about Jerry Rice with one of the agents. The agent was surprised: "I thought all you dudes like is soccer down there." "Soccer is for sissies," Jesús responded, and the agent laughed and patted him on the back.

By now he was beginning to understand a little better how the country worked inside the border. It was like a huge, clumsy giant. And like all giants, it had certain vulnerabilities that weren't immediately obvious. But when you uncovered one, it was easy to take advantage of it. When a policeman saw in him the eyes of a frightened child, they could be moved to sympathy. The old ladies, the young couples, they practically left their doors open so that Jesús could do his business. The pawnshops never asked him for documents. The government claimed that they had tightened measures against immigrants, the country wouldn't stand for an invasion of illegals, but he never felt any restrictions. Despite how much they complained, the country needed people like him. They preferred to look away instead of arresting him.

He still suffered bouts of dread, but at least the apocalyptic visions of fires and floods that had beleaguered him for such a long time no longer tormented him. He might even find it in himself to reconcile with María Luisa. What might she be up to now?

In Juárez, Jesús went out most of the time: the round of taverns, the Plaza Monumental bullring, or the dog races. He watched wrestling on television and went wild when he saw how Mil Máscaras cut the ponytail off some *idiota* who had tried to provoke him.

One day Miguel, a coworker from Braulio's auto body shop, told him he didn't like wrestling.

"It's all fake, hermano, just playacting. I mean, you can't possibly believe all those chokeholds, cross-bodies, and flying kicks are real and not staged ahead of time. It's a good show *a veces*, but nothing more than that, güey. The Arena Mexico capitalists meet the wrestling dudes before the show and they all decide who's going to win, what moves they'll do, and when. Get it?"

Jesús pushed Miguel to the ground and started kicking him. The other mechanics had to jump in and separate them.

The next day, Braulio chewed him out and told him he didn't want problems between his employees. He forced him to apologize.

Eventually, though, Jesús realized Miguel was right, and it ruined everything. Now he watched the same wrestlers on television and tried to enjoy the show, but it wasn't the same anymore. Mil Máscaras circling the ring, his aerial technique, the signature throw, that special hold . . . Now he felt cheated. He'd been such a devoted fan for so many years, only to find that in the end it was nothing but a big sham. Like movie stars. Better to cheer on Jackie Chan.

He took his masks from the closet, stacked them one on top of the other, doused them with kerosene, threw a match, and felt better watching them burn.

He starting running with a group of *chavos* called Los Satánicos, who squatted in an abandoned house in Colonia Bellavista. They had pool tables, foosball, and a jukebox on the first floor; Jesús sniffed glue, listened to heavy metal turned up full blast, and frequented the whorehouses on Mariscal and Acacia Streets. He also went to cantinas looking for chamacas from the maquiladora who were living on their own. There were a few rapes. He said it was their fault for flirting with him and then trying to act all prissy.

He got liquored up, smoked weed.

He sold the hot jewelry in Revolution Mall and hid the money in a locker at the main bus station; he kept some clothes there too, and a pistol he had nicked in Detroit.

He spent three weeks a month across the border in the summer. He stole a new car every two weeks; the rest of the time he traveled around in freight cars, robbing bigger and bigger houses. That's how he came across the pistols. He bought drugs with some of the money. He quit smoking weed and cultivated a cocaine habit. His face swelled, and his cheeks got red and blotchy. He sweated a lot at night and started having visions of fire and rain, gaping abysses that opened on the earth's surface.

One time he cut a finger while breaking a window to burgle a house. He stared, hypnotized, at the oozing blood, letting the coppery odor carry him away; he put his finger in his mouth and it tasted like metal. He improvised a bandage to stop the bleeding by tearing the pocket off his shirt, but all it did was make him realize how much he craved new blood. He threw the strip of cloth away and decided not to enter the house.

Jesús was making an effort to keep his darker, more violent impulses under control. He'd been choosing empty homes deliberately. He noticed how much harder it was to restrain himself now. Robbing cars and homes was too easy, it didn't give him the same buzz, that cold euphoria of having a knife in hand, about to end some useless person's life. Deadwood.

Someone had given him a mission; he was doing what he was meant to do.

One summer he jumped a freight train to Florida. It ran slower than usual, which allowed him to jump off a number of times, raid houses, and jump back onto the same train on its way out of town.

The train had stops in St. Petersburg, Boca Raton, Fort Lauderdale, West Palm Beach.

He rented a locker in the West Palm Beach station to stash some necklaces and other trinkets along with the stolen cash, and jumped the train to Miami.

Jesús finally hopped off again at around six p.m., as it was riding through a neighborhood on the outskirts of the city. It didn't take him long to find an empty home. It was a wooden two-story residence painted sage green with a fussy manicured lawn.

The automatic garage door had been left open, which gave Jesús an easy way in. There was a dented red Toyota in the garage and space for another car; maybe they'd gone shopping or out for dinner? There was a lawnmower on one side, and two yellow bicycles, carpentry tools piled high on an aluminum shelf. The trashcan was full, there were random things lying around, tote bags from a shopping mall, a drawer full of last year's Christmas decorations.

He scanned the photographs in fancy metal frames hanging on the first-floor wall. She was brown-skinned with jet-black hair, a little on the plump side. Her eyes were the exact shape of almonds. He was a freckly blond, tall and athletic (he was playing tennis in a number of the photos).

The living room was equipped with a stereo system and television. They had a whole collection of horror movies on DVD with a particularly robust selection of Dracula and Wolfman films. There were CDs of Gloria Estefan and the Miami Sound Machine, Luis Miguel, and Stevie Wonder.

In the second-floor office he read their credentials hanging on the wall: she was a dentist, he an ophthalmologist. Their computer screensaver showed a photo of the two of them sitting in a boat, beholding a violet-tinged sunset.

Jesús walked into the master bedroom.

He had only taken a few steps when suddenly a figure jumped up from the bed and ran to a door on his right and slammed it shut. It was a woman. He immediately shot after her and grabbed the handle of the bathroom door before she could lock it. He charged her, tried to knock her to the floor, but she slipped away and ran back into the bedroom. Jesús turned around and followed her.

He felt something crack his head. The impact sent him reeling and he collapsed, dazed. He tried to stand up but couldn't: the woman pounced on him, biting and yanking his hair. Jesús had to fight hard to get free of her. He was smaller than she was, but stronger. He shoved her as hard as he could and managed to escape. He got to his feet, panting. She ran for the stairs, screaming hysterically, and grabbed a bat; he took off after her.

Then he lost her. Could she have run to a neighbor's home?

Jesús grabbed the car keys that were on the dresser by the phone. He ran to the garage and opened the Toyota's door. He jostled the key in the ignition and the motor turned with a cough of shocked gears. He backed out of the garage hesitantly. Where was he going to go?

Just out of the driveway, he turned right and drove for three blocks until coming to an intersection with a main road, where he took a left. The signs and traffic lights aggravated him; they were all around him, pointing in every direction. Nothing compared to the easy riding of a freight train, where everything else moved while he lay stationary on the ground watching the parade of landscapes blinking through the slits in the door. Usually Jesús drove only in familiar territory, a few streets in cities he knew intimately, and the freedom of the highway.

The police stopped him a few hours later on the outskirts of Miami. He had driven ninety miles.

Two months later, a Florida state court found Jesús guilty of aggravated assault, breaking and entering, and grand theft auto. He was lucky: they didn't connect him to his prior crimes in Texas.

He was sentenced to twenty years, his exact age at the time.

6

Landslide, 2008

I was working on a new version of "Luvina" with zombies when my cell phone rang. It was Fabián. "Am I interrupting you? If so, I can call back later."

"You won't call back later. What's up?"

"Just reminiscing. Want to come over?"

It was midnight; I had already dressed for bed, in shorts and a T-shirt, and the lights were out except for my desk lamp. The day in Taco Hut had been exhausting; after a restorative nap I had just gone back to work.

I asked if he was OK.

"It depends. I had a few gin-tonics and they went straight to my head."

"Oh, that's it."

"That's not only it."

He could have tried harder to justify the phone call.

"I'll be there in half an hour."

I hung up.

The front door was slightly ajar when I arrived. It was raining: the leaves of the plants in the yard were slick and shiny. I got off my bike and stepped in a few puddles along the gravel path that led to the porch and got my boots muddy—being back in this territory that had once been mine gave me the jitters.

The house was over a century old. It had been restored a decade ago, but even so the wood floor and the walls never stopped creaking. Woodstock, Fabián's ash-colored cat, looked at me apathetically from its perch on the front porch. I took my boots off and left them on the mat; Fabián's black bicycle was in the stairway entry, and I leaned my bike against the wall. The kitchen light was on, but nobody was on the ground floor, which wasn't unusual since Fabián only came down when he wanted to cook something. I nearly bounded up the stairs. I could hear Billie Holiday's wistful voice coming from the room at the end of the hall, crooning a song of unrequited, flawed love, the kind of song that Fabián knew by heart.

He was sitting on the bed staring at a pile of books on the coffee table. He looked up and saw me, though I'm not sure he actually registered my presence. His eyes went back to the coffee table. I slowly looked around the room, checking to see if everything was still in place, whether my absence had changed anything. There were the blurred telescope shots of a lunar eclipse and comet. The *Saturday Evening Post* cover from 1932, with the Norman Rockwell illustration of a little girl who is drawing. Fabián collected examples of "meta" in diverse art forms: drawings of drawing, texts that referred to another.

There were two table clocks on the nightstand, the one from his bedroom and the other from the living room, both of which were smashed to bits. "What's up with that?" I asked, pointing at them.

"The incessant ticking was driving me nuts, so I clutched a hammer. Then I realized how idiotic it was. Time still goes on.

The underlying message was that perhaps I shouldn't sleep. Seriously, never, ever sleep. Three, four hours a day and that's it. Things may be tough when I'm awake, but when I close my eyes it's worse. So between one bad thing and the other, maybe the best thing would be to keep my eyes open. But don't be concerned; I'll do my best to let you sleep."

His eyes held the tired promise of someone who is trying to be charming but knows deep down that he's no longer able to engage in these games, who doesn't believe his own words or gestures because they're no more than the exercise of habit, activated by the body's memory. There had been nights when his flirting brought results. But I didn't want to open myself to melancholy, so I erased the images from my mind.

Fabián twitched his nose as if he were rearranging his nostrils and lay back on the bed. I walked over to a chair that had a stack of books on it, moved them to the floor, and sat down.

"You have an awful lot of books for someone who thinks they're a bunch of crap. You could use a Kindle."

"Habit is the hardest thing to break. Once I finish my manuscript, I'll never crack another book in my life."

"No reason to be so categorical."

"Why not? It's the only way to get somewhere in life."

"My, aren't we being earnest tonight."

"Don't fuck with me, peanut," he said and pulled a baggie full of white powder from under his pillow. "I thought it would take you longer to get here. Here," he said patting the bed. "Lie down next to me. There's space, even if there isn't space."

"So we can both look up at the ceiling?"

The storm shook the walls. A bolt of lightning lit up the night sky, and through the window I saw a flash of the trees in the neighbors' yard, their branches thrashing about like dueling swordsmen.

I needed Fabián to show some sort of deep feeling toward me, even if that feeling was negative. But I knew he was toying with me, that what moved him was indifference at best, disguised as cordiality. Any passion in him had gone into deep freeze a long time ago. I had to figure out how to make sure the same thing didn't happen to me, how not to allow my feelings for Fabián—a mixture of desire and rage—to turn into some personal myth that overwhelmed the other areas of my life.

He handed me the baggie. "Want some?" I didn't want any, no, but why is it always so hard for me to say no to him? I dropped the baggie on the table, cut a few lines on a magazine, and snorted them.

"Oh dear, dear little Michelle. She who still believes in literature. In the novel. In poetry! I had that kind of faith once. Do you remember that poem by Martí? The poet worked at night, by candlelight. And Cuba passed before his eyes like a black widow. He asks whether he'll have to choose between Cuba or the poem. Or are they one and the same thing? I thought they were the same. I once believed they were the same."

"They aren't."

"But Martí realized that words were insufficient. And for that reason he turned his back on literature and went in search of freedom for his people, and death, on horseback. And that's how he found what he was looking for."

My nose burned.

"I don't get what you want to achieve. For nearly a decade you've been reading all the books you can get your hands on, in order to concoct a complete theory. That tells me that you haven't lost faith yet. So you don't like the novel as a form, so what? García Canclini, Sarlo, Ludmer, González Echevarría, Molloy, they're the stuff of literature too. Their theories are pure fiction. And when it comes down to it, what does it really matter anyway?"

He sighed. "You know something? I've always considered myself paranoid, yet I never went so far as to think there was a reason that certain things were happening to me here. But now I do. The deans are against me and they've decided to make my life miserable."

"Oh, so they're crazy?"

Fabián had trouble getting up. I followed him into the living room. This was the same room where he tried to teach me how to tango a while ago, and we couldn't stop laughing at how clumsy we both were. We used to watch DVDs here and give tireless play-by-plays (he introduced me to the work of Lucrecia Martel and Philippe Garrel, and I pestered him into watching everything by Miyazaki and the new *Battlestar Galactica*). I shouldn't let myself get carried away by such memories. The past is not a good map for the present, I tried to remind myself, and yet . . .

"Oh, they have cause, yes. But not enough to put a tap on my phone."

"What are you looking for? Can I help you with something?"

"I have to go out, will you wait here for me?"

"You're crazy, where could you possibly be going at this time of night, and in this weather? And why would the deans want to do something like that?"

"I have to see a friend. The deans take my trash in the mornings to analyze what I've eaten, written, and bought."

"I'm sorry, I'm not going to let you go out there. What do

you mean, your trash? Why would they do something like that?"

"Because I'm too good to be here," he said as he tied the laces of his brown suede shoes with the black spots. "They don't want to give me the raise I deserve, and prefer to fuck me over instead of letting me go to a better university than this piece of shit one. Come morning, the previous night's trash is always gone."

"It's called a garbage truck. Maybe you forgot that you had taken it to the curb for pickup because you took it out so late. I saw you take your trash out at times when you were exhausted and half-asleep."

"The garbage truck comes around once a week, get it?"

"Got it. And no. Maybe you did something to seriously aggravate the deans?"

"Oh knock it off, you feisty little girl." I could see the tremble in his lips. "If you doubt me, there's the door. Unless you're a spy."

The lights went out in the house. I walked over to the window. There was a blackout in the whole neighborhood.

"Are you going to blame the deans for this too?"

"Why not? Anything's possible."

"Whatever, Fabián. I'm on your side, I just want you to finish your book and . . ."

The lights came back on around the neighborhood. Fabián sighed.

"Oh, all my theories, my big book. You're truly on my side, huh? If anything gets out, I'll know who the traitor is. There's my book. Read it. Tell me what you think."

There was a manuscript on the desk. I laughed cautiously but was excited.

"Seriously? You're letting me?"

I picked the manuscript up and held it on my lap. I quickly calculated about five hundred pages. I read the title: "Regarding the Absent Everything."

The first paragraph was somehow familiar to me, like a paraphrased excerpt from *Facundo*, which I'd read in Fabián's class my first semester in Landslide. The second paragraph changed rhythm abruptly, and the prose seemed to want to capture an oral cadence, Fabián's voice. I remember when we studied the testimonies of nineteenth-century Cuban slaves in his class, how they struck a certain rhythm in the body of the text. The voice was close on the subject, and for that reason, testimony is the narrative discourse par excellence.

I allowed myself to be carried away by the rhythm of the prose. It was like being transported to one of Fabián's classes. Then it dawned on me. It wasn't merely a good attempt; it was a literal transcription of one of Fabián's classes. He always carried a tape recorder with him during his classes, and the first thing he did was turn it on and set it on the desk.

It went on like that until page 83. Two, three, four classes, one after the other. Next came a list of last names. First A, then B . . . I jumped to page 115. 271. 362. 420. It was a copy of the Landslide white pages.

"I don't understand. I don't get it."

"That's all there is. All the truth I wish to tell."

"But the book you've been writing . . ."

"Utopia: there's no such place."

"So much for all the excuses. You never had time for anything else. I had to let the genius work in peace."

I threw the manuscript on the floor. He walked out onto the balcony. It was one of his favorite places, we used to sit there and talk while he showed me everything he'd planted in the yard. One plant after another until there was no more space— lush vegetation that today I imagined pulled up or withered.

A few minutes passed. Fabián didn't come back, so I walked over toward the balcony. Fabián stumbled in. He shouted for me to get out of the way, and then he shoved me and started insulting me. I wasn't in the mood for drama, so I bolted down the stairs, grabbed my bike, and left. Fabián called my cell phone but I didn't answer. He left apologetic messages.

Things were fine until the calls stopped. I started to think that I might have been too hard on him, too awkward and proud. Should I call him back? Maybe I should go back over to his house.

I tried to write but couldn't concentrate. I tried to put myself in Fabián's shoes, comprehend his feelings of despair, imagine myself sitting in front of a laptop for years, incapable of moving forward on my book. I failed. Lying on the sofa, I picked up an anthology by the Hernandez brothers and flipped through the pages as I waited for my cell phone to ring.

My dreams were restless that night.

7

Starke, Florida, 1988–1994

Jesús spent his first night in the Starke, Florida, prison with three other men. Their skin was covered in tattoos; they hadn't shaved for days and stank to high heaven. They talked among themselves, and when he entered the cell they had looked at him askance but didn't say a word. Why would he have been put in the same cell as them?

He lay back in his assigned bunk. He felt cold; they had taken his blazer away and told him they'd put it in a bag and give it back when he got out. In exchange, they gave him an orange uniform. He wanted his blazer back.

One of the men approached him and spat at his feet. He smiled at Jesús but kept still. There was no use picking a fight; they were burly men, he was better off avoiding a scuffle. Much of his cunning lay in his ability to discern when to attack and when to get lost in a crowd, avoid drawing attention to himself. Fighting was justified only when he was sure he could win. What about the incident in Miami? That was something different, the woman had surprised him in the bedroom. It was a costly mistake for Jesús. Let it serve as a lesson: never let your guard down.

He looked down at his hands. A twenty-year sentence. Sons

of bitches, it was overkill. How the fuck am I going to survive in this place for such a long time? He wanted to keep his spirits up, but it wasn't easy. He might disappear and nobody would be the wiser. His mother must have given him up for dead by now; María Luisa had gone on with her life without him. Anyone else would have done the same. And Papá? What had become of him? Maybe he's in a different prison in this country that's as wide as it is foreign.

A shiver ran through his body. A chilly wave that rolled down from his head to his feet, like an ocean swell of anxiety, of panic. He needed a few lines.

It was a windowless cell. The bars on the door were made of reinforced iron. He was used to coming and going as he pleased, right through houses, through cars. This place was a whole different story.

There was a constant murmur running through the building. Sudden screams from other cells, moaning, shrieking, the loudspeakers barking commands or instructions. He wouldn't be able to sleep.

That's what he was thinking when he closed his eyes and fell asleep.

Around two in the morning, a disturbing feeling woke him up. He opened his eyes enough to peek through his eyelid slits. From the darkness he could just barely make out the presence of someone kneeling beside his bed. One of the men was sucking his dick. He tried to sit up and scream, but the other two men covered his mouth and held his hands down. Someone punched him in the eye. His sight clouded and little strings of blood dripped down his face. The pain was intense, as if they had broken a bone. His right eye swelled shut.

A few more punches knocked him to the floor, where he received a barrage of kicks. He tried to protect his face but it was useless. His lips were split and bleeding.

He was still conscious when they pulled his clothes off and turned him over. He felt like screaming when the first cock penetrated him violently, but he knew the guards would never come. He had been put in the cell intentionally. This was how they initiated newcomers.

He lost consciousness when the third man sodomized him.

The majority of Starke's three thousand prisoners were black. Cubans predominated among the Latino population. In the shower one morning, two of them took turns raping him. Jesús didn't resist this time; at least he was spared a beating like the one he got that first night.

The guards rarely intervened in rapes or brawls. He used to think he was strong and agile, but not in prison. Nearly everyone lifted weights, and they were tough and muscular. Jesús was easy prey. He was in no condition to confront anyone: he was taken to the infirmary after the first night and given three stitches in his right eye. He could hardly open either one.

One morning a guard approached him and told him in Spanish that he could offer "protection." Jesús asked what that entailed. The guard, named Orlando, took him to a utility room full of cleaning utensils. He told him to drop his pants and sit down on a plastic drum. The guard sucked him off.

Jesús closed his eyes and let him.

His sleep was terrible. The slightest noise would wake him up. When new prisoners arrived, it prompted memories of his own first night and he would start shaking uncontrollably.

He was finally transferred to his own cell during his third week in Starke, but he couldn't relax.

Orlando got him an appointment in the infirmary. There was a photo of President Bush on one of the walls, and posters of *Saturday Night Fever* and the 49ers on another. Jesús sat on the examination table and waited.

The doctor who attended him knew Spanish, though Jesús made an effort to speak in English. Orlando had told him that everything would be easier if he could speak English. The rapes hadn't ceased altogether, but at least they had dwindled in frequency.

Jesús pointed at the 49ers poster. "Joe Montana is great," he said.

"Really? I prefer baseball. I don't know who put that poster up."

"*Qué?*"

"So what's your problem, son?"

"I not sleep. Everything hurt me."

"Where does it hurt?"

"Everything."

"You mean everywhere."

"Yes."

Jesús let out a gush of words in a confusing blend of Spanish and English. He told the doctor everything that had happened to him since arriving in Starke that first night. He gestured with his hands to make himself understood and opened his eyes as wide as he could to show how he couldn't sleep. He pantomimed unzipping his pants to explain the rapes. "Violate," he shouted over and over again. "I raped!"

The doctor had a hard time understanding him, but the

panicked expression on Jesús's face conveyed everything he needed to know. He took pity on Jesús and gave him pills for the anxiety, and to help him sleep. He told Jesús to hide them carefully and not to abuse them. He removed the stitches from his right eye.

Jesús considered suicide several times. He witnessed brawls between rival gangs that left prisoners toothless and with stab wounds; every night the gangs pulled out all kinds of new weapons, regardless of how often the guards inspected the cells, from rudimentary knives made with wire or pieces of metal to pistols that had been smuggled in during a visit.

He saw a prisoner stab a guard with a screwdriver; the blood spurting from the guard's chest prompted him to think that skin is just a wrapper holding the red liquid inside. Mesmerized, he watched it gathering in a puddle on the floor. It made him miss having his knife, the thrill of puncturing other bodies, making them burst like tires.

Jesús saw one of the burly, tattooed guys from his first night push a black prisoner from the second floor. His head split open on impact. Jesús was given the task of cleaning up the blood and wiping the floor down with a cloth and alcohol. He couldn't help stopping when he came across little pieces of brain, and staring at them for a while. How easy it was to break through someone's skin and spill out everything that's inside.

Jesús saw people being raped frequently. He was forced to have sex. At least now he didn't do it for free; he'd learned how to get things in return, like food or protection.

He spent most of his time in his cell. He learned that the 49ers were invincible in their bid for the Super Bowl; they'd only lost two games—against the Falcons and the Rams. Montana and Rice were having an outstanding season. He drew a portrait of María Luisa on a sheet from a paper roll and stuck it to the wall. At night he masturbated thinking of her. Orlando asked who she was, and he said my wife.

"Does she know you're here?"

"Ain't talked to her in many years, *buey*."

"I could help get a letter to her. Or a message. Whatever. Just tell me where to find her and it's done."

Jesús thought about it. "Is OK," he said, "don't worry. She no cared about me these years, I no care neither."

"It's a big country, man. You're like a needle in a haystack. Even if she looked, it wouldn't be easy to find you."

He had given an alias when they arrested him. Someone in the consulate had asked him for next of kin to communicate his detention. Jesús said he didn't have any family.

The medicines helped him feel better. He stopped having suicidal thoughts. The dreams came back again: he was the sole survivor in a world where ash rained down and the rivers flowed with blood.

They'd release him for good behavior before he served his full twenty-year sentence. Maybe even before serving ten if he was lucky. Then they'd see who it was they'd been fucking with. They'd be sorry for pissing him off.

He'd make them all pay for humiliating him, and it'd be a bitch.

The 49ers took the Super Bowl that year (they were down 16–13 in the last quarter, but then Montana threw a ten-yard pass to Taylor and clinched it).

A year went by. Two years (the 49ers won the Super Bowl again, 55–10 against the Broncos), and a third (the Giants eliminated the 49ers in the playoffs).

During his fourth year in Starke, Jesús worked his way into the protection of a white supremacist from the Aryan Brotherhood named Randy. By that time the photo of Bush in the infirmary had been replaced by one of Bill Clinton.

Jesús knew that Randy was one of the leaders of the Brotherhood, the most powerful and feared gang in Starke; they controlled the drug smuggling and responded viciously when anyone dared to encroach on their territory. At lunchtime Jesús would line up behind Randy in the cafeteria and do things like offer to pick up anything that fell to the floor. Randy appreciated how naturally Jesús accepted his subservience. He was lanky, with bad teeth and tattoos covering his arms and back. He wore studs in his lips and nose.

Once the prison guards and other prisoners saw Jesús hanging around Randy several times—in the prison yard they were two contrasting figures, a tall blond beside a short, brown-skinned *cholo*—they didn't dare mess around with him. In exchange for Randy's protection, Jesús had sex only with him. The members of the Brotherhood made fun of Jesús: they found out his name was Jesús María José, and so they started calling him María. María the Spic they called him, and he would try to correct them: "I no Puerto Rican." "María Speedy," they said, and Jesús accepted the nickname.

One afternoon Randy asked him if he believed in God.

"I not stop believing," Jesús responded. "But I don't go to mass for long time."

"For Christ's fucking sake, bro, a name like you got, you should be behaving a hell of a lot better! Lemme show you a little bit about fucking God. Follow me, Speedy."

Randy led him to the chapel beside the infirmary, a tiny room that smelled like jasmine room freshener. A Christ whose legs and arms were just a tad too long hung on a wooden cross above the altar. Prayers written by prisoners begging for intercession were painted along the green walls.

Randy sat down on a pew, Jesús sat beside him.

"This world is the work of a lesser God," Randy said looking him hard in the eyes. "Ain't no other explanation for it. And the lesser God—he don't have a name, see? He's the Unnamed."

Randy unzipped his fly.

"You want here? *Por favor*, no here."

Randy grabbed Jesús by the nape of his neck and shoved his head into his crotch until Jesús's lips gave and encased his cock. It was meaty, covered in black spots like a birthmark.

"Repeat after me, Speedy. Our Unnamed Father who art *not* in heaven."

"Our Unnamed Father who art *not* in heaven," Jesús said. He shut his eyes and let his tongue tickle Randy's dick cautiously; he knew how Randy liked it.

"Holy be the absence of your name."

"Holy be . . . the absence of . . . urmph . . . your name."

"Thy kingdom of blood come."

"Thy kingdom . . . of blood come."

"Thy will be done."

"Thy . . . will be . . . done."

Randy pressed down hard on Jesús's neck so that his mouth sucked in the whole cock down to its base. Jesús was blowing him, trying to concentrate on what Randy was saying. It was hard to breathe.

"On earth as it is without heaven."

"On earth as it is without heaven," Jesús repeated and got stuck midsentence.

"Give us this day our daily bread!" Randy said in a threatening tone, and Jesús knew he had better not make a mistake with the following sentence. He lifted his head a little and said:

"Give us this day our daily bread."

"Forgive us not our trespasses."

He moved up and licked the tip of his penis, stopped.

"Forgive us not our trespasses."

"As we do not forgive those who trespass against us."

"As we . . ."

He got stuck again, but then continued: "we do not . . . forgive those who urmph . . . trespass . . . against us."

"Lead us into temptation."

"Lead us into temptation."

"And do not deliver us from evil."

"And do not deliver us from evil."

When he finished, Jesús spat Randy's cum out and wiped the spittle from his inflamed lips with the back of his hand. Randy zipped up his fly and started laughing, his mouth gaping like a black hole that could swallow Jesús whole. He clutched his stomach as if it hurt. He made such a racket that one of the guards approached and tapped the floor with his billy club to alert Randy of his presence.

"If you don't know how to behave in here," the guard said, "you'll have to leave."

Randy apologized but broke out into hysterical laughter again the second they left the chapel.

Wasn't it a contradiction allowing Jesús to spend the majority of his time with the Aryan Brotherhood when they were ruthless against blacks and Latinos?

"Nah," Randy would say. "They make good slaves."

Jesús thought he was right. He didn't like the blacks, and the Latinos were filthy and abusive, worse than animals. Whenever one of them tried to approach him, he pretended he didn't speak Spanish.

He stopped spending all his time in his cell. His uniform hung loose on his frame since he hardly ate—the gruel they served for dinner made him sick, a blend of chicken, cornbread, and grits—so he started lifting weights and hanging out in the yard during the day.

Thanks to Randy's influence, he began reading books and newspapers from the library. He read about Richard Ramirez, the Night Stalker. Talk about a potent Latino: he'd committed thirteen rapes and murders in California. No compassion for his victims whatsoever. He read up on the First and Second World Wars, about Vietnam. After listening to Randy, he agreed that Hitler was right. He reached the conclusion that wars were necessary for human survival. Life was a constant struggle. Only the strong survived, the most cunning, the best.

"When you get outta the can," Randy told him, "remember to join the Libertarian Party. The government's a piece of shit. They gave niggers too many rights."

That was what he'd do.

When Waco happened, when the FBI killed the leader of the Branch Davidian sect and several children, the Aryan Brotherhood in Starke took it personally. Jesús heard Randy say that it was a big government conspiracy to get rid of powerful white people like them. "They better be prepared for a fight when we get out. We ain't gonna let them rest."

And Sarajevo? Clinton sent planes to the Balkans to take advantage of the war and bomb cities and decimate entire populations. "That's where the whitest races of all came from," Randy explained.

Jesús decided it had been naive of him to think the government ever gave a hoot about them. Randy was right to suspect everything.

He would leave Starke prepared for the coming fight. But which one? The Aryan Brotherhood might be right, but they didn't think much of him. He wasn't really interested in joining their struggle anyway. His interest was merely provisional, circumstantial.

His was a solitary fight. Against the government. Against everyone.

One night Jesús dreamed that a sinister force arose from the deepest part of the darkness and came looking for him. It surrounded him and enveloped him entirely, then stole his heart. His cell lit up with a blinding flash of light. He saw himself covering his eyes and rising from his bunk, while at the same time he could feel himself lying there without moving, without opening his eyes, as if he had split into two.

The energy had no face or body. But it said that he belonged to it now, that he no longer had a will of his own and he had to do what it said. The voice said it was half man and half angel and couldn't die. He told Jesús it was time to prepare for the deluge of fire and ashes to come down, and the rivers of blood that awaited him upon release. He had been sent there to fulfill a mission of purification. This was part of his journey through the desert, in preparation for the final battle.

Jesús woke up trembling and drenched in sweat. He was convinced that he had just been visited by the Unnamed.

He thought about going to talk to the prison chaplain, tell him what happened. No, Jesús thought, he would never understand.

He did tell Randy, who gave him a few pats on the back.

"What a lucky shit, Speedy, Son of fucking Christ! I been waitin ma whole life for the Unnamed to appear. Mysterious are His ways, bro. He goes and calls upon a fucking Mexican. Ain't that just proof of His greatness!"

"What I gotta do, *buey*?"

"Get yerself some toilet paper and write the gospel down same as the Lord shared it with you."

His comment pissed Jesús off: he's making fun of me and thinks I don't know.

Orlando got him a few sheets of rolling paper. He wrote BOOK OF REVELATIONS at the top of one, followed by a few lines describing Unnamed's visit.

It took six years for Jesús to finally be released from Starke Prison on good behavior.

When they gave him back his belongings, the blazer was missing from the bag, so he complained to the officer who walked him to the door. The officer laughed at him and suggested that he file a complaint with the prison director.

The Migra was waiting for him outside, to escort him to the Mexican border for immediate deportation.

THREE

1

Landslide, 2008

Fabián called back several times. I didn't always answer, and when I did, I would barely listen to what he said. The more I rejected his calls, the more fascinated he became. He wrote emails. One of them said: "i love you but i'm not in love with you. i love you but I love many people. i wish I could write poetry and tell you how i feel but i can't. you shouldn't feel bad. someone like you can't feel that way. but maybe you're fine and it's just the wee hours, the three o'clock silence that makes me have these thoughts, or maybe it's the silence of six o'clock, because there are silences and there are silences, and nothing matters to me as much as you do." Another one read: "angst, my companion, but i survived and that's why i'm prepared for the abyss. i have little faith and plenty of reasons. it's what destroys me because i want to be with you."

And that's how we started meeting in cafés again and going to bookstores together—in Comics for Dummies we bought bound collections of Betty Boop and Krazy Kat—and got lost in the dive bars on Sixth Street that always reeked of weed. He would show up for lunch at Taco Hut and interact with my coworkers (Osvaldo was Panamanian and tempted to join the army; Sabrina came from Lubbock and read Nora Roberts novels on her break; Mike made fun of Fabián's accent and was obsessed with Faith Hill).

Once I prepared a *majao* for him with dried beef my mother sent to me. It wasn't as tasty as the ones my Aunt Vicenta prepared in Santa Cruz, but Fabián seemed to like it, and luckily he'd never tried the dish before to know the difference. We went to the movies one Saturday at the university theater, bought the biggest bucket of popcorn they had with an XL Coke, and watched a double feature of Hitchcock movies, sneaking furtive kisses in the darkness. Thanks to those rare moments of fulfillment, I slipped back into the world I had abandoned, back to a place where the man I was so desperately attracted to would spend days at a time in bed, struggling to control his panic attacks, and others when he would return to his office and his writing desk, determined to reimmerse himself in his work, still teetering on the verge of a collapse.

Sam called to apologize, and I said forget it, but when he suggested we have a coffee I begged off. La Jodida stopped by the restaurant to say hello but then just stood there in silence. I had nothing to say, so she left and then I felt bad.

I tried to develop a storyboard for a piece I had in mind, set in a town of vampires and zombies who coexisted peacefully—except for a few skirmishes between fundamentalist vampires and purist zombies—but then Samantha showed up. I wanted to blend my readings of Hamilton with Rulfo and use a touch of the imagery from the Silent Hill video game. I hadn't figured out yet how to work the perspective with the squares on the page, and the colors; I was trying to innovate, but I didn't quite know how to go about it.

Chuck had recommended a stack of magazines with supernatural themes, variations on superheroes. I drew Samantha wearing black boots up to her knees, a black jacket, and gloves, and thought that what I was really drawing was some man's wet dream. I threw the notebook in the trash. Fabián told me not to get discouraged, my drawings had more spirit to them than before; he kept giving me ideas so that my story would be "truly apocalyptic."

We decided we weren't going to pretend this time around, and attended department receptions together. Konwicki, the Pole, seemed bothered to see me, as if he were making good use of his moral superiority to make assumptions about me (or maybe the reason was simpler, he remembered my paper mocking "Agustín Yañez, precursor to Agamben" the semester I left). I couldn't care less what he thought now; I wasn't a student anymore.

One day when I was in the hallway leaving Fabián's office, Ruth Camacho-Stokes approached and greeted me warmly, as sweet and affable as ever. She was dressed in a red-and-white checked skirt and horrendous orange Crocs. Her shoulder drooped with the weight of a bagful of books from the library. She told me she wanted to give me something.

"I'll never forget those papers you wrote for my class," she said. "Admittedly, they lacked a bit of theoretical depth, but your voice was strong and it made me forgive the other shortcomings. I'm preparing a dossier for the Martín Ramírez exhibit next semester, and I thought you might find the time to write a text inspired by one of his drawings. It doesn't have to be academic, that's why I thought of you."

She pulled a hardcover book out of her bag. It was an expensive coffee-table edition full of color reproductions, some of which were 3-D popouts.

"This might help motivate you."

"To be honest," I steeled myself, "this type of illustration doesn't really appeal to me."

Ruth wouldn't take no for an answer. "Just think about it, maybe you'll come up with something. We have until January, you still have a few months to think it over."

I accepted but without committing myself fully. She smiled and then whispered: "You're good for Fabián, you know, I admire your patience, though as colleagues we've been more lenient with him than we should."

"It must not have been easy. Knowing him to be so brilliant and then, once his wife left him, watching the shipwreck . . ."

She looked at me, flabbergasted.

"Oh that's not the chronology of things, my dear," she sighed. "Fabián left her, it wasn't the other way around. When we hired him, he'd already been having—um—problems, but he could hide it well. His book was published, the reviews were spectacular, and we decided to look the other way. Little by little, we started hearing about some messy stuff going on with Mayra. So yes, the cause and effect gets a little complicated. It's not so easy to decipher, maybe his anxiety is what led him down this path. Maybe it was the early success. Or maybe neither one, maybe it's just something in his personality. We're all addicted to something, aren't we? It's just that some more than others. Who knows?"

After Ruth left, I kept thinking about Mayra. Till then I had thought Mayra was the culprit, the one who'd opened this black hole into which a despairing Fabián had been falling. Now there was a different version: him as perpetrator.

The professor had said she admired my patience. Maybe she really meant something else: she was amazed at my stupidity.

I was sitting on a bench in the Arts Quad, reading *Black Hole* and waiting for Fabián to get out of a meeting, when Sam showed up. His hands were buried in his jacket pockets; he was chewing gum and made an effort to appear unconcerned. I had been avoiding him, trying not to let him get to me, the gloomy unrequited lover bit, his splendid bravura of despair and complete surrender to a lost cause. But it was too late now, I was already infected, we were being cast in similar life roles. And in his case, I was the perpetrator. Maybe I had infected him with my own virus. It made me able to understand him better and not feel so bad; you believe you're praying at the right altar and the strength of your prayers will bring the miracle that transforms reality into what you want it to be.

He told me that Oprah had chosen a novel by Roberto Bolaño as the book of the month. "It'll be good for Latin American literature. Readers will be curious to know what else there is besides Bolaño."

"It will do a lot of good for Bolaño," I said. "Readers will want to read more of his books. This country doesn't allow for more than one 'great foreign writer' at a time. Murakami and Sebald already had their turns."

"You're being unfair."

"Have you seen how they talk about Bolaño?" I responded. "As if he were a Beat writer, a Latin American Kerouac. Always romanticizing. 'In Latin America they are still producing the type of writers this hyper-professionalized country isn't able to because of what's being taught in the thousands of creative writing programs.' It goes something like that. I read it in *Harper's*."

"We're good at creating legends, that's for sure," Sam said. "But also at destroying them. Did you read the *New York Times*?

Now we know that Bolaño didn't shoot heroin and he wasn't in Chile for the Pinochet coup. Pretty soon we'll find out that he never went out, and was more of a bibliophile recluse than Borges. Anyway. I'm thinking about doing my thesis on a chapter of *The Savage Detectives*. When it's published, I'll have to compete with a whole slew of other doctoral theses on Bolaño. I should have been quicker. He's created an industry."

"Bolaño, Inc. A brand name."

He talked about an essay comparing Bolaño with Philip K. Dick, and I remembered some scenes from *Ubik*, though I didn't see any connection between the two writers.

"So, how's he doing," he asked abruptly.

"You're his student. You should know better than me."

"My dear. Your level of dedication never ceases to amaze me. You're blind where he's concerned. Fabián is never going to change. There's no way out, it's been too many years. His colleagues have covered up for him the whole time; they've substituted for him in his classes, kept information from the deans about his cancellations, his missed faculty meetings, forgotten students, unwritten letters of recommendation. People are just fed up, which is understandable."

"He'll publish his book and you'll see how everything is going to change."

"And you'll go live happily ever after in a cabin on a deserted beach in North Vancouver?"

"Don't be mean, Sam."

"And don't tell me it hasn't crossed your mind. How romantic, to run off and live beside someone tormented by the furies. An older man, too. How many years is it? Eleven, twelve?"

I let myself daydream, contemplating my Converse, until he finally changed the subject to his weekly radio program. His analysis of what he called "the psychopathology of everyday violence" in the US had been very popular among his listeners. He drew up a theoretical framework to the discussion, composed of the usual suspects: Freud and the death drive, Nietzsche and the Superman, Sade and Bataille and the attraction to evil. But the listeners really got hooked on the program's tabloid feature, the way Sam covered the most extreme cases of serial killers and school mass murderers. His most popular program had been the one dedicated to Columbine.

"The listeners began a discussion about whether a fifteen-year-old boy, even one as dedicated to evil as Eric Harris, could truly be considered a psychopath. I tried to stay out of it, but to me it's obvious that he is one. Cultural conditioning of course plays a role, but in cases like Harris's, nature is so strong there's no way of treating the psychopathy."

"Why don't you ever talk about your thesis with this kind of enthusiasm? Maybe you should change your project."

"Too late. I'll be good, finish my thesis, and when I'm finally hired, I'll teach classes with titles like 'Killing Machines' and force my students to read *Natural Born Killers*, and I'll give quizzes with questions about who was the Railroad Killer or what is *The Book of God*."

"Why not? To each his own."

I wish we had been able to find more subjects like that, things we felt passionate about. He wanted to hurt me with the issue of age, but I'd already dealt with it a long time ago and had to admit that the difference attracted me. He said nasty things about Fabián, which only succeeded in getting me to defend him to an absurd extreme; why in the world, for example, had I lied about Fabián and his book?

Sam got up, winked at me, and left.

December rolled around, the end of the semester, the temperate part of winter. We spent a weekend together in San Antonio as if we were a normal, stable couple. We stayed at the apartment of a friend who was in Argentina on a research grant. It was a small, minimalist apartment with a futon thrown on the floor and bare walls and science books everywhere, and an empty fridge. Not a single photograph. "He's a strange type," Fabián said. "I met him at college in Buenos Aires. He doesn't like to accumulate things, and I mean neither possessions nor relationships. He makes a lot of money, but his belongings fit in a single bag."

"You should've been more like him. You might have avoided a number of problems."

"Don't think I didn't try. But it's a little too late now, don't you think?"

Fabián was thin and his eyes were sunk deep into his skull; he did what he could to keep his mood light, and devoured his favorite dishes—devil's shrimp, chilaquiles—displaying an appetite I hadn't seen before. He washed it all down with Coke Light and didn't touch any alcoholic beverages.

We spent another weekend with some friends in El Paso (we were surprised to see the waves of Mexicans pouring in from Juárez, trying to escape the cartel wars and the Mexican government's desperate attempts to control them). He returned to teaching, resumed his office hours.

I went back to work in the restaurant, but only part time. I worked the night shift. Luckily I was scheduled along with Mike, who immediately started spouting bad jokes, making me laugh whenever he saw me a little down. When my shift ended, I'd go to Fabián's house. They were wild times, we experimented a lot with uninhibited sex. One morning he asked me to slap him in the face with all my strength; I was surprised but complied. He told me to stop holding back, that I should let myself go. I slapped him hard; his cheek turned a shocking tone of red and I could tell he had liked it.

I knew the whole thing was dangerous, but I hadn't gauged to what extent. I found out one Wednesday when I went to his house from Taco Hut and found him drunk, watching a porno film on television with the volume up full blast. He was lying back in bed without a shirt, his hairless chest dusted with birthmarks. I looked at him and he laughed as if I'd caught him in the middle of a prank.

"Turn that off, please," I said.

"Don't be such a fucking prude. Why don't you come and sit here next to me."

"At least let me turn it down."

"Why? What's there to hide? You remind me of a girl I had in Yale. The poor thing was shocked when she came to my room for the first time and saw a *Sports Illustrated* calendar on my wall and my *Playboy* subscription. As if it were a big deal, for Christ's sake. She said it turned women into objects. We didn't last ten days after that."

On the screen I could see a man lying back on a sofa and a woman dressed only in high-heeled boots jiggling around him.

"Her name is Tory Lane and she's one of the nastiest bitches. You can't imagine the things I've seen her do; once she let them tie her to a cross and penetrate her with a lit candle."

I grabbed the control and turned the television off.

"Some other time this just might be fun, but not now."

"You're more naive than I thought, peanut."

I sat down beside him. On this same bed: him, me, a few years ago. Days I thought were foretelling a new period of happiness and growth in my life. It takes talent to make that big of a mistake, and youthful naiveté that I hadn't lost yet, despite all the discouragement.

He lit a cigarette and set off the smoke alarm. We had to open windows and air the place out.

Fabián started humming a Dylan song.

"Last night I saw myself sitting in a chair beside me," he said suddenly. "I got bigger and then I shrank as if I were made out of sponge. At first I thought I had overdone it with the uppers, but no, it was all me. I wanted to get up and shake my hand but I couldn't. I felt inebriated but I hadn't drunk anything, so I said it would be good to drink something so that my body would feel the same way again, it would balance out. I tried to remember my name, but I couldn't and that scared me, but I remembered other things, like the old watch I had left to be repaired and forgot to pick up a long time ago, when Mayra was still living with me."

"What am I going to do?" he said, and I realized it wasn't a rhetorical question: there was real anguish in his expression. "Seriously, what?"

"You're going to get better. I'm going to help."

"I can ask for a year off and we can go anyplace where there's a beach. I would love to go to Mar del Plata; my parents used to bring me there when I was a kid. You can draw, and I'll watch movies."

"You'll write your book, this time seriously. Go on now, get into bed. I'm feeling so generous tonight that I'll even let you have the whole bed to yourself."

"What about you?"

"Don't worry, I'll sleep on the couch."

He opened the closet and took out a tiny plastic bag. He cut a few lines on the cover of an anthology of new Latin American literature that was on the desk. I sat on the bed, left him to it while I tried to gather my strength. The shadows of the objects in his room seemed to be swelling threateningly.

"Want some? My dealer showed up today, I couldn't say no. It's the good shit at the good price."

I couldn't take it anymore.

"It's either that shit or me," I said, staring at him.

"You're out of your mind. Come on, join me."

"I said I'm done. If you want my help . . ."

"If you put it that way then, sweetheart, it would be best if you left me alone."

I immediately stood up and walked out. I could hear his insults as I walked down the stairs.

"*Cobarde*, go on, just leave. Don't bother coming back till you learn how to fuck, silly bitch."

Once I was on the street, I breathed in the chilly night air and hopped on my bike.

I had to concentrate on my illustrations. On my stories.

He never really loved me. The sooner I accept it, the less time it will take for me to get over him.

And yet.

Three blocks later I stopped. Did I know what I was doing? It didn't matter. I wanted to go back to Fabián's house.

Fabián went back to Buenos Aires three days before Christmas. I went to Houston. I returned to Landslide the day after

Christmas. The restaurant paid a bonus for working during the holiday season, and I needed the money.

The nausea first came a little while after that. I would throw up for no reason at all.

It took me a week to figure out what was happening.

2

Ciudad Juárez, Villa Ahumada, 1994

He'd gone to prison with a slight limp, and it had become more pronounced. Jesús let his hair grow long and a downy mustache had sprouted too, so when he arrived in Juárez wearing grimy, worn-out clothes—dingy coffee-colored boots and a pair of skin-tight jeans he'd been given in a Goodwill store in El Paso—he didn't expect anyone to recognize him. Yet his face and body type were still perfectly identifiable.

Miguel was the only one in the body shop left from back in the day, before he'd gotten lost on the other side. He greeted Jesús warmly and took him to a cantina where a blind fiddler was playing a bolero composed by Agustín Lara to an absent audience. In La Querida—where a sign on the mirror read: "I'll trust you tomorrow"—they drank sotol and caught up. He told Jesús that Braulio's headless body had been discovered one morning in a field. The body hadn't been easy to identify.

"*Qué cabrón.* They say it was a payback hit. Messed up with the cartel. The city's getting more dangerous all the time. Worst thing is the dead ladies they keep finding. Cops say they ain't no clues, bro. Say it's some satanic cult. Like some foreigner's doing it or something."

"Yeah, gotta be a seven-foot-tall albino dude or something.

Didn't they say the Subcomandante was a foreigner too? On account of them blue eyes and shit."

"Guess so. Gotta be more than one dude, though. Nobody can razor up fifty women that way on his own, güey."

The fiddler stopped playing and approached them, extending his hat for some coins. They ignored him.

Jesús rented a room on Guerrero Street. Tony's Burritos (made with watered-down mole) was a block away, in front of Borunda Park, where a rusty Ferris wheel went round and round, squeaking at the hinges. Worms with long coiling tongues and bulging eyes adorned the seats. The bumper cars spat showers of sparks, as if demon drivers were pushing them from behind. The twirling teacups spun so quickly the faces of the people inside looked deformed. Children shot plastic ducks with BB guns, fished in basins that were painted to look like ponds, threw rings at glass bottles.

Jesús liked to ride one of the wooden merry-go-round horses, the bright yellow one with a broken ear. It made him feel like he was suspended in the air, hanging on to the metal pole that skewered the little horse like a pin so it wouldn't get away. The tinkling sound of the music helped liberate his mind, let it wander. From time to time he'd come across a tight bitch and consider stalking her till he could jump her from behind on an empty street and fuck her brains out and gut her with a knife. But then he talked some sense to himself: better not get into trouble, *carajo*, just chill out.

While spinning round and round on the carousel, he thought about what had happened to Braulio, which neither surprised nor hurt him. Fate had its own way of dealing with things; better to let it work itself out. The hardest part, the crucial thing, was finding the voice of fate and listening to it.

Starke belonged to his past now, but what was in store for his future? What to do?

One afternoon he saw the Unnamed sitting on the horse next to his. There were no eyes in the creature's skull-like face, and its mouth was frozen in an expression of perpetual terror, ready to howl in the presence of something much more sinister than itself.

Jesús wanted to jump down but couldn't. Ants with huge pincers for jaws were pouring out of the yellow horse's mutilated ear. He hid his hands behind his back, afraid the ants were going to bite him.

The Unnamed got off the horse and walked in front of him, transformed into the figure of a man with a hat and a handlebar mustache. He felt someone tap him on the back. It was María Luisa.

"What are you doing here?"

"Sir, would you please dismount? The ride is over."

It was the woman who operated the merry-go-round.

Jesús hopped down and apologized.

Jesús knew enough to avoid being caught up in the city's new surge of random violence. He had nothing to do with the cartel, but feared someone might remember his prior connections to Braulio.

Miguel put him in touch with a guy who dealt in stolen cars on the other side of the border. It'd be a snap, he still understood their language. He'd make Juárez his center of operations, though he'd try to spend as little time there as possible.

At first he concentrated his efforts on El Paso, staying as close as possible to Juárez. But after an arrest and a brutal process of interrogation, he realized it would be better to distance himself from the border area. He avoided crossing the line at the same stations; he wasn't protected the way he used to be.

Soon, without even meaning to, he gravitated back to jumping freight trains. He came and went, came and went, as if the border held no secrets.

He spent a few months in the Kentucky tobacco fields, and worked another month in San Diego for a company that supplied Porta-Potties for stadiums, parks, and highways under construction. His job was to clean out the latrines, which made him vomit constantly. Fucking shit job, he'd say under his breath, happy with his double entendre. What got into people in these shitcans? he asked himself. So clean in their own homes and so disgusting in public.

He reported to different parks or streets around the city at dawn, the sites where people went to find illegal workers for underpaid labor. *Compañeros* would confide their stories to him, their rabid fear of the Migra, how much they hated the coyotes who brought them across and kept their savings, their belongings. One person had spent thirty hours in a fruit crate. Another crossed at Tecate through a hole in a metal curtain and had to wade across sewer canals full of shit. Another snuck through the cyclone fence in Tijuana, then followed the coyote to a van parked on the side of the road, with the Migra flies in hot pursuit the whole way. After they dropped him off, he had to hightail it across a freeway. One Salvadoran crossed in Tijuana on a moonless night through snake- and rat-infested brush, climbing into the hills till he found the bridge where a pickup truck with a camper shell was waiting. A skinny white man hid under a train, crouched in the corner for ten hours, praying he wouldn't fall and be sliced into bits. A woman with trembling hands had been detained by the Migra and deported twice, then raped by the coyote. She finally made it on her third try. A Oaxacan man had crossed in a van with no seats, squished in a nook in the back. The dogs came sniffing, but he prayed hard and they left him alone. A Colombian got lost in the desert with his wife and watched her die of thirst before the coyote showed up and saved him. Another who crossed the wilderness was spared by a well that had a puddle of stinking mosquito-infested water near a cave with a picture of the Virgin of Guadalupe.

"That's bullshit, cabrón," the fat man next to him exclaimed. "I might buy the well story, but no Virgin."

"I swear on my old lady, who'll get crippled if I'm lying, buey."

"Well, now she is."

"What about you, hermano?" they asked. But Jesús kept his mouth shut. He had stories to tell that were a hell of a lot more interesting than theirs, but they had nothing to do with crossing the border. If anything, he identified more with the coyotes, who went back and forth across the line like it was the most natural thing in the world. He was like them, not this pack of *imbéciles* who had no clue what real life on the border was like, they'd all been swindled and were lucky to have survived. It's about having guts, not being scared. Fear makes people smell differently, and the Migra hijos de puta knew it.

Jesús found work as an electrician, a gardener, a bricklayer. He hated doing grunt work for the gringos. It wasn't fair that he only had twenty bucks in his pocket after a full day's work. He shot it on booze and bad coke and stayed in homeless shelters for food and lodging. They were run by different religious organizations, the Salvation Army, or other human rights groups. He grew accustomed to a diet of lentil soup and fried chicken. At night he stretched out on camping cots; he was a light sleeper, restless, there was always noise in the background of men masturbating or fucking each other when the lights went out. There were blacks, whites, Latinos. Every once in a while someone tried to have their way with him, lured by his baby face and slight build. He'd have to sneak out and sleep in an alley on pieces of cardboard. A few times he had to negotiate being left alone by masturbating black guys; one time a big, beefy dude raped him repeatedly, and Jesús denied that the pain also gave him pleasure.

"No no no no NO. don't get noplace with pasience of saints. ebryone has to DIE. what you think animals don't know who you fucking with. who you think you are. can't do nothin to me, want to destroy but can't do nothing. i am the ANGEL OF REVENGE. One day only me left on earth. the imortal one is me. animals, all animals. KILL THEM ALL."

Occasionally he would sit on a bench next to a lilac tree in Borunda Park and write down sentences in his notebook like "my hart is shatterd" and "pane melts in my insides" and "the steel man find him the kriptonite, it melt him, him it melts" and "i mark of my chest and point and shoot the bulitt to the middle of the unicorn."

The pages of the notebook were filling up. How many times had he begun so carefully, with precise sentences, before his rage took hold of him and everything became a monologue with no punctuation or accent marks? Yet another notebook for the growing pile of, how many were there now, nine or ten? Each one was dedicated to María Luisa, who didn't deserve them.

When there were no more blank pages left he quit writing, his hand stiff and cramped. He hid the notebooks in secret places around Juárez, scattered like clues that when unearthed would chart the process of his breakdown. He hid the first one on a shelf in the Municipal Library, tucked between copies of Porrúa's "Sepan Cuántos" collection of classic literature (*Joseph Fouché: Portrait of a Politician* by Stefan Zweig and *El fistol del Diablo* by Manuel Payno). Another was in Miguel's basement, concealed by photo albums that nobody ever consulted. A third had been placed in a metal box and buried in a hole he'd dug with his foot at the bottom of an acacia tree near the climbing path to Monte de Piedad. What to do with this new one?

The collection of notebooks constituted his *Book of Revelations*. He couldn't explain how, but the time always came in the writing when visions appeared of burning towns, forests engulfed in flames and smoke, children drowning in storms and floods, horses dying, women in epileptic seizures, retarded children, and rivers of blood. Everything was covered in ashes, as he imagined the world after the end. Then came the incarnation of a prophet with long black hair who shepherded the sole survivors to a promised land. He was the Unnamed.

When he was so broke that he couldn't drink or buy coke, his cheeks would flush and his body shake so much that at times he couldn't hold anything in his hands. His mouth got dry and cottony. Anything—dog crap, a headless chicken at the butcher— would make him nauseated and sweaty. He missed the doctor at

Starke, who used to give him tranquilizers. The pharmacies on the other side wouldn't give him anything without a prescription, and in Juárez the generic drugs weren't cheap and didn't last very long (at one point he was popping five alprazolams a night), so he preferred doing lines of coke instead.

Jesús had a hard time sleeping at night. He would dream with his eyes open: he saw *alebrijes* that came to life and tried to devour him. He listened to the Unnamed's voice and copied out in his notebook the sentences dictated to him. "BUTCHER ALL IDIOTS. Women and children first. WOMEN and children FIRST. half man half angel. manangelmanangel."

Only alcohol and drugs could calm him down. He had to get some money.

He went back to breaking and entering houses near the train station. He selected the houses as carefully as possible: they had to be empty, the only thing he wanted to do was steal.

He started accumulating money and jewelry again, hoarding them in a locker in the Juárez bus station.

The Niners were back on their way to the Super Bowl. The quarterback, Steve Young, wasn't half bad, but Jesús missed watching Montana throw and soon got bored with the games.

He tried to write a letter to María Luisa. He didn't know what to tell her. He mixed sweet childhood memories—playing together in the hollow tree—with insults for having treated him badly, for being so rude to him.

He wanted to focus on other things, but the urge to get a few things straight with María Luisa wouldn't be appeased. Maybe it would be easier to see her face to face and talk. What's she like? A hot babe? How's she different?

The idea made him anxious. She might not want to see him. Would she shut the door in his face if she opened it and saw him standing there?

He'd faced worse fears. He'd get over this one.

One early morning a bus dropped him off on a street in Villa Ahumada, and his steps steered a straight course to his childhood home. Would it still be there?

Yeah, there it was. The one-story home with a tin roof and stucco walls, with a hundred-year-old tree in the patio. He nudged the door open; it was unlocked, as if they had been waiting for him. The hinges squeaked. There was noise coming from the kitchen. His mother, wrapped in a black shawl, was preparing a pot of beans and warming tortillas in a skillet. Jesús sat down in a chair, waiting for her to turn around.

A plethora of crosses hung along the walls, in all shapes and sizes, as if his mother had begun collecting them: made of tin, wood, or aluminum; big ones and small ones; some in flamboyant colors and others funeral black; with agonizing bloody Christs hanging, or else empty.

No cross should have Christ nailed to it, he thought. He was as absent as his father before him.

She turned around: she didn't look a day older. She saw him, and there was no hint of surprise in her expression. She brought him his breakfast, sat down beside him, asked if he wanted anything else.

He didn't answer, just bit into the tortilla.

She ate in silence. He did the same, his gaze fixed on his plate.

She looked at him as if she could see straight through him and fix her gaze on the soot-stained wall behind him.

"You took off just like your father," she finally said. "Everyone runs away from this place. In the end, all that remains are voices."

"María Luisa?"

"She left too. She lives with Jeremías, he's a hardworking man. She has a son. All I ask is that you don't hurt her."

Jesús felt a pang in his heart. The trip had been useless, then.

He asked where she lived.

"In New Mexico. I don't have the address. Jeremías's brother might know."

Jesús stood up and carried his plate over to the sink, then walked into the bedroom. It seemed smaller now, and the walls were bare, stripped of the flashy colors of his wrestling posters. The floor where his mattress had been was now split in two, as if an earthquake had wanted to pull one side of the room away from the other. As if someone had cast a spell, a hex strong enough to turn this tiny paradise into a grimy black hole.

His mother and father's bed was still there. His mother and María Luisa's bed. His and María Luisa's bed.

Nobody, nothing, never. What if that's all the truth there ever was? What if he had never really lived there and his mother was right to behave as if his visit wasn't really happening?

He walked out of the bedroom and turned for one last look at the bed. Whatever tricks reality was using to mess with his head, they didn't stand a chance against his memory: it had been true, all of it.

He didn't want to approach the bed but observed it from the distance, feeling edgy, as if what had gone on there had the power to take him places where the best thing he could do was clutch a knife.

His mother escorted him to the door.

He asked her for Jeremías's brother's address; she gave it to him. He said a silent goodbye with an embrace. She let him; her limp body offered no resistance, but neither did she receive his hug with warmth.

Jesús walked out onto the street. The sharp daylight blinded him for a moment before he slowly recovered the sight of things.

Once he'd visited Jeremías's brother and secured his sister's address, Jesús went on a sotol bender in *cantina* Paso del Norte—a Chinese couple waited on him, the jukebox was stocked by someone with an abusive passion for Los Tigres and Juan Gabriel, a cat snoozed on a table beside an old fart playing solitaire—and spent hours reminiscing over that glorious afternoon he spent at the circus with his father and María Luisa. The only thing he remembered of the show that day was a stubborn goat that wouldn't budge despite the menacing lashes of the tamer's whip, and two clowns parodying a wrestling match. The three of them sat perched on rough planks; his feet were sunk into the layer of straw thrown over the ground, and he stared obsessively at María Luisa, captivated, hypnotized by the reactions on her face. He couldn't have cared less about the trapeze artists, the sword swallower or dwarf contortionists, what compelled him was watching how María Luisa experienced the spectacle. She expressed awe, fear, tension, sorrow, wonder. He had thought, or at least now in the cantina Paso del Norte he believed he had thought, that he should never, ever part from her for the rest of his life. Everything would be as it should be, as long as he could continue relishing the way she relished everything so passionately.

How would she react when she saw him? How would he react?

He had imagined this reunion so many times when he was in Starke that he hadn't really considered the implications. Was he prepared for her rejection, her disappointment, her aversion? He was no longer that little boy with the mischievous twinkle in his eye who liked to play outdoors with his sister. Nor was he the restless boy of those few days spent together before that night when, though their lives were moving in different directions, they had shared secrets and complicities.

At times he was consumed by rage and thought that perhaps the knife was the best thing for her too. Fucking sow. What was she doing with that cabrón Jeremías. What was she doing with a son?

He asked the Chinaman for a paper and pencil. He started writing a letter to her right there at the counter.

"Dear litle sister I see all is good I alway want to see yu and hab think that"

"Dear sister all I wan say to yu is that"

"Litle sister lots a things hapen I wan yu to no I keep yu in my hart"

"Sister sister life seprate us but mie fist is ful of"

"Dear sister is good see that lif is good to yu, I just"

"Fucking sow *idiota* kill idiots KILL THEM ALL."

He staggered out of the cantina boozed up and once he was outside, the street rushed straight at him. He tried to get back onto his feet but wasn't able to; eventually he just passed out. Two adolescents who were passing by pushed his inert body to the curb so he wouldn't be run over.

Jesús came to around midnight, numb from the cold.

He had a tough time getting up. When he finally did, the first thing that popped into his mind was how he was going get to Albuquerque to find her.

Jesús no longer cared about what happened years ago. It was time to concentrate on what lay ahead.

When he arrived in Juárez, he gathered all the money he had hidden in the station locker and, taking Miguel's advice to heart, went to live in a town called Rodeo, in Durango, some two hundred kilometers due southeast. It wasn't easy to get there—the only way was by a winding mountain road—but that's just what Jesús was looking for, at least for the time being: isolate himself from the world, get lost. Begin a new life.

A simple home, white walls, one story, and two rooms, it didn't cost more than a thousand dollars.

He started wearing glasses because his eyes hurt. He was drinking less and managed to get his drug use under a modicum of control. He was sleeping better, and the red blotches on his cheeks had disappeared. He wanted to make a good impression on his sister when he saw her.

Soon he got a job as an English teacher in a small school run by the Fray Bartolomé de las Casas convent. The school stood just in front of the town's only police station. It made Jesús smile: if they only knew.

3

Auburn, California, 1948–1952

Did he like it, or didn't he? They had transferred him to a bigger building. They said he'd be better off here, he'd have more space. It was true enough, there were more than a hundred spacious buildings connected by roomy hallways with nice tall windows looking out over the surrounding gardens and the walls that separated the building from the roadway. But there were more people here too, wandering around aimlessly. Many of them had some kind of physical deformity—crippled or one-eyed, amputees, missing chunks of their faces, their big tongues lolling. All of them were survivors, he understood, of someone else's war, some war that had been waged far away from Martín's home. He was now in a great nation of warriors who would soon go to the aid of *señor gobierno* to burn churches there, just like they had sailed the oceans to attack other nations.

The nurses and orderlies, dressed in blood-spattered white uniforms, were constantly obliging Martín and his companions to stand in line while they dispensed remedies for this and that. Never gave them any peace. They were like soldiers. Yeah, he reckoned, they were enemy troops after all, and he'd best keep that in mind despite their good manners.

Early in the morning they roused them with a shrill alarm that went off in all the rooms, and the patients were assembled into rows. Young ones over here, elderly ones over there. Men over here, women over there.

Fluids and more fluids. Everywhere fluids. In all shades and colors. Reddish, greenish, yellowish. He knew it plain as day now: everything on the inside of a person was liquid, and skin was the outside, like the wall of a dam. Gooey rivers flowing around with every heartbeat. They'll open his noggin and there'll be liquid inside there, too.

He gave nicknames to the orderlies. Whitey, Gitupboy, Little Stepbackwards, Coyote, The Shack, Whachusay. They brought them to the two bathrooms in each of the halls and made them take turns bathing, showering, and dressing. They doled out the meds. They counted constantly to make sure nobody had gone missing or was hurt. Three times a day, twice from sundown to midnight, once in the wee hours.

Breakfast was served when they were finished in the bathrooms. They were sent back to bed and food was brought on carts. They gave them plastic knives, forks, spoons, and plates. Martín helped collect the dirty dishes and utensils.

He liked Whitey. Not so much Gitupboy. Little Stepbackwards was OK. Coyote was too, but could get moody; it depended on when you caught him. The Shack was plain nasty. And Whachusay was a nurse, and she was the best of all.

Order was essential. The doctors came to check on them at specific times. Lights went out at appointed times. In the afternoons they were allowed to play board games or cards, or do crossword puzzles. There was a small movie room. If they behaved, they were allowed to spend time outside in the garden.

Martín didn't care for cards and board games. He found a secluded table where he could draw by himself. People approached him to talk every once in a while, but when he didn't answer they'd leave him alone. Sometimes they'd ask to be drawn. That was the best.

He sketched the room where he spent most of his time. Walls with windows. He liked to draw what he had inside his skull more than anything. The cinematographer inside his own brain, like that one film he had seen with María Santa Ana a couple of times in Los Altos. The images in his head projected endlessly, but he stopped them and mixed them up with the ones he had seen in magazines, full-color pages with women advertising soaps and washing machines and cars and trains. He drew horses and cowboys. A man sitting at a table by a huge window like a tunnel with a train passing through— everyone thought he was the man in the picture. Crowned virgins, saints in red robes, landscapes with trees, churches, and animals; trains coming and going, endless tracks that criss-crossed the hills. Cars, trucks, and wagons driving through tunnels, lightning bolts everywhere. Diagonal lines, vertical lines, horizontal lines. Undulating wave after wave, enough to make you dizzy, bottomless black on white paper, softer black on brown paper. He liked to create mood, symmetry.

At times he used charcoal. Other times he preferred colored pencils, graphite, watercolors, wax crayons. He'd sit on the floor and glue loose pages together to make a surface space that was big enough for his drawings. He cut figures out of the magazines to create collages.

He missed Mr. Walker. He wondered what would be of María Santa Ana.

What about his daughters? And Candelario?

One of Martín's pavilion mates roamed around wearing a blue cape tied around his neck. He would bare his teeth in an evil-looking grin. Another would race around in his wheelchair and spray everyone with an aerosol can. Martín went to great pains to talk to them in the hall or outdoors in the garden, but all he could do was grunt and babble. Then he would laugh. But his laughing annoyed The Shack, who always came running over to tell him to shut up, even though it was hopeless; nobody could make him stop laughing.

The man with the cloak would cry "I am a hero!" over and over again, and Martín wondered what "jiro" meant. The one in the wheelchair shouted, "My spray will make you invisible!" Martín understood the words, but no one ever disappeared after being sprayed.

Martín, on the other hand, was able to close his eyes and make them all vanish. Whenever an orderly would take him to one of them rooms where the doctor connected him to cables, he concentrated real hard and the doctor would disappear. The electricity shook him and he tried to keep the pain from existing, but that was impossible. It was easy to make the orderlies and doctors and walls and gardens vanish. It was much harder to make the pain go away. It was always there, somewhere. If not stabbing his head, it was like a hammer bludgeoning his chest, or in the cold water in the bathroom where he stayed until his skin got pruney, or the hot water that turned it pink, or the electricity that shocked him in the room of walls so white that all he wanted to do was draw.

"Eeeeeeaaaaaa."

Martín attended pottery class once a week. He met people from other areas who were interested in drawing and sculpting. He made friends with a güero who relentlessly drew soldiers and cannons, parachutes and airplanes, and a cross that looked like a propeller. He observed the drawings, which were never very good, and they made him think of María Santa Ana's war. Things were different there. Atanacio had talked about razed churches and horses, destroyed houses and crops, but he never mentioned airplanes and parachutes. Is María Santa Ana still running with the Federales? At times the thought kept him up late into the night, wondering whether she had joined up of her own free will or if everything had been part of her strategy to get behind enemy lines and fight from inside, shouting, "Viva Cristo Rey!"

He shouldn't kid himself. He was a prisoner of war. María Santa Ana: a lousy traitor. Maybe he was there because she had alerted the Federales, and señor gobierno was a friend of the United States of the North's señor gobierno.

The güero would sit beside him without saying a word. He clapped a lot though, that's for sure. He clapped whenever he liked something, and when he didn't like something too. Martín had no idea what the güero really thought of his drawings, but he never seemed to stop applauding them.

After class Martín liked to go outside. He could spend all his free time with his friend there, in silence. Gitupboy took a photograph of them. Martín didn't like it because he was smiling in the photo and he'd lost a few teeth. He'd learn how to smile with his lips pursed together for the next one.

The pottery teacher decided to show some of the drawings by his class. A gentleman would come to see them with students. An art professor who wants to build ties with the community, Martín heard them say. He's from Romania, Whitey said one day when Martín was taking a bath. "Transylvania, ha ha," he said. The joke circulated throughout the building: Dracula was coming for a visit.

They arranged the drawings on the solarium walls. There were colorful ones, and others in black and white; some were done using watercolors, and a few with crayons. There were plenty of yellow suns, windows, and little girls floating on cottony clouds, coddling teddy bears and holding balloons.

When the gentleman and his students arrived, they remained standing before Martín's drawing for a long time. It was of an armed horseman riding across wavy hills with a deer at his side. He asked whose drawing it was. The pottery teacher pointed to Martín.

The man approached him. Dracula, it's Dracula: Martín's mind raced. "You have talent," he said. "You know that?" Martín didn't respond.

Dracula asked him through gestures if he could take a drawing as a gift. Martín agreed.

The art professor left with a satisfied grin.

From that day on, the man visited him regularly. Martín anxiously awaited the visits, because he brought drawing books and other supplies like crayons and colored pencils. He couldn't rule out that this was all part of the enemy plot, but he had to admit it was stronger than him. He didn't want to make the teacher disappear. Though he'd keep on his toes, and the moment he saw anything suspicious, Martín would close his eyes and send the teacher to face his wrath and annihilation.

A. Ny-ah. Lay. Shun.

When the professor saw that Martín had new drawings, he'd date them in the lower right margin. "It's good to record when you did them," he said. Martín smiled. The drawings were carefully stored in the pottery workshop. Martín was allowed to come and go freely. He was no longer expected to make beds and clean rooms. Now all he was supposed to do was draw. And he drew. He couldn't stop drawing. Little sketches, colossal illustrations, some bursting with color, others in various shades of gray. He asked them for magazines, and he cut the illustrations out and glued them to the drawings. He didn't want the professor to come for a visit and find him empty-handed.

One day the güero didn't show up in pottery class. Martín waited for him the next week, but he didn't come then either. He approached the teacher, holding one of the güero's drawings. He gestured frantically. Where is he? The teacher brought his hands to his neck. Then he drew a noose on a piece of paper. He expressed grief in his face.

Martín made the sign of the cross.

One day in pottery class, they told him he had a visitor. He was a strong, brown-skinned youth. He identified himself as his older brother's son. Martín didn't want to see him.

The director called him into his office and made explanations for things that Martín didn't understand. In the end, the only thing that was clear was that he had no option but to receive the young man.

Little Stepbackwards supervised the visit.

His brother's son was so moved that he began to cry and embraced him. He said he was working in San Francisco and a *paisano* came with news that he might have kin in a hospital upstate. He followed his hunch and did some research, and the doctors verified that they had institutionalized him around the same time the family had lost track of him. He had to be his *tío* Martín.

"*Calma, calma,*" Martín said. "What do you mean San Francisco? Where's that?" He was in the north, way up north, he knew that much. When he came, he remembered, he had passed through a state called Texas with his traveling buddies, and eventually they migrated to California, and slowly but surely they got separated and he was sent up north, up and up, until he finally stopped. The train, it had to be built. The rails, the tracks, the crossties. The steel, the wood, the sweat in the afternoons under the scorching sun out there in the desert and in El Picacho. Sometimes his whole body hurt, though not like now, and accidents had happened, once a steel beam fell on his leg and he limped for a spell, and once a dynamite explosion threw him to the ground and his ears kept on ringing, for how long? A long, long time, in the faraway, that place he wasn't now, with other folk like him, everyone hoping to go back, never going back, that's right, that's right, something in this country made them not go back, made excuses to stay, happy to send money home, but even when no more money, no more job, no nothing, and now what, hey, what, now it's war, hey, war in Mexico, that's why he didn't go back, blame it on señor gobierno, blame it on María Santa Ana.

His sister's son explained what had been happening in the faraway place. Martín was distressed; he didn't want to know about his traitor wife. He didn't want to hear about the war, he said. Little Stepbackwards was shocked: Martín was able to speak?

"There's no war on, Uncle. It ended over twenty years ago."

The young man wouldn't stop talking, something about how much his daughters and Candelario missed him. Something about it being time to go home. Something about how he would do all he could to help him.

His daughters? Candelario? How could he ever trust them now, no doubt the Federales had raised them and filled their heads with ideas. He jumped up, frantic, began kicking the walls. Little Stepbackwards tried to calm him down, reassure him.

"You have to return to your family, Uncle. We're waiting for you. Please, Uncle."

Martín pleaded with Little Stepbackwards in sharp gestures to be taken back to his bed. He extracted the last letter he'd received from Atanacio from a bag and returned to the room where his sister's son was waiting. He handed the letter to his nephew and asked him to read it. When he did, Martín turned his back and stared at the wall.

"I don't understand, Uncle."

"Traitors," he said. "My wife, the Federales."

"That's not what it says, Uncle. You misunderstood. It says that she fought beside Uncle Atanacio to defend the ranch, and that the Federales apprehended both of them. But that happened many years ago, and now she's waiting, all your children are waiting."

Martín's affliction grew into frenzy and he started punching the wall. By the time Little Stepbackwards could get to him, he had knocked his head hard against it, too. Martín brought his fingers to his scalp and saw that he was bleeding. He stared at his hands and saw fluid, fluid was leaking from his body and now it wouldn't stop. The skin hadn't worked as his dam, what was he going to do? He was going to die, to die! He started bellowing.

Little Stepbackwards called for other orderlies, and together they subdued Martín, wrestling him to the floor. He felt someone's knees jabbing into his back, and somebody had grabbed him around the neck.

He closed his eyes. They vanished. But the pain persisted. "Aaaaaahhhhh."

Little Stepbackwards told the young man his visit was over.

Martín was terrified. They'd transfer him to another prison and he'd be put in a dark Mexican cell. The Federales in his country were sons of bitches; they had no respect for life. It was so nice here.

He made an effort to calm himself down. Would the blood stop? A nurse bandaged his head, they were going to take him to another room, "estiches, estiches" he heard someone say.

His sister's son stood up and walked over to Martín before the apprehensive gaze of Little Stepbackwards and the others.

"Uncle, Uncle. *Por favor*, don't do anything to him. It's all right, I understand. Do you have any message for your wife and children? They're anxious for news about you."

Martín drew a valley with wavy hills and Jesús on the cross.

The blood dripped from his head and stained the paper. Little Stepbackwards told the young man in a bumbling Spanish to tell them they'd see each other in the next life.

The young man hugged his uncle before leaving, and never returned.

Shortly afterward, Martín learned that the professor would be coming to live in the building for a few months.

4

Landslide, 2008—2009

First I got a bad headache—it happened just after Christmas when I was walking around the mall. Then came the nausea, always at strange times like after having a cup of tea or eating a salad. I attributed everything to the stress of my relationship with Fabián. He sent emails and called me from Buenos Aires, but I already had an inkling that our affair wasn't going anywhere, not now, not if we tried again a thousand times over. Fabián was losing his way, adrift in his hallucinations. One of his emails read: "it's the ice-cream i like the most, nobody can compete with the kind they make here. the dulce de leche, it's a poem. i had a panic attack on the airplane and felt as though I had jumped out with a parachute. i split in two, one of me watched everything from the window of the plane and the other me raced like a bullet toward the ground because the parachute wouldn't open. this morning i woke up around six and felt compelled to go out into the yard. when i got there, i heard a buzzing sound and looked up in time to see an object coming straight at me. it was me and the unopened parachute. i fell to the ground to avoid the impact. late, late. i shut my eyes and when i opened them again nobody was there. i took off lickety-split thinking i had survived, that from now on everything would be different. but then i saw the mangled body of the skydiver, and i was filled with dread."

I wanted to help him out, to feel as though I were an indispensable part of his life. But in the end I realized that none of it was really up to me, and I started feeling asphyxiated by him. Sometimes I thought it was just my pride and stubborn character: I wanted to go back to him because I couldn't accept being dropped so brusquely; I'd rewrite the narrative of our affair, and this time I would be the one to leave, coming out on top. Other times I was overwhelmed by a desire to surrender entirely to him, sure I'd never find anyone else like Fabián; our moments happened in fits and starts, but they did happen. We both bought into that dynamic, we were incapable of cutting ties completely, incapable of surrendering completely, lost in the ambiguity of loving and not loving.

A week of vomiting gave momentum to my growing hunch, and a visit to the pharmacy and a pregnancy test established the fact. I found truth in a bathroom bedecked with Jeff Buckley concert posters. I couldn't sleep: I was terrified of Fabián's reaction when the time came to fess up. I didn't want to give him the news by phone or email. It was better to wait till he got back in January.

Fabián returned on a Monday. I let him rest on Tuesday morning, then plucked up the courage to go to his home. He opened the door and led me upstairs, and I told him to please sit down on the couch. Woodstock curled up next to him. I told him the news and it left him speechless. When he caught his breath, he said that he was happy for me and that he would be responsible for the baby, but that he wasn't about to let himself feel "tied down" to me. Then he remarked on how little we had actually slept together before he left.

Maybe someone else had been there in his absence? He saw the expression of rage on my face and tried to apologize, but it was too late: in those days a single word out of place was enough to flip my switch, and yes, there had been many words out of place.

Later, when we talked by phone, he suggested that I go to Planned Parenthood and wanted me to know that having the baby wasn't obligatory. I hurled the phone across the room.

I had considered telling La Jodida and asking her to accompany me to Planned Parenthood, but I no longer trusted her the way I used to. So I went alone and felt miserable. A plump black woman with a gummy smile courteously explained that what I was considering now was more common than I realized, one out of three women under the age of forty-five in the United States had terminated a pregnancy. I winced at the thought of an infinite cemetery of unborn children. They gave me brochures with photos of fetuses from illegal abortions. I learned how the morning-after pill worked. I had a bout of dry heaving in the parking lot on my way out.

I met with Fabián in the Chip & Dip. I told him I refused to have an abortion. He was more resolute now and said he forbade me to have the child. He told me again how he had lost his wife, how it triggered his depression, and the idea of bringing another life into the world was intolerable.

I asked Taco Hut for time off. My nights were restless. I obsessed over Fabián's words and inflexibility, wishing I could make up my own mind, but his attitude carried too much weight. I began worrying about my own future, thinking in his terms, seeing things from his vantage point: I wouldn't be able to study if I had to take care of a child, I told myself; I'd have to give up writing and drawing.

I was trying to convince myself that it was the proper decision. But I couldn't, not entirely.

Fabián called again late into the night. Better not do it in Landslide. We should go to El Paso next weekend. He'd make the inquiries.

Two weeks later, we headed for El Paso. We found a room at the Holiday Inn, and Fabián spent most of his time in the cold water of the swimming pool, hiding away from me. We took a cab to the clinic and got lost in the tiny streets near the border; the skyline of Juárez cut a silhouette into the distant sky, a darker sky than the one over El Paso, choked as it was by the factory smog.

There were two benches in the clinic's waiting room. The nurse attending me had thin, bony arms, and her black hair was tied back into a long braid.

"Who referred you to us?"

"A friend who teaches in El Paso."

"Honestly, I just don't get you. We could have done this in Landslide. It's sheer paranoia. I mean, don't you think we're a little old to be sneaking off? Anyway, Planned Parenthood was clear about how strict their privacy code is."

He shrugged his shoulders as if to say well, too late now.

Once I was in the room, the nurse told me to get undressed and handed me a gown. I hopped onto the examining table and waited for the doctor to come in, Ana Carranza at your service. Fabián sat next to me, I squeezed his hand apprehensively.

Dr. Carranza gave me an injection, I closed my eyes and when I opened them again a few hours later, Fabián was no longer beside me. I was still woozy when the nurse approached and helped me sit up, which I did with difficulty. I located

Fabián sitting on a nearby bench. He was leafing through a magazine; he came over and embraced me. I would have belted him if only I'd had the strength.

Fabián remained withdrawn the rest of the way back, and he hardly spoke. My whole body was sore, but the cramps in my stomach hurt the worst, I felt frail. I slept a lot.

The next few days I stayed in the studio convalescing—took it easy, tried not to worry, to get back on my feet. No strong painkillers, just a few Tylenol. At times the cramps got so bad my eyes would water and I'd fall to the floor writhing in pain. I took advantage of the time to reread the first volume of Neal Gaiman's comic-book series *The Sandman*; I was still so impressed with the blue of "Sleep of the Just," the phantasmagorical atmosphere in "Imperfect Hosts," a sentence in "Dream a Little Dream of Me"—*Dream dream dreeeeam . . . whenever I want to. . . . All I have to do . . . is . . . dreeeeam . . .*—the dark colors and the way he framed the vignettes in "A Hope in Hell."

I should devote myself to reading and nothing else. Yeah, I could be a professional reader.

5

Rodeo, Mexico; various US cities, 1994–1997

Jesús woke up with a nasty toothache and went out to find a pharmacy. A sign taped to the frosted glass at the entrance of La Indolora read "Injections 3 Pesos." The woman who attended him had butt-length black hair and was sporting electric-blue nail polish. She wouldn't stop talking and he could see her chipped front tooth every time she smiled. The yakkety-yak grated on Jesús's nerves, but luckily he found a distraction on his way out: there was a scale just beside the door. For three pesos they also took your blood pressure.

Jesús was short of change; he looked back at the woman and took off his glasses as he approached her. She had already guessed his intentions, though, and held out a few coins before he even opened his mouth. Jesús thanked her and asked for her name, eyes lowered and rubbing his hands nervously.

"Renata. You just passing through?"

"I live here now. Only been a few weeks."

"What brings you to this two-bit town?"

"I like two-bit. I get tired of having people around all the time."

"People here aren't grateful for what they got," Renata said. "I was in Juárez for a while, but had some trouble and came back home. Now I got a good job and I'm not complaining."

Jesús walked out of La Indolora with her telephone number stuffed in his pocket.

The next day they went to see a Jackie Chan movie together, but Renata didn't care for it—"I know it's just a movie and not real life, but it's so violent"—and afterward he took her to have dinner at Restaurante Veracruz, following recommendations he'd been given when he asked around for a classy joint. The floors were decorated with mosaic tiles and there were flower arrangements on the tables. Two men locked in a heated argument were busy draining a bottle of mescal. A redhead was fully concentrated on a guidebook to Mexico; her backpack rested on the chair beside her.

Renata was wearing a long blue dress and had done her hair up in an intricate weave—arabesques that had taken over an hour to braid when she got out of the shower. She was so impressed by Jesús's manners and that he was spending so much money. When he told her he was teaching at the nuns' school, she said they must pay awful good.

"Two hundred fifty pesos," he said.

"Really? That's hardly anything."

"When I need *plata*, I head across the border for a few months. I worked on a tobacco plantation and in gas stations. I've done things like pick oranges in California, planted asparagus, harvested rice in Texas. The worst thing was cleaning latrines. It ain't such a bad life."

"Why don't you stay then?

"'Cause when I'm there, I miss being here."

The following weekend they went on another date. They kissed under the dim lights of a karaoke bar where a pot-bellied dwarf in mariachi garb sang Pedro Infante songs. It was

June, but the Christmas decorations were still up: a plastic Santa wiggled on top of a speaker, a dried-out tree covered in gaudy ornaments withered in the corner, a garland hanging from the ceiling spelled out MERRY CHRISTMAS.

Jesús tried to squeeze her breasts out on the dark street, but she wouldn't let him. He invited her over; Renata said no.

"I like that," he said. "I like that you ain't like those blonds up north."

"My *madre*, may she rest in peace, taught me that a man should respect you before you let anything happen."

Stupid old bitch, Jesús thought. But he was in no rush—not like he had too many options in Rodeo anyway, and Renata wasn't half bad. He had concocted his plan over the past few days, and a stable partner was an essential part of it. Someone in town to dispel suspicion. Provide respectability. Someone who occupied his house when he was away, took care of his stuff. One thing was sure: the journey had to continue. Staying in one place the rest of his life wasn't an option.

A little while later, Jesús contacted a black-market dealer who moved hot cars. He told him he could open a new supply line. He had no intention of crossing the border: all he wanted to do was exploit some of his contacts in Juárez to float the cars, resell them, and make some cash in commissions.

Jesús soon became a little big shot in Rodeo thanks to his thriving car business. Buyers from neighboring towns and cities contacted him. He relished the local notoriety, however minor, and was convinced that his dry spell had come to an end. People got to know him in the bars, he hooked himself up for cheap coke, and in the bordellos putas fought over him because he was flush and he paid in cash.

He took Renata with him to Juárez. They went shopping in Futurama, Renata swooned over the sparkly brand-name shops. "It's your lucky day," Jesús told her, "someone just paid back a debt, so I can buy you anything you want." She hugged him gleefully and began her march through the stores "quick, before you change your mind." Jesús sat in overstuffed arm-chairs and waited while she tried on dresses and shoes; he answered in monosyllables when she came out to show him a pair of pants or a bag, and kept quiet when she chose something he thought was too pricey. They left the plaza laden with bags; Renata was chatty and cheerful, he kept repeating under his breath, "It's over, *puerca*, it's over."

They finally slept together on the trip, it was the first time. She was flat chested, and he offered to pay for new tits. Renata blushed: the operation frightened her, but she'd think it over.

Jesús suggested she move in with him. Renata said no: what would people say? Things should follow the proper order. Jesús thought, who the fuck do you think you are, *imbécil*, be glad I'm letting you live. But then he figured it didn't really make a big difference anyway.

Within two days he proposed and she accepted. Two months later they were married.

"FUKING HORE IF YOU ONLY NEW. i cant stand you i cant STAND YOU. ain't your falt coz I HATE ALL. They talk and talk and say no respec me but they all craizy. I now is my money, no money no atention, $$$, oh yeah, they all like that. FUCKIN opinions all the time, rats ain't got brains. Judgement Day is nie, im a angel im God im KILL THEM ALL"

The Book of Revelations was growing. The notebooks were hidden in secret spots all over town. He sent some of them to María Luisa's address in Albuquerque.

On one of his first trips to Juárez after getting married, Jesús fell into temptation and crossed over to El Paso. He found a telephone booth on Santa Fe Street and called his sister's number. A deep voice answered the phone.

It was her. It was her.

He hung up.

Jesús ran straight over to the Freight House and jumped the first train leaving the station. There were two stinking, dirty-faced bums in the wagon, their hands were cracked and dry; they were on their way to Missouri, one of them explained.

The train lurched forward. Jesús had missed this ritual of being on the tracks. He stretched out on the wagon's creaky floor and tried to catch a little shuteye. He'd figure out how to get to Albuquerque in a while.

"Holy be the absence of thy name. no no no no NO."

A big burly man holding a gun surprised him in the first house he tried to burgle, in a small town near St. Louis. He took off like a bat out of hell.

Worried the man might try to identify him, he went to

apply for a new social security card in St. Louis, under a false name. The woman in the social security office picked up that something was peculiar. Reyle, Reyles, Reyes? The name didn't sound right.

Jesús was still in the waiting room when two INS inspectors showed up with a cop, who read him his rights and made the arrest. He was taken to a holding cell where other illegal aliens like him were kept.

He was accused of trying to solicit a social security card under false pretenses, of lying to the Social Security Administration and entering the country illegally. The public defender worked his case without much conviction, limiting the defense to attempting a lesser sentence. Jesús begged to be deported, promising that if they left him at the border, he'd never come back again. They didn't believe him.

He was sentenced to twelve months in prison.

He served the time in solitary, fanning his growing hatred for the people in this country. The guards beat him and punished him under the slightest pretext; his fellow inmates spent all their time stabbing each other, buying coke and weed from the guards, and raping each other like dogs.

Jesús was allowed one phone call a week, and instead of calling Renata, he dialed his sister's number in Albuquerque. At times nobody would pick up and he imagined her off working somewhere. When a voice answered on the other end, he would panic and hang up.

Nights were restless. The doctor prescribed a number of different medicines to reduce his anxiety: Librium, Tryptycil, Valium, Clonazepam.

It was impossible for him to write.

Jesús started having nightmares about his first victim, the puta from the California—how many years ago was that? The whore's face would morph into María Luisa's face, and then back.

He was released from prison after serving five months of his sentence. He walked out edgy but determined. After Starke, he'd done his best to keep the dark Jesús tucked deep inside and under control, while quietly preparing for the final battle. But not now, not anymore. He would pour out his indignation like a burning river of fire upon the earth until there was nobody left but him, standing atop a mountain of toothless skulls, all that would be left of the wretched who brought down his wrath with their coruptionignoranseprejudiceinferiority.

When he got back to Rodeo he found Renata at home. She had decorated the place with pink curtains, and there were stuffed animals on the sofa, in stark contrast with the football posters—Montana, Rice—that he had taped to the walls.

She gasped when she saw him. She sat down on the flowery couch, not wanting to hold his hand, but then she tried to hug him. Jesús wasn't sure how to act either. He took his glasses off, put them back on again, and finally said: "What the fuck have you done to my house? What's up with the fucking curtains, *vieja*?"

Renata burst into tears, catching Jesús off guard. Moron, he thought, idiot, puerca. But he adjusted the way he was thinking. It wasn't worth getting into a fight with her. He apologized for being inconsiderate; "It's just nerves," he said, and encouraged himself to come up with some explanation: he had found work on the other side, near El Paso, but didn't have a way to get word back to her. Renata believed him; she wanted to believe him, all she needed was for him to tell her something convincing. Slowly but surely she calmed down. She moved closer to him and gave him a kiss, told him the next time he should warn her in advance, she had been so worried.

"It's just not fair, Jesús. My brother comes over here and asks where you are and I don't know what to say. Then the neighbor comes, and I have to put on a brave face and act like I know. And you hear so many stories of fathers and brothers and husbands who are fine one day and gone the next, skipped across the border. At first they send money, then they vanish off the face of the earth. I know you're different: look at me, Jesús, you would never do that, but still it's not fair."

Stupid bitch is gonna get what's coming. Right now he needed her though. And to stop people's running at the mouth, he'd leave her some cash next time, open an account at the local bank and let her take out 150 bucks a month if he was away.

But the fucking curtains had to go.

Over the next few years, he spent very little time in Rodeo. He went back to jumping freight trains and burgling houses in cities and towns in Texas and New Mexico. Renata accepted their implicit pact: Jesús always brought her some gift when he returned—watches, earrings, chains, dresses—and his pockets were stuffed full of dollars. She agreed that what else could he do if there was no work in Rodeo, what else but cross the border every once in a while to keep up their lifestyle. She got used to being alone in the house, to seeing him for a week every three or four months.

But Jesús finally worked up the nerve again to hunt down María Luisa's specific whereabouts in Albuquerque, make sure she hadn't moved. His quest had been interrupted when they threw him in prison, and it was high time now that he reached his destination. Clinton had just been reelected and Jesús was in a pissy mood because of it. It meant there'd be more Wacos, more bombs over Sarajevo.

It was a Friday afternoon when he showed up on her doorstep, a house in the suburbs near a K-Mart. The house was smaller than the others on the block; it was painted deep purple. There was a tricycle in the yard.

He rang the doorbell. A woman came to the front door. María Luisa? She was a little plump and wearing a roomy dress that made her body into a rectangle, like a piece of furniture. What happened to her slim figure that used to make him so giddy? There were the green eyes, but they didn't engage squarely (now they were dodgy and evasive, the way he always looked). Her cheeks were pockmarked and there was no shine to her hair. Her thin lips looked like piecrust. Where was her glow? She looked even older than him now.

"Jesús . . ."

He wanted her to invite him in. He had to tell her about the *Book of Revelations*, there was a place for her salvation.

"Maria Luisa . . ."

"Don't just stand there, please come in, come."

A wave of intense emotion short-circuited his capacity to react; he turned around and ran away.

They were dangerous months for Jesús. The Migra was relentlessly tightening its control along the border, the prisons in the desert Southwest were full of Mexicans and Central Americans waiting their turn to argue their case and avoid the inevitable deportation—my wife and children are here Your Honor, I'm a political refugee from my country Your Honor, if you send me back the narcos are going to kill me Your Honor, Your Honor, Mister Lawyer, sir, mister, mister sir, please, please, please.

In California the police stopped the freight train Jesús was riding in, and he was arrested together with four hoboes. He was pardoned and sent to a city along the border and released.

Another time he boozed up in Texas and was arrested for public disorderliness and not having papers. They released him three weeks later. When he got back to Rodeo, he told Renata that he had been arrested. It gave her more faith in him: Jesús didn't hide anything from her, not even the bad things.

Christmas was just around the corner. He was exhausted; he wanted to get back to Rodeo in time for the holidays. He would rest for a few months, his body was begging for it. One of his knees ached, it got excruciating at times.

Dusk had fallen. The city's lights were coming on. The train was sliding through the suburbs just outside Houston—cars lined up at the crossings, waiting for the signal bar to go up—when Jesús spied a three-story house perched beside the tracks. The sheer size of the structure called his attention; it was much larger than the neighboring homes.

His body started to tremble. He jumped off without thinking twice.

The back door was unlocked. The house seemed empty, but he armed himself with a knife from the kitchen just in case. It was a serrated knife, the kind for cutting meat. Jesús went up to the master bedroom on the second floor. He jumped onto the bed and immediately sank down deep: it was a waterbed. They say you sleep better on them, but he didn't buy the spiel. It was like floating on Jell-O—it jiggled too much, like having a thousand twitchy worms underneath. No way he was gonna close his eyes on that thing.

The pictures along the wall told the family story: a married couple together for about a decade, three kids. She was a doctor who worked in the university, a typical white lady; he looked like a bank executive or something. Jesús came across pamphlets with images of fetuses on her desk, and there was her name: Joanna Benson. He read a few lines of the pamphlet, in English. He thought he understood that the doctor did experiments with fetuses.

He'd better hurry.

He'd stay there and wait for her.

Jesús took some of the ceramic pieces from the dresser and stuffed them into his canvas bag. He snatched a wooden box decorated with mother of pearl that was full of necklaces and earrings; he found three crisp one-hundred-dollar bills in one of the bedside drawers, along with a watch that wasn't running but looked chichi. In one of the girls' rooms—decorated with posters of Mel Gibson, Tom Cruise, and Bon Jovi—he found a baseball bat in a toy chest near the bed. He batted an imaginary game of baseball and realized that in fact he'd never actually played the game. He should. There must be a league in Rodeo.

He took the bat with him back down to the first floor. He considered pinching the stereo set but decided against it: too heavy. There were more ceramic knickknacks in the dining room, but they were too clunky and would probably break his canvas bag.

Jesús sat in the living room, waiting. He started when he heard a noise, readied himself, alert. It was the garage door. He still had time to get out.

He followed the sound of the car's engine as it entered the garage. The driver turned off the ignition and the engine sputtered, then stilled. Jesús positioned himself beside the door between the garage and the house, looming there, waiting.

The woman walked into the room with grocery bags in her arms. The shock of being blindsided and the force of the blow sent her headlong to the floor. Tin cans, butter sticks, a milk carton all went flying; her low-heeled black sandals skidded across the carpet.

"Oh, oh please, no. I have three little ones."

"You shut the fuck up, Joanna."

He sat down on top of her and punched her in the right eye. The crack juddered her entire face. He hit her again. This time he felt something snap, as if a bone had broken. KILL THEM ALL, Jesús intoned and plunged the serrated knife deep into her thorax. He grabbed the bat and swung it hard, until her face was nothing but pulp. One of her eyes was driven from the socket and landed on the kitchen floor, next to a tin bowl full of water for a dog that was nowhere to be seen (maybe he's at the vet, or maybe they're doing experiments with it, too).

Satisfied that the woman was no longer breathing, he got up and went into the kitchen. He picked her eye up and threw it in the garbage. He returned to where the woman's body lay and sliced off her tongue. He should do this to Renata. That'd get her to shut up.

Jesús undressed her. She had peed her pants, the puerca. He folded her clothes into a pile, threw them in the garbage too. He sat back down on top of Joanna. He masturbated in front of her. He penetrated her. He fixed his eyes on the bloody mess that had once been her face. He moved rhythmically, feverishly, until he felt that electric flash gathering somewhere deep inside. He pulled his cock out and held it over the gaping orifice and finished himself off.

The spurts of semen mixed with the blood. He was trembling. His heart hammered in his chest, relentless.

With one of his bloody fingers held high, Jesús approached the white kitchen wall and wrote: THE UNAMED.

But he caught his spelling error, and wrote again: THE UNNAMED.

Fatigue slowly crept in, and his throat was scratchy and parched.

Jesús used the first-floor bathroom to wash up, first his face and arms, then the drops of blood splattered across his pants and shirt. Then he took them off and went upstairs looking for a change of clothes. He found a blue shirt that was a few sizes too big, but he put it on anyway. Not the pants: they were so big that even with a belt he couldn't stop tripping over the cuffs. He put his jeans back on and convinced himself that it was no big deal. He'd have to buy himself a new pair.

Back in the kitchen, he opened the fridge and prepared himself a ham sandwich and washed it down with a glass of milk.

He shot a quick glance from the corner of his eye at the naked body in the next room. The blood on her chest was drying quickly. Her color was draining, the skin was turning ashen and pale.

He threw the laden rucksack on his back and went out the back door. He left the bat and the knife lying on the kitchen floor.

6

Landslide, 1997

That morning, Sergeant Fernandez was in his office doing paperwork. A few of the thumbtacks holding the map of Texas on the wall behind him had fallen, and part of the territory had curled over itself as a result.

He thought about Debbie and wondered what it must feel like to live so many years in one place yet always fancy you'd be better off someplace else. Whenever he brought up the subject, she would sigh in that heavy way that defines an entire manner of seeing the world, expelling the air she'd been hoarding in her lungs for just such an occasion. He'd notice the condescending curl of her upper lip, the tetchy angle with which she held her arms to her waist, but even so he insisted that she articulate the words these gestures were meant to define.

He ran his fingers over his two-day beard. "It scratches Rafa, you really need to shave," Debbie had said. So many things he was supposed to do, according to her. Moisturizing cream around his eyes so his crow's-feet don't deepen. Serum on his cheeks and forehead, lotion before bed. She was obsessed with staying young. In her teens she had been a model for shopping centers and department store catalogs; during college she'd been an actress in an amateur theater company. She'd shown him the photographs, the posters where her aloof, captivating smile was the main attraction for luring spectators.

He ran into Jackson on his way out of the office, carrying a folder and talking to McMullen over the phone.

"Did you read the dispatch from Houston? Heinous murder in a Houston suburb. Yesterday afternoon. The killer may have jumped a train to get away. They asked us to tighten up surveillance at the station."

Fernandez stopped cold in his tracks. "Wait a sec. Give me the details. Slowly, please."

"Here, read it for yourself."

McMullen handed him the folder. There were copies of police emails from Houston, the INS, Texas Rangers, and the FBI. Fernandez read that a Baylor University professor had been brutally murdered in her home. Three stab wounds to the chest, her face had been smashed in with a baseball bat. She had been raped after death. Two words were written in blood on a kitchen wall—or two attempts to write the same word. The killer's fingerprints were found at the scene of the crime, taken from the knife and bat. Sperm samples were sent for analysis. The INS hadn't found a match yet, though there was a profile of the suspect: a young male, probably Mexican or from a Central American country.

"OK then," Fernandez said, "if he can't spell in English he must be Mexican. So we can all sleep peacefully now."

"Not so quick," McMullen said. "What if he strikes again?"

Ah, McMullen never catches the sarcasm.

"Why do they think he jumped a train?"

"The house was in the vicinity of the station. It's the most likely scenario."

"But he could also not have taken the train, right?"

"Sure. Right now anything's possible, he could even be on a bike."

"He wrote on the wall, you say. Must watch *Night Stalker.*"

"Just what we need. Psychopaths who study other psychopaths."

He met up with Debbie at the Best Western in downtown Landslide. They drank a bottle of red wine and she got a little tipsy. After having sex, Debbie jumped into the shower while he read a copy of *Newsweek.* She came out dressed in a red robe; she took it off in front of the mirror in a corner of the room and rubbed her body with a creamy lotion. Almond-scented, Fernandez noticed, distracted from his reading and watching her sideways. She was struggling against the ravages of the aging process, her body doing all it could to resist what was happening inside, the tissue that was losing elasticity and loosening, the skin that was drying out, the spots showing up on hands and cheeks, the joints that creaked and threatened to give out any second.

He should go find himself a twenty-year-old whore instead. He had to admit it would be tough now: he had a weakness for her. Their habitual rendezvous had begun on weekdays, sometimes in hotels, others in his apartment. She stopped charging him after the third month, though he continued to pay; it preserved a sense of freedom and allowed him to fool himself into thinking this wasn't a stable relationship.

The way she walked around the room naked, so willowy and uninhibited. She called herself an escort, not a hooker, and insisted there was a difference. Sometimes she accompanied men who wanted just companionship, no sex. Fernandez would have liked to meet them, he wisecracked. Ask them how they did it. How it worked for them. Must be the same kind of men who bought *Playboy* for the articles. Anyway, what mattered was that as long as she was hooking, she would continue to be a whore to him. They could spend all their time together, but he refused to consider them a proper couple. Sometimes when he was out doing his nightly rounds on the streets of Landslide, he would catch himself wondering what she was up to. If she was out somewhere with another man. He would have liked her to quit, but he was too proud to ask. It had to come from her. Who knows, maybe it was exactly what Debbie was hoping he would say to her.

She lay down in bed and quickly fell asleep; he thought about leaving the money on the nightstand and taking off, but didn't want to be curt and decided he'd hang around for at least a few more hours. Sleep never came: he was too sober, overwhelmed by the lack of coherence to the whole murder story. The Baylor professor, slain near a train station . . . The worst part was finding the FBI telegram in McMullen's folder. The Federales were taking over the investigation. Sons of bitches always got the interesting cases.

From time to time Fernandez still visited Joyce, the daughter of that elderly woman who had been murdered by the "Train Killer." Early on he'd shown up at her workplace—a preschool—asking questions about her mother. Had Joyce considered any possible scenarios, did her mother have people working for her, gardeners or plumbers? He followed all possible trails. Joyce never disclosed anything of consequence, and he wasn't surprised. He kept visiting her anyway, as if he were a doctor making a house call, someone who took care of family members who had experienced a close encounter with death. Joyce told him stories about her mother. Once they even went to see a movie together. It was unprofessional of him, he knew, but loneliness is a poor counselor.

He sighed and turned the television on, flipping through the channels. He watched the end of a Bruce Willis movie, a *Seinfeld* rerun, an infomercial on slutty blonds during spring break. Before letting himself doze off he turned to Fox News.

Dawn Haze Johnson, the anchor of his favorite news program, was complaining about a pedophile in Wyoming and sermonizing about how young parents don't look after their children properly, don't supervise their games or friends closely enough. Dawn Haze was an expert at crying over spilt milk; always zealous about finding culprits, she'd go so far as to blame the parents in the case of a daughter who was abducted from her bedroom at three in the morning because they weren't awake and watching over her while she slept.

After the pedophile bit came a segment of breaking news about a couple who had been brutally murdered in Weimar, Texas, a town of some two thousand souls. Reverend Norman Bates and his wife Lynn had been bludgeoned to death with a hammer taken from the reverend's own garage. The killer had entered their home by slashing the screen door with a knife.

Dawn Haze fondled her blond locks and fiddled with the silver buttons on her shirt before informing her listeners that she'd share her exposé just after the pause. Fernandez let himself be drawn in by the woman's performance. The commercial break seemed to go on forever.

He should call McMullen in the meantime to see if there was anything new on the case.

She was back: the INS authorities have identified fingerprints at the scene of the crime as matching those taken a few days ago in a Houston suburb. The face of Jesús González Riele appeared on screen, a Mexican illegal who had been arrested twice and deported.

He felt like waking Debbie up. Letting her know about the blurred black-and-white photograph. The brown skin, the downy mustache, the prominent cheekbones, the scruffy black hair. Could it possibly . . . could it be him?

He looked at her lying next to him, lost in her dream. She wouldn't much care about the things he had to tell her.

Dawn Haze was foaming at the mouth: "Immigration laws are so lax that our country is being invaded by Mexicans who are spreading the same type of callous violence they practice over there. It's time we build a wall and keep them out!"

Fernandez coughed and got out of bed. He tried not to disturb Debbie while getting dressed. He belonged to only one country, and that was the United States. He had arrived with his parents from Calexico at the age of twelve, and his love of the country and conviction ran deep. Even so, it made him uncomfortable to hear people slander Mexico or the Mexican people. It was so easy to make sweeping generalizations. True, there must be some vicious narcos and thieves coming in, but the vast majority were normal people looking for a new lease on life, for decent jobs. And while we're at it, what country can outdo the United States when it comes to creativity in violence?

He regularly got into arguments with Dawn Haze. In truth, the only reason he watched her program was to let himself get all riled up.

Now he was outraged. But not with Dawn Haze, with Gonzalez Riele, or Reyle, who had just gone and fucked them all over. When Fernandez was eighteen, he had worked as a security guard in the Gap store in downtown Landslide. A kid had come in once to try on some clothes, and as he was exiting the store, one of the other guards on duty noticed he had jeans on under his pants. The guard stopped him and marched him to the back of the store, where they smacked him around a little bit. The kid started bawling, he didn't have papers, "please don't arrest me, please don't." Fernandez had a hard time convincing the other guards to show mercy, he was just a kid. Fernandez told the boy he'd better not ever do it again. He let him walk. How many times on his beat as a Ranger had he stopped a car for a broken taillight or an expired inspection sticker, to find that the driver was a frightened illegal? He felt sorry for them and let them go. He'd give them a break, and who knows, maybe now they were doing as well or better than he was. But did any of it matter now? All his effort, and the hard work of so many other people, would be eclipsed by the media frenzy and people who wouldn't remember anything else but the one illegal who was a killer.

What would Dawn Haze say if she knew that this man might have killed not three but as many as five people? He'd find out soon enough.

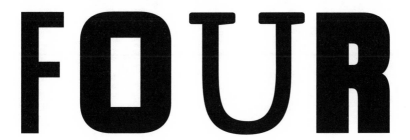

1

Auburn, 1952–1959

The professor was now residing in the white building. Nobody would have confused him with the other doctors or nurses. His head was shaved bald. Even when the heat pinched, he always wore long-sleeved shirts and a black, gray, or coffee-colored suit, elegant but boring, Martín thought, though surely they must think the same about his own uniform, this sky-blue pajama-type thing with pants so loose they'd fall straight to his ankles if he forgot to tie them nice and tight.

In the mornings the professor would keep Martín company in the pottery workshop when nobody else was there, so he could spend some quiet time drawing. Martín would sit down on the floor under the professor's watchful eye and comb his mind for memories. When something finally caught his attention, he'd observe it through the filter of the magazines he loved to read and shape it together with the drawings and photographs that filled their pages.

The professor tried to strike up a conversation in Spanish with him one day, but Martín didn't answer. He changed over into English and continued on about how he'd dedicated his life's work to studying art made by people who were *loco*. He used the

Spanish word *loco*, which Martín understood. He said he spent all his time researching "skitzofrenic" art, or "autsaider art," something like that. The words just kept trickling and dribbling out of his mouth, no way the professor's teeth could hold them all back, and so it occurred to Martín to draw a pair of long incisors on one of his jockey's faces, an open mouth like the professor's that spewed little drops of spittle. Or better: he could draw the words themselves. A man with a stomach chock-full of words that had to be expelled, as if he had swallowed a bunch of rabbits. A puking gush of vowels and consonants floating in green phlegm. Why did people insist on using that other language, it's like a can of worms. Did they want his head to burst open? Where was their compassion? All he asked was to be left alone to draw. Go take a hike and shut the door behind them.

Rabbits. He used to hunt them in Picacho. Every once in a while a shot to the stomach would rip one of the tiny bodies apart. But María Santa Ana knew how to cook them fine, following her mother's recipe. Oh, and that meat she'd cook smothered in onions and beans? And her oven-roasted suckling pig. Aaaahhhhh.

The professor said he had faith in Martín's talent. He admired him. He believed he'd found the Mexican Jenri Rusó. Who? Jenri. Russsssaaauuuu. Yes. That's it. He brought Martín notebooks, magazines, and colors. That made everything bearable. The professor could go on chewing words as much as he wanted, as long as he kept fetching art materials. And Martín drew. He came up with a painstaking ritual that began with removing the pages of a notebook and placing them along the floor to glue them all together and make enough space to draw. Then he'd make his own paste from things like shoe polish, crayons, charcoal, red juice he extracted from certain fruits, and his own spit, with lots of phlegm whenever possible. He mixed it all together in bowls he had learned to make in pottery class. Once everything was ready, he'd painstakingly cut out illustrations and photos from his magazine collection. He liked the soap advertisements best of all, because they always had faces of beautiful women in them that reminded him of María Santa Ana, even though they were white. Sometimes he would glue a face to the far end of some railroad tracks, as if it were a destination, or the promise of one. "Are you homesick?" the professor asked him in English. "Would you like to go home?" But Martín couldn't understand what he was saying. "Is . . . your . . . wife . . . waiting?" the professor asked in Spanish, and this time Martín could sort of catch what he was trying to say.

The professor could spend three or four hours at a time just sitting there and watching Martín work. Martín once drew something that looked like a cat, and the professor asked in Spanish if it was a cat. "Sí, gato," Martín answered and kept drawing.

The professor then spoke in English: "I thought you were mute."

"Miut?" Martín didn't understand the word.

The professor left and came back with an English–Spanish dictionary. He showed Martín a series of illustrations. He asked if this were a *zapato*.

"Sí, zapato," Martín responded in a voice so low he could barely be heard.

"And this is a *perro*?"

"Sí, perro."

"And this house is *tu casa*?"

"Sí, casa."

"And this woman is *tu mujer*?"

"Sí, mujer."

"And this building, *iglesia*?"

"Sí, iglesia."

"You aren't mute, Martín."

"Miut?" Martín didn't understand what the professor said.

The professor looked in the dictionary. *Mudo*, he said a couple of times. Martín didn't respond.

"You don't speak because you prefer not to, isn't that so?"

"Perro," he said. And then: "Casa, mujer, zapato, gato. Aaaaaaahhhhhh."

He closed his eyes. Everything was much better that way. The professor vanished. He should just stay in this peaceful place, in this dark room where he could be all by himself. He felt panic. What if the professor was still there when he opened his eyes?

A long time passed before he finally dared open them again, and when he did, the professor was gone.

The professor asked his permission to show his drawings in an art gallery in Sacramento. Martín didn't really understand what was being requested of him, but he signed the page Whitey handed to him anyway. His signature was undulating and serpentine, the *M* stretched out like the hills of his town.

On occasion the professor would bring someone along who translated what he said in English into Spanish. But Martín decided he wasn't going to speak anymore. They had betrayed his trust.

The show had been a "success," the professor told him. Martín now had several visitors dropping by to meet him, local artists, critics, and teachers. Some were sculptors or painters themselves, and of course the professor's students. The hospital director allowed the visits; he'd even tag along every now and then, proud that one of his patients was fetching so much attention. Martín received his visitors but would have preferred they not come. Why couldn't they simply drop off their gifts and leave him in peace?

One patient handed him a pen and paper and gestured for him to scribble something down right then and there. Martín drew a miniature train. The cottony wisps of smoke looked like they wanted to float right off the page. The fat man looked at it and pointed his finger at Martín and fired. Martín smiled, and the fat man burst into tears. Gitupboy and Little Stepbackwards ran over and tried to calm him down. They took him outside.

What was Martín supposed to do? Throw himself to the floor?

From then on, the director restricted Martín's visits. Only the professor was allowed access to him.

There was another show in a place called Berkeley. And another in a place that was farther away called Syracuse. The professor brought news clippings back with him, and Martín read the headlines: "Wonderful Insane Art." What was that? The photos showed the professor giving a talk at a university near Syracuse, in a little town called Ithaca. Martín's drawings could be seen behind the professor.

There was another show in some place called Oakland. The professor arranged a special leave for Martín so that he could attend. He lent him his black suit, though the arms of the jacket were a little too long for him. One of the orderlies gave him a yellow belt that didn't really match, and the director gave him a checkered tie that looked like a napkin.

Martín left the building in a van, accompanied by the red-haired orderly he had nicknamed Firecracker. The professor sat up front.

The redhead spoke a few words of Spanish and he asked Martín if he knew what year it was. Martín understood the question but didn't answer.

Uno nueve cinco cuatro, the orderly said. Martín understood, without understanding.

When he approached the blue building where his paintings were hanging, Martín read the big letters on one of the walls by the entrance: "The Art of a Schizophrene: Drawings by Insane Artist Martín Ramírez."

Schizo, schizo, schizo . . .

He walked through the rooms in the building accompanied by the professor and the redhead. People came up and asked to have their photo taken with him. He smiled and let them. Then he remembered his decaying black teeth and tried to smile while keeping his mouth closed.

He liked how clean and well lit the rooms were. His drawings could be appreciated. But the walk took less than ten minutes. He wanted to leave now, go back to his building. His home. Didn't they understand?

There was another show in a place called San Francisco. It was going to be even bigger, with more visitors, and the professor explained that his drawings would be displayed in a small room, but there would be the work of other *artistas locos*.

Martín ventured to ask: "Locos?" He wasn't *loco*.

"Schizophrenics," the professor said in English.

That damn word again.

"Psychotics," the professor continued, but Martín couldn't grasp what he was saying.

"The sculptures of a patient after a lobotomy."

"*Lobos*. Wolfs?"

He wanted to draw wolves. They used to prowl the outskirts of his town.

"That's right," the professor said. *Lobos*.

The show was one of his all-time best experiences. The professor gave him a folder stuffed with news clippings. He blacked out the photos where his teeth were showing. He wanted to read them but kept getting stuck: that damn language still got in his way. Important people called and asked for an appointment to meet him, but the director said no. One or two were allowed to come with the professor, and he made the introductions, then stepped aside so that they could talk. But Martín never opened his mouth, Martín closed his eyes and made them disappear, and when he opened them again, the important people weren't there anymore.

He kept at his drawing. The professor didn't live in the building anymore, though. No matter: he still came to see Martín three times a week. He scrutinized his drawings, made comments, cataloged them, and then he'd leave. He'd take some of the work with him after asking permission; Martín said yes, assuming he was borrowing them, though truth is, he never brought them back.

The professor would get irritated with him if he didn't have anything new. "Martín, we make it so easy for you." Martín had no idea what the professor was saying, but the tone of voice frightened him. He didn't want to offend the professor. So he would start drawing, and sometimes the professor would watch and say something like "More of the same, we need new things." And the only thing that Martín absorbed was that they wanted him to continue drawing. No complaints.

He still suffered from a chronic cough and was so accustomed to the headaches by now that he only noticed them in the scarce moments when he felt relief. At times he'd grow anxious, agitated, and the only way the orderlies could calm him down was with morphine injections or immersing him in cold water, but luckily there were no more treatments with cables.

The Federales had won the war with the help of the United States. He would forever be a prisoner now. He had to get used to the idea. He could find a way to make peace with his situation and everything else, as long as they let him draw. Like María Santa Ana's betrayal, not seeing his daughters. And Candelario. Aaaaahhhhh.

The professor showed up one day looking very solemn. Martín got upset: had something happened, did someone die? The professor guided Martín outside to the patio. They walked along the main path, lined with freshly pruned trees whose trunks were painted white. The sky was marine blue, and the glowing sun had dropped below the hilltops, infusing them with a golden aura. Martín thought about the bare hills of his own town, the muted colors of its landscape.

Judging by his gestures, the professor had something important to say, but Martín couldn't decipher the words. He had grown a thin mustache and it itched. He'd ask Little Stepback-wards to shave it off for him. Or maybe Firecracker instead.

The professor wrote out a word for him. Europe.

He knew that Europe was a big country and that it was far away. Did he want him to draw it? The problem was he'd never been there.

The professor gave him a big bear hug. It felt good, and Martín didn't want to detach himself from the warm body holding him.

They walked into the main hall. "Take care of yourself, Martín," he said in Spanish.

"*Cuídese, cuídese*," Martín repeated.

The professor turned around and walked away until he disappeared altogether.

Martín never saw him again. Now he spent all his time alone. Wasn't that what he'd always wanted?

He stopped drawing at the same pace as before.

Truth is, he missed him.

They rotated the orderlies; sometimes they kept him company, but it was never the same. The doctors talked and wrote things down on papers for the orderlies, but their visits were fleeting. His building companions screamed at each other and fought, and there wasn't a single moment free from bodily fluids oozing and dripping everywhere. He couldn't stand it. If it wasn't blood, then someone was pissing in the hallway or vomiting on the tables or over the beds. They stank to high heaven; he probably smelled the same, though, a blend of stale sweat and piss and medicines. If it were up to him, he'd have lived with his eyes closed the whole time. Make everything around him vanish, only keep the images of his life on the ranch that he turned into illustrations.

He was friendly with some of the people in the pottery classes, but he knew he irritated them.

What if he started talking? Wasn't he old enough by now?

A new doctor came along, short-sighted and flat-footed, and he said that Martín should get to work, start helping out, what was the meaning of this privileged life he was leading doing nothing but drawing and not lifting a finger for anyone else? He wasn't really sure if that's what he said, but in any case that's what happened.

He went back to working on the grounds. He watered the plants. Cut the grass. Looked at the hills and thought about his hometown. He imagined himself riding around Picacho on horseback, alone or with Atanacio, looking for rabbits and deer to feed the family. He thought of when he and María Santa Ana would go to the market to sell eggs and tomatoes they grew on the ranch. When he'd attend mass with his wife and daughters but not with Candelario. Without his son? Yes, that's how it was because Candelario hadn't been born yet, and if Martín hadn't left San José, he might never have been born.

He got tired so quickly. His chest hurt. The orderlies talked to the administrator. The new doctor's orders were revoked. He was to stop helping outdoors. He was allowed to dedicate his time to drawing again. He didn't think it was because the doctor liked his drawings so much. He figured it was because he was afflicted with sadness.

He missed the professor.

2

Landslide, 2009

*Of the mountains in the south, Luvina is the highest and rockiest.
It's infested with that gray stone they make lime from. They call
it crude stone there, and the hill that climbs up toward Luvina
they call the Crude Stone Hill. And the ground is steep. They say
in Luvina that one's dreams come up from those barrancas; but
the only thing I've seen come up out of them was zombies. Sad
zombies, scraping the air with their thorny howls, making a noise
like a knife on a whetstone.*

*That man who was talking fell silent a while, staring out the
door. And outside night kept advancing.*

*Another thing, sir. You'll never see a blue sky in Luvina. You'll
see this: those hills silent as if they were dead and Luvina crown-
ing the highest hill with its white houses like a crown of the dead.*

*I didn't want him to tell me about the hills. I wanted to hear
more about the zombies.*

*Well, as I was saying. Wherever you look in Luvina, it's a very
sad place. You're going there, so you'll find out. I would say it's
the place where sadness nests. Where smiles are unknown, as if
all the zombies' faces had been frozen. When the moon is full
you can see the figure of the zombies sweeping along Luvina's
streets, bearing a black blanket.*

I left my life there. I went to that place full of illusions and returned old and worn out. And now you're going there . . . All right. When I got to Luvina the first time, the mule driver who took us didn't even want to let his animals rest. As soon as he let us off, he turned around. "I'm going back," he said. My wife, my three children, we stayed there, standing in the middle of the plaza, with all our belongings in our arms. Just a plaza without a single plant to hold back the wind. "What country are we in, Agripina?" I asked my wife. And she shrugged her shoulders. "Go and look for a place where we can eat and spend the night." She took the youngest child by the hand and left. But she didn't come back.

Did the zombies eat them?

We found her in Luvina's church with the child asleep between her legs. "I came to pray," she told us. Nobody was there to pray to. It was a vacant old shack without any doors, and a roof full of cracks. "Did you see anybody?" "Yes, there across the street . . . some women . . . I can still see them. Look, there behind the cracks in that door I can see some eyes shining watching us."

That night we settled down to sleep in a corner of the church behind the dismantled altar. That's when we heard zombies with their long howls coming in and out of the hollow caves of the doors, whipping the crosses of the stations of the cross with their hands full of air. The children cried because they were too scared to sleep. And my wife, trying to hold all of them in her arms. And me, I didn't know what to do.

A little before dawn they calmed down. Then they returned. "What is that?" my wife said to me. "What's what?" "That, that noise." "It's the silence. Go to sleep."

But soon I heard it too. It was like bats flitting through the darkness very close to us. Bats with big wings that grazed against the ground. Then I walked on tiptoes over there, feeling that dull murmur in front of me. I stopped at the door and saw them. I saw all the zombies of Luvina, their black on the black background of the night. I saw them standing in front of me, looking at me. Then, as if they were shadows, they started walking down the street. No, I'll never forget that first night I spent in Luvina. Don't you think this deserves another drink?

It seems to me you asked me how many years I was in Luvina, didn't you? The truth is, I don't know. Time is very long there, as if you had lived an eternity. Because only zombies live there, and those who aren't born yet. And they're still there. You'll see them now when you get there. You'll see them pass as shadows, clinging to the walls of the houses, almost dragged along by the wind. When the sun pours into Luvina, the zombies appear and suck your blood and the little bit of moisture we have in our skin. I left Luvina and I haven't gone back and don't intend to.

But look at the way the world keeps turning. You're going there now in a few hours. Maybe it's been fifteen years since they said the same thing to me: "You're going to Luvina." In those days I was strong. But it didn't work out in Luvina. The name sounded to me like a name in the heavens. But it's purgatory. A dying place where even the dogs are zombies and there's not a creature to bark at the silence. And that gets you down. Just look at me. What it did to me. You're going there, so you'll soon understand what I mean . . .

He kept staring at a fixed point on the table. Outside you could hear the night advancing.

We were sitting in my apartment on the living-room rug. We had opened a bottle of red wine and had been chatting for a while. Night had settled on the windowpanes; a moth fluttered around the yellow halo of the lamp beside my laptop on the folding table. Sam's face glowed; his body was in shadows and it appeared as if a floating head were talking to me.

"It's great, it has verve. It respects the original but at the same time turns it into something else."

"You really think so?"

"But it's supposed to be a joke, isn't it? I mean, I think we've had enough of zombies for a while."

"Don't you think a book of classic remakes is a good idea? Aureliano Buendía as the Werewolf, for example. And maybe add a few cartoon strips, like Piglia's anthology *La Argentina en pedazos*."

"I know where you got the idea, my dear, I'm familiar with that novel *Pride and Prejudice and Zombies*. But none of it convinces me. I mean, I expect more from you. I'm willing to concede all the paraphernalia of monsters and gothic scenery, as long as the ideas are fresh and original."

Fabián was feeling better during those few weeks and had returned to teaching, but I wasn't in the mood to see him. When my shift ended at Taco Hut, I headed back to my studio hoping to lose myself in my own world. I had been blocked; nothing was coming out right and I couldn't draw, so I fiddled with versions of classic tales, introducing zombies and vampires. I needed to talk, to feel that someone was really listening to me, so I let Sam come over to hang out again. I made it crystal-clear that I wasn't interested in getting involved, and he said drop it, although it didn't take long to realize he hadn't yet resigned himself to the fact that it was over. "No big deal," he quipped. I was plenty aware of my shortcomings and knew that his idealized version of me, of what I was capable of being and doing, was hyperbolic.

I lit a cigarette, reaching up to disconnect the smoke alarm. A cruel idea crossed my mind: why don't I tell Sam all about what happened with Fabián, about our little trip to El Paso. That would put him off all right, make him stop chasing me. But I guess I didn't really want him to stop calling. His company was better than nothing. I ended up confessing everything to my mom, but all it did was make her worry. She called me every day now, insisting I go back home for a while, or let her come and stay with me till I'd convalesced properly. I'd change the subject and ask myself why I had to open my big fat mouth. What was it worth? She wanted to give Fabián a "talking-to"—"the jerk's going to hear what he's got coming to him"—but I told her not to even think about it.

I should be in the thick of my novel by now—well, graphic novel that is, calling it a "novel" seems a little pretentious. But well, since I've failed to come up with anything original . . .

"Give yourself a break. You've had a rough couple of weeks. After all, you can always count on zombies."

"Until you can't."

I opened the window and flicked the cigarette butt out, then we smoked a joint. I thought about my daughter who would never be, and my whole body ached. I would have named her Ana, and she'd have worn her hair in a long braid, like Dr. Carranza, and she would have brought some focus into my life. Coffee-colored eyes with the look of strength and determination that I lacked. I wouldn't have been a perfect mother, I wouldn't have known what to do in that world of bibs and diapers, but she'd eventually have turned seven or eight, and then . . .

The lights in the neighborhood glowed serenely in the night; a neighbor's panicky voice searching for her cat could be heard against a background din of cars traveling like flashes of lightning along the highway. I refused to let the despair of loneliness get the best of me. I should have been out with my friends in College Station; it was just the time of night when we'd have been trying to make up our minds whether to hit a bar, or maybe a club instead. Always the same old routine, tired of everything and ready for our next adventure.

"La Jodida called me the other day," Sam said. "She's back with Megan, but I suspect she's also seeing Nissa. Have you ever met her?"

"Once, at a rave. She's a very pretty black woman."

"She says the sex is great but when they fight it's atrocious. And she's noticed that at times her memory fails. She's going to kick it all on her birthday: the alcohol, the cigarettes, and the coke."

I remember hearing Fabián make similar promises the first few weeks we started hanging out, when we'd go bar hopping on Sixth Street. We barely knew each other yet, so he was still trying to impress me. He made it seem as though there were other things more important to him. It took me a few years to finally realize that I had lost the battle way back then, on the second floor of a deserted jazz club when I threatened to leave him if he didn't lay off the drugs, and he just laughed at me and I caved.

The world: a place full of highly flammable materials. I was getting burned.

La Jodida had called me several times too. She'd wake me up early in the morning to tell me she was in bed with Megan, sleeping naked by her side, girl, she's so hot, and I'd doze off again without answering and wake up a few minutes later and she'd still be talking, I have a squeeze, I'm happy, we're going to San Juan over break and I'll introduce her to my parents, they'll be happy. I didn't answer, and after a while she'd say you piece of shit, bitch, you're going to rot in hell, you got me into this and then you wash your hands, and I'd answer what exactly did I get you into, you're old enough to make your own decisions, and she'd say you made me try it the first time, you think I don't remember, bitch. I'd hang up but wouldn't be able to go back to sleep, and I'd walk into the bathroom to take a cold shower and sit down in the tub and let the water wash over me until my skin turned pruney.

The woman was still looking for her cat, the pitch of her voice growing more and more desperate.

We returned to the living room. We finished the bottle of wine and he suggested opening another one. A sudden cramp racked my body. I grabbed my stomach with both of my hands and fell to my knees.

Sam helped get me up and onto the couch. I lay back on the cushions to catch my breath, wait until everything returned to normal.

"Y'aint getting rid of me, peanut." He smiled and brought me a glass of water. "My turn."

"For Christ's sake, Sam. Give me a break. I'm tired and everything hurts."

His radio show started in an hour. We had agreed that first we'd read my story and then we'd go over his script together. He handed me the folder he'd dropped on the table when he came in. That night's show featured a list of the top one hundred serial killers. It opened with a reflection on Maldoror, "the first serial killer in Latin American literature." The music: a few songs by Kasabian—a band that paid tribute to Charles

Manson—and a song by Guns N' Roses composed by Manson himself.

"I'm not sure about the idea behind the whole thing," I said. "Doesn't it seem a tad frivolous to you? I mean, it's fine to make a list of models, of songs, of rock bands, even writers, but serial killers?"

"Well, it's too late to make such big changes to the script, a few small adjustments is all I can do."

I was moved that he'd go to such an effort to seek my opinion, that he too had a frivolous side and was more than just a wooden academic. He did his first radio show a few months after we met. Might he have been trying to impress me, to convince me that I was mistaken about him, and I simply missed it?

I read: "Pedro Alonso López, the 'Monster of the Andes,'" more than three hundred murders throughout Colombia, Peru, and Ecuador. His mother was a prostitute. He was expelled from his home at eight, sodomized by a pedophile, and then raped a number of times while in prison . . ."

"I don't see why you're giving all the dirty details. Are we supposed to feel sorry for him?"

"Of course not. But we do have to put things in their context."

I didn't feel like continuing.

"Do you mind if I stop reading? To tell you the truth, I'd prefer to listen to it, to be surprised. I don't feel very well and I'm going to lie down in bed and listen to you quietly."

"Whatever."

He stood up and grabbed his coat. Was he upset?

"Why don't you come with me? We could hang out at Underground after the show."

"It's Monday, Sam."

"Who'd have believed the day would come. You staying home."

"Are you out of your mind? Can't you see how bad I feel?"

"Sure. And over some fucking idiot who's not worth a second of your time."

"Why are you so obsessed about it? If you're so sure, why don't you kick him off your committee?"

"Believe me, I've tried. But it's not possible."

"Then you understand me more than you think."

I walked him to the door. His goodbye kiss just lightly brushed my lips. I looked at him reproachfully. He pretended not to understand.

As soon as he left I called Fabián. I asked him to come over. No, he was catching up on his mail and it would him take the whole night. His words slurred a little and I suspected that he'd been drinking. I asked.

"Everything's peachy. I'm old enough to take care of myself. I can't talk right now, the deans have tapped the line. Sons of bitches. They're looking for reasons to get rid of me. But you know what, they fucking can't! I have fucking tenure! They're fucked."

He sent me a kiss: "Tomorrow I'll cook something special, and you're invited." He hung up.

I tried to forget about it. I had to read the book about Ramirez and only had two weeks left to deliver the essay, Ruth had written an email asking how it was coming along.

I read halfway through an essay and leafed through the reproductions of his work. He was a talented illustrator. It would be hard to live a more wretched life than his. How bizarre that his drawings were now hanging in places like the Guggenheim and the Smithsonian.

I closed the book. Something in his work was trying to speak to me, but I wasn't in the mood to listen.

I ran through the conversation with Sam a few times. I didn't want to agree with him, but I knew he was right. I ripped up my version of "Luvina." I went to bed, switched the radio on, and checked my emails one last time before I fell asleep. There was one from Fabián in my inbox: "all i want is for you not to disappear, that you be infinite. that we walk together hand in hand among the ruins of buildings as if nothing had ever happened. that we eat dulce de leche ice cream on a deserted beach and laugh at the Deans. and dance. i always feel as though the best is over. I don't want to feel as though the best is over."

The next day I phoned Ruth and told her not to count on me for the show catalogue. It didn't seem to bother her; her tone was calm and understanding, as if she had expected it. That hurt my feelings. I would have liked her to fight for me, not to give in so easily, even if it were only so that I could refuse once more.

I hung up feeling as though she didn't want me to participate in the show catalogue any longer, when I was the one who had just abandoned ship.

3

Houston, Texas, 1999

Jesús fell to his knees. His hands had sunk into the gravel at the side of the tracks; one of his palms was cut and bleeding. The train's silhouette shrank into the night. The sound of the whistle persisted but eventually faded out, and the soft resonances of summer settled back in: the chirping of crickets and cicadas; children shouting in the distance, delaying the time they'd have to go indoors, put away their bicycles, say goodbye to the neighborhood kids.

He stood up. His limp was getting worse. He had jumped from the moving train even though it hadn't slowed down. It wasn't the first time he'd done that, and he had the scars to prove it: on his right hand, his left forearm, his right wrist, his forehead.

The house that had caught his attention was on a corner lot and had a chimney; there was a well-worn, faded green couch on the porch and strings of carnations hanging from wires. A wooden sign with gothic letters decorated the front door window and read MI CASA ES SU CASA.

He peered in and saw a couple arguing in the kitchen. The man wore overalls and a straw hat that reminded him of the Mennonites he had seen near his hometown when he was a boy.

He was in no condition to challenge someone a full head taller than him. Fucking white people. Even the women made him seem small by comparison. No matter, they didn't intimidate him anymore, not like they used to. He could come and go as he pleased, as if this whole gigantic territory belonged to him alone. He knew how to get around: his size made him more agile than them. He had fake social security cards he'd bought from the coyotes, stolen driver's licenses, even cards for libraries and gym memberships. He knew their weaknesses: there were guns everywhere; violence was an everyday affair. Like in Mexico, but different. The police and the law enforcement didn't function there; here they tried, but whenever a sexier crime came along they'd get distracted and forget.

He spat.

A young woman wearing butterfly barrettes in her coal-black hair stepped out of a blue Honda Civic in front of an ochre-colored ranch house. The yard was delicately landscaped, with luminous rosebushes and a lemon tree that looked as though it had popped (there were lemons scattered all around the ground). She glanced over at him quickly but continued on her way inside as if in that split second she had gauged that his was an insignificant face, that saying anything to him was a waste of her time, that he was just another of her paisanos walking the streets in search of a job: carpenters, plumbers, construction workers, anything to earn a few bucks. Why didn't they all just go back to Mexico?

Fucking puerca. They were the nastiest, the bitches who changed their clothes style and accent, took on snotty airs, tried to hide their origins. He walked over and snuck around the house, peeping through a back window. The woman was alone; she had switched on the lights and was pacing back and forth, barefoot, talking on a cell phone in English. She was wide-hipped, with fat legs and a plump ass. Meat everywhere, the way he liked his women.

She set up an easel in one of the rooms, pulled up a chair, and sat down in front of a sheet of onionskin paper, holding a paintbrush in one hand and a box of watercolors in the other. Her back was to Jesús. He knew he needed to hurry, but he preferred to wait just a little bit. He was curious to see what she was painting.

A figure appeared on the paper: a man running across a dry riverbed.

He had better enter through the front door this time. He went into the kitchen and opened a drawer beside the sink, trying to find some instrument. There was a pair of scissors but they weren't sharpened. He found a wooden block in a corner beside the microwave that held five knives lined up according to size; he grabbed the biggest.

He stood motionless in the hallway between the room and the kitchen. She finally caught sight of him standing there, and stopped painting. There was a tiny hint of defiance in her expression. He had expected her to scream the second she noticed him.

"I haven't done anything wrong," she said in perfect Spanish. "Take whatever you want. Just please don't hurt me. My name is Noemí . . ."

Fucking asshole bitch. Would it hurt to be a little original?

Jesús saw her lip tremble slightly, as if a sense of dread was finally coming over her. Her cream-colored skirt was embroidered with little flowers, and there was a smudge of lipstick on the collar of her white blouse.

"I'm illustrating a children's book," Noemí continued.

He took in the walls around the room: movie posters (*Toy Story*, *Ice Age*, *Monsters, Inc.*).

"It's about a man who leaves his wife and his children to cross the border and look for work."

He coughed.

"Don't think I like it," Jesús said.

"Excuse me?"

"Ain't believable."

"I can change it if you'd like," she said quickly. "I don't know what's going to happen next. Maybe one of the sons will cross the border to look for his father. I saw this show by a painter not long ago . . . We've been crossing the border for a long time."

"You mean the border crossed us. All this was ours first."

Jesús moved in a little closer, till they were only a few feet apart. Noemí glimpsed the knife, the blade glinted in the room's overhead lights. "Please don't hurt me," she said, her voice reduced to a whisper.

He consented with a quick nod. And sprung, plunging the knife deep into her chest. She struggled to defend herself and fell to the ground, clinging to the knife handle with both hands. "That's right, puerca. You stab it in." Jesús straddled her, bent down, and pulled the knife out of her chest, smearing his hands with the blood as it gushed from the wound and formed a puddle.

Before continuing, he walked over to the window and lowered the blinds.

Then he gouged the knife into one of Noemí's eye sockets. He messed around with the white, viscous substance as if operating on a life-sized doll. When he was little, he had operated on one of María Luisa's dolls without asking her permission, the only doll she'd ever been given for her birthday. He sliced the head off.

This time he stabbed Noemí in the other eye. The blade cut a chunk out of her right cheek and sunk back in to the left one, shattering the bone and leaving shards in its wake. He drove the knife into her forehead, but the blade broke off and Jesús was left holding the handle. "Fucking puerca, even your knives are cheap."

Nah, he wouldn't fuck this one.

He went to one of the walls and wrote in blood: UNNAM

The word was too long; he'd leave it like that.

He washed his bloody arms in the sink and threw the knife handle in the kitchen garbage bin. He reheated a bowl of pozole that he had rummaged from the refrigerator and chased it down with a cold Corona. He found some necklaces and silver earrings in the bedroom; no cash in the wallet, but he pocketed three credit cards. He dumped Noemí's DVD collection in his bag. The only movies she seemed to like were animations; who knows, might just find something good.

He stopped to observe the painting of a smiling skeleton in a cowboy hat sitting in a chair and playing a guitar; bingo cards were strewn about its feet (the mermaid, the soldier, the drunk, the valiant, the rose). There was a book of photographs of the Mexican Revolution. One of them caught his attention: a man standing before a firing squad, smiling, holding a cigarette in his hand. His attitude expressed a complete lack of fear. Courage.

That's the way he'd go when his time came. With a smile on his lips, a cigarette in his hand—even though he didn't smoke—and a bottle of sotol in the other.

Noemí's cell phone rang and he was tempted to answer it but refrained. He grabbed the keys to the Honda on his way outside, jumped into the car, and drove off. He stopped at the first gas station he saw. He bought beef jerky, Doritos, a six-pack of Corona.

He called his sister from the public telephone at the entrance to the gas station. As soon as he heard her voice, he hung up.

He drove south. The closer he was to the border, the more secure he'd feel.

Two deer crossed the road and he slowed down to watch them. The whole region was teeming with antelopes, coyotes, and snakes. They said wolves can only be found on the Mexican side now; ranchers in Texas and New Mexico had killed them off to protect their livestock.

He passed a jeep parked on the dirt shoulder of the highway, in the shade of a cedar tree. Jesús moved into the right lane and drove by slowly. A middle-aged woman was trying to change a flat tire.

Our unnamed father who art not in heaven.

Jesús pulled over. He grabbed the knife out of his bag, stuck it between his belt and the back of his pants. He stepped out of the car and strode over to the jeep with a firm step. From his repertoire of possible expressions, he chose the most humble, solicitous one possible, the same one that had saved him from being arrested a few times when the police had detained him. A few cars passed by without stopping. The sun was relentless; it burned his neck, his arms.

"Hi, need some help?"

The woman was surprised to see him. She was short and stout and barefoot, with cropped brown hair and a pierced lip. Her face was tough and weatherbeaten, as if she spent the greater part of her time outdoors. Her arms were smeared with grease. The jack was next to the flat tire, under the jeep, and she held the wrench in her hand. She had taken her rings and bracelets off and set them on the ground near a can of beer.

"Hi, thanks," she said in English. "The lug nuts are really tight, they won't budge forward or backward. I was thinking of just calling a tow truck."

"Lemme give it a try," Jesús said in English.

"My name's Peggy. Want a beer?"

Jesús said yes to the beer, more out of politeness than because he really felt like drinking one. Peggy went to the back of the jeep and fetched one for him from a cooler.

KILL THEM ALL.

Jesús grabbed the wrench and tried to loosen the nuts. Three of them came off quickly, without much of a struggle; the fourth and the fifth required more of an effort, but eventually he worked them off too. He fought with the sixth for a long time. Sweat ran down his forehead and cheeks, soaked his armpits. He took a swig of beer and nearly spat it back out: it tasted like piss.

"No luck?"

Holy be the absence of thy name.

"Just gotta keep at it, güey," he said in Spanish. Then he jumped back into English: "Just a shame I don't have the time. There are people waiting for me."

"Thanks anyway. I'll just call a tow truck."

It wouldn't take much. The road was deserted; he could jump her now and knock her over. She was more or less his size, probably stronger than she looked, but he could overpower her. The knife would do the rest.

Jesús asked her what was the best way to get to Highway 10. He was playing for time while he decided what to do. It was easy, just keep driving straight ahead for ten minutes and he'd see the signs.

Peggy didn't have a cell phone. She'd have to walk some three hundred feet where the CALL BOX was on the side of the road. Jesús walked alongside her. Once there, he stared at her a moment, surprised to see the sparkle in her green eyes, and said:

"You're very lucky."

"I guess so. Seeing as things could be a lot worse."

Peggy fidgeted in place, a little antsy now, and lowered her eyes.

"Well, guess I should call for the truck now. Thanks again."

Jesús turned around and walked back to the car. Peggy glimpsed the knife as it flashed in the sun, but she pretended not to and concentrated on making that phone call.

4

La Grange, Texas, 1999

The elderly woman lay in bed with her skull crushed in. The blood had soaked into her hair and run down her forehead and cheeks, staining the comforter and forming a puddle on the floor. The shovel the murderer had used was visible at one side of the room. The television was on, tuned into a Spanish-language soap opera.

Sergeant Fernandez heard the FBI agent just outside the bedroom, in the hallway. Apparently she had been asleep, the agent said. At least she didn't suffer.

"Any leads?"

"The report just came in from Houston. They confirmed our hunch. Now it's official. The fingerprints taken from the shovel's handle are Reyle's, and they match the ones taken from the house in Houston yesterday. Ditto the other crime scenes. Drops of blood now tie him to five murders. So. Not to state the obvious, but I'm afraid we've got a serial killer on our hands, folks. He doesn't even bother to cover his trail."

"He never really did," Fernandez said. "He's just been very lucky. He's been incarcerated, he's had run-ins with the police a bunch of times, and the only thing INS did was deport him to Mexico."

"What else could they do? They arrest illegals every day. All they want is to haul them back to Mexico, clean and quick."

"But this is different," Rafael said. "With a record as long as somebody's arm, they should have been more careful. These murders could have been avoided."

Fernandez brought his hands to his forehead and tried to conceal his annoyance. Nothing ever functioned the way it was supposed to. Starting with him: the FBI databanks tied Reyle to at least five murders; for a long time he'd had a hunch that a single person was tied to the other unresolved deaths, and yet he never actually acted on it. He never bothered to bounce his intuition off anyone else. If he had, maybe now someone up the chain of command would be congratulating him for his sharp instincts, cussing their own carelessness. And his fellow agent was right, you can't blame the INS: Reyle had used a series of pseudonyms, he was in possession of several fake social security cards, and he was remarkably elusive, you had to give him credit for that. It was true what others liked to say said about the Rangers, famous for their arrogance toward other federal agencies and local police: how they loved to turn things in a Hollywood film. Somehow they had begun to believe their own legend. It's also what the Rangers said about the FBI.

The FBI had dubbed the Gonzalez Reyle manhunt Operation Stop Train, the agent studying the walls in the hallway said, as if he might find some clue that would lead him straight to the killer. The media gave Reyle a nickname: Fox News was calling him the Railroad Killer. Some clever FBI agent must have fed the name to the journalists, the type of agent who spends the day profiling serial killers.

They might have made an effort to be a little more original, Fernandez thought as he walked out of the house. If all the murders had taken place next to a football stadium, they'd have called it Operation Touchdown, and the murderer would have been given the nickname Quarterback Killer.

The elderly woman's son and his wife sat in the back of a police car, in a state of shock. The son blew his nose into a Kleenex; the woman's head was shaved, and Fernandez wondered if she was undergoing some kind of treatment. She reminded him of one of his cousins after chemo; she had put up a good fight, but the cancer won out in the end.

Annie Tadic's lifeless body had been discovered by the two of them. She lived alone on a ranch in Fayette County, near Highway 10. They were supposed to have breakfast together that morning, but she never showed up. When they phoned over to the house, she didn't answer. They went to her home and found her there, already dead.

Fernandez walked by and bowed his head slightly in greeting. He heard them express surprise at the idea that the deceased would have been watching a Spanish channel; she didn't speak the language, which had been a problem with the occasional hired help. Fernandez concluded that it must have been the killer who had changed the channel. So after murdering the elderly woman, he sat down next to her and watched a soap opera. He'd done similar things in other houses: after committing a heinous murder and often a postmortem rape, he'd calmly prepare a sandwich, drink a beer, or heat some dish in the microwave. An FBI psychologist from Quantico who was an expert in profiling serial killers wrote in a preliminary report that this astonishing equanimity hid a calculating personality, a rational mind with a delusion of absolute omnipotence. Fernandez agreed with the omnipotence bit but not with the rest of the report. You couldn't always draw such a neat correlation between cause and consequence. The murderer could have been so nervous after the fact that instead of fleeing, he needed to sit down and have a beer. Rational and calculating? Not necessarily. Although in truth, who knows? Psychopaths like Reyle were cut from a totally different fabric. A serial killer case was way beyond anything he'd ever had to deal with as a Ranger.

He went back to his car, behind the yellow tape that cordoned the house off.

The Quantico psychologist's report made him think how much of what the FBI agents worked with was fictional, and they were often wrong. They profiled murderers, wrote reports full of childhood abuse and rape, developed procedures for observing the world through trivial acts. The fictions helped fill in the blanks, allowed them to speculate aloud and feel more confident about reaching a positive outcome, that the rule of law that had been broken would be restored in the end. All murderers can be reduced to a limited set of attitudes, obsessions, and compulsions. But all these narratives lacked a fundamental element: "the inexplicable," that little detail that doesn't lead to anything else. How easy to appreciate that evil can be titillating, it fascinates, seduces. How much harder to accept that evil, horror, the abyss are a fundamental part of life. Remarkably, the FBI had someone in charge of getting into the head of serial killers: someone had to do it. But Fernandez had come to the conclusion that it was better not to understand them at all. They just were, period. One had to arrest them, get rid of them by lethal injection.

The midday sun fell ruthlessly over the plains and scattered ranches, the cedar and oak trees with parched trunks and cracked branches, the cacti leaning heavily as if they could no longer endure the burden of the heat. There was a single, drawn-out cloud hugging the horizon, with metallic-hued trimming. Fernandez gnawed a piece of beef jerky.

Annie Tadic hadn't been made to suffer. That was the only good thing.

For weeks Rafael Fernandez stood by helplessly and followed the unfolding of Operation Stop Train. The state police and FBI doubled their vigilance in train stations and patrolled the tracks of the country's rail systems, looking for places where the killer might be hiding out. They raided care centers, town squares where illegals gathered to look for work, and homeless shelters where vagrants were given shelter for a night. The Railroad Killer's photograph was made public and appeared in all the national and local newspapers and television broadcasts. In some counties they printed WANTED posters with the word in capital letters, together with his picture and a cash reward for anyone who gave information leading to an arrest.

Eight days after Noemí and the elderly woman were murdered, they found Noemí's Honda Civic near the train tracks in a small town outside San Antonio. That prompted a frustrated FBI agent to say on camera: "Everything indicates that he crossed the border and escaped into his own country. Which would be a shame for us. They don't have capital punishment over there, and you see how well that's working."

Dawn Haze took advantage of that comment to devote two whole episodes of her show to badmouthing the Mexican justice system and attacking the "liberal" states that didn't have capital punishment. Fernandez belly-laughed at her arguments, but then chastised himself because he knew it wasn't a laughing matter, it was all miserable and pathetic, and there were a lot of people who agreed with Dawn.

The following day, Dawn broke an "exclusive" on the show: the Railroad Killer had been detained by the INS near El Paso before his latest murder spree, and despite running a check on his file, they had still deported him to Mexico. The INS must have been perfectly aware that the detainee was a murder suspect. The INS responded lukewarmly: "The INS computer network was not connected to other agencies and had no way of accessing information from the FBI or Texas Ranger systems. What's more, the suspect used a series of aliases, which complicated things."

"Excuses, excuses," the anchor railed. "Not only did they show negligence by releasing him but also in failing to connect their computer system with other agencies'. Nothing can bring the victims of these murders back to life, which is the result of your gross incompetence."

Fernandez had to admit it, this time Dawn Haze had nailed it.

Back in the office, Fernandez compiled a list of the Railroad Killer's victims (the nickname had stuck, even he was using it now).

Victoria Jansen. Mrs. Havisham. Joanna Benson. Noemí Dominguez. Norman and Lynn Bates. Annie Tadic.

Seven murders. Surely there were more. Almost all of them were women. Two of them were elderly women. He was a spineless killer who looked for easy prey. He remembered the lyrics of a corrido: "Gregorio Cortez said / with a pistol in his hand: / no Mexican / would run with a gutless Ranger swine." It was funny to think that now the Ranger was him and he was pursuing a gutless Mexican. Several years had passed between the first two murders and the more recent crimes. What could have happened? Quantico's updated psychological profile was like something straight out of a manual on psychopathic behavior: the killer was driven to commit the crimes to quench his thirst for blood, but he had grown more accustomed to killing and quickly became bored with less vicious behavior, so the time between murders was decreasing. After several years of successfully restraining his impulses, the Railroad Killer was now rampaging out of control; the next crime was likely to take place very soon.

Did the victims have anything in common? Something that might determine who was next in line? The murders occurred in the vicinity of train stations, but who would be the next ill-fated soul to encounter the predator in the confines of a living room, a kitchen, a bedroom? Who next would find herself eyeball to eyeball with an illegal alien bristling with years of amassed rage and a butcher knife in his hand?

Sergeant Fernandez pitied the next victim.

That night he and Debbie rendezvoused at the downtown Ramada Inn. He felt her fingernails dig into his back during sex, as if in desperation. As she straddled him, he glimpsed her face, concentrated, the cascade of chestnut hair that hid her eyes. His imagination took over and he floated in and out of the moment, when suddenly the image of Annie Tadic's crushed skull flashed through his mind. He had to get that image out of his head.

She came, but he didn't. She kept working on him, but to no avail.

"What's wrong, Rafa? Work getting to you?"

"Sorry, gorgeous. You know what's on my mind."

"Yeah, I know," she said and desisted. She got up and lit a cigarette, then lay back down by his side. "It's still frustrating though."

He pulled her over and kissed her. She leaned against his chest.

"I don't want to stay in Landslide."

Fernandez contemplated her straight nose and prominent cheekbones, the cigarette dangling between her lips.

"I have a cousin up north, in Ontario."

He shouldn't let the veiled threat get to him. He had to take her as she came, understand it as merely the strategic maneuvering of a woman who wanted more than she had. The truth is, something about the comment had disturbed him.

"Canada? Why so far away? That's north of north."

"Yeah, I know. You once said you'd follow me to the ends of the earth. Why don't you come with me?"

"Sounds like a great idea, but what about my job?"

He got out of bed to use the bathroom, hoping it would bring a change of subject. When he came out, she was already dressed and zipping up her boots.

"Something wrong?"

"No, everything's peachy. Just that time's up. That'll be a hundred and fifty dollars."

He grabbed his wallet from the nightstand and rummaged for the bills, but she didn't give him enough time: she walked out and slammed the door behind her.

Fernandez didn't know whether to run after her, to wait for her, or to call her. Eventually he just lay back down in bed, telling himself that she'd come back. But she didn't.

She'll calm down. Just give her a little time.

McMullen told Fernandez that the FBI had been researching the suspect vigorously, and all leads pointed to a small town called Rodeo in Mexico. Reyle was married and that was where the wife lived. The Mexican authorities sanctioned extraterritorial jurisdiction for the FBI to operate in their country, and they staked out Reyle's house in Rodeo. The Mexicans wouldn't allow them to take the investigation a step further by alerting the wife; they were afraid she'd find a way to warn her husband.

They had to sit tight and wait for Reyle to fuck up, try to return home.

Fernandez broke down and called the FBI offices in Houston. Agent Johnson got on the line, the person in charge of Operation Stop Train. Fernandez was friendly with the robust, affable black man whose favorite pastime was fishing in the Gulf. They'd worked a couple of cases together.

"Hey there Wayne, how's the fishing?"

"Depends on which kind we talkin' about . . ."

"Listen, I have an offer to make. It's not official Ranger stuff, I'm out on a limb here. You know I speak good Spanish, no gringo accent. So in a place like Rodeo I wouldn't call any undue attention to myself. I could get close to Reyle's wife, tell her about her husband and ask for her help. Earn her trust."

"Too risky," Johnson said without thinking twice. "What would we gain? If he's organized a double life for himself, sooner or later he's going to let down his guard and return home. It's better just to wait it out."

Fernandez insisted: "The alternative is not better. We sit by and stake out his house and wait, but he's not going to return willingly, he's gotta know we're on his trail. But he'll find a way to get a message to his wife. And when that happens, just maybe, if we earn her trust, she'd be willing to surrender him in exchange for something."

Johnson said he'd let him know. He wasn't entirely convinced, but he'd put it through the channels.

Days went by. Fernandez imagined long meetings to discuss his plan. The FBI wanted to be in full control of the cases they were investigating.

That weekend Johnson finally called back. They accepted his offer, but an FBI agent would accompany him. "We considered just doing it ourselves, but it felt like we were stealing your idea. So now you're coming with us."

If it didn't work, at least they could say they tried. What else could Fernandez do? Accept. If he didn't, they'd go talk to her themselves.

He told them it was OK by him.

5

Landslide, 2009

I returned to my normal shift in Taco Hut; I carried my Moleskine with me to work and spent my breaks illustrating my adaptation of "Luvina" or doodling ideas for my story. I sharpened the main character's profile, Samantha, a Latino woman obsessed with cleansing the world of vampires, zombies, and werewolves after one of them killed her baby girl. The postapocalyptic territory called Marcela was divided into the North and the South and separated by a river. I told the story to my coworkers; Osvaldo and Mike liked it, but Oksana, a Russian girl who had recently started working with us, didn't get it.

I went on creating my universe, even the tiniest details—the chemical waste that turned men into zombies, the abandoned mansions that alluded to gothic literature and suggested the end of time—but it was hard for me to really let myself go, get the story to flow like lava. Ana haunted me at all hours of the day. I couldn't face her, or the person I imagined she would be—a long black braid, a shadow who turned its back to me. I was paralyzed and failed.

Reading was the thing that gave me a little peace. But I couldn't read just anything, only the first few chapters of *The Sandman*.

Over and over again, I'd finish reading and then start all over again.

Fabián wasn't good working company, either. He would sit in front of his computer answering emails, perusing blogs, or rummaging around in the hard drive, paranoid that the deans had introduced some spyware virus that sent them copies of his communications. I took stock of his defects. He wheezed now, and it was hard to tell if it was asthma or an allergic reaction; he locked himself in the bathroom, and I could hear what sounded like retching. He'd come out as if nothing had happened, open a bottle of wine, snort a few lines on a mirror or a credit card. I always refused to join him and preferred to look the other way. Later we'd watch a B movie from the 50s—*Attack of the Killer Tomatoes, The Fifty Foot Woman*; he knew how much I liked them and had bought an eighty piece DVD collection (a Home Shopping offer he saw once at three a.m.). Sex was irregular due to the drugs: a few fiery nights would be followed by others when he couldn't get a hard-on.

Fabián could be very tender at times, like when he'd write tacky emails from the office telling me how much he missed me, how he couldn't imagine his future without me. There were moments when I felt moved in a very deep way, when I could see his fragility peeking out from behind a few sentences: "i was standing beside myself dressed in a black suit that looked like it belonged to an undertaker. i put some cables to my head and pressed a button and received a shock. the person that was me said you're not well you're not well you're not well you're not well. he grabbed my hand and said that he would take me to an amusement park and i told him yes, of course, and i turned into a child. I had a balloon in my hand and suddenly i wasn't with myself anymore and i felt very lonely. would you like to go to an amusement park? six flags isn't very far away."

Some evenings we'd stroll around the neighborhood, walk by the baseball diamond in the park whose perimeter was all lit up in bright white lights. We'd often see the groups of people there who gathered regularly: business professionals who played softball after work, foreign students from the university chasing after a soccer ball. We'd stretch out on the grass and watch the games. These were times when I would make an effort to project some sort of shared future, despite knowing full well the limits we'd established where that was concerned—I'd try to imagine myself in a home near the sea, writing and illustrating until dawn while he slept. I always failed to conjure a clear image of it.

There were days when I'd call after my shift in Taco Hut and he'd tell me he didn't want to see me, and his stony, detached, measured tone of voice conveyed just how far he'd shut himself away. Other times his tone would turn suspicious and he'd ask if I was a spy for the deans. At those times he usually sounded drunk or stoned. The weeks slipped by like that, following this manic, bipolar rhythm.

I still hung out with Sam, who offered to read what I wrote and kept trying to make sense of why I rejected any deeper kind of relationship with him. Every once in a while I'd check in with La Jodida, but all she ever talked about was alcohol-drenched affairs and coked-up bed-to-bed encounters with near strangers (she only began cheating on Megan after she found out that Megan had been cheating on her). I ran into her at a bus stop one afternoon—her pants were sagging, she had a black bandana on, and her shirt was all wrinkled and filthy; she told me she might have to go back to Puerto Rico.

Her grades had plummeted and she had a bunch of incompletes in her classes; her adviser said she was at risk of losing her scholarship. She didn't seem that worried about it, though. We parted with an ambivalent embrace.

Sam invited me to go with him to the inaugural cocktail party given by the university museum for Martín Ramírez's retrospective. I didn't want to go with him, so I convinced Fabián to accompany me.

Fabián made an effort to dress elegantly, though his jacket was scruffy and his pants too short. There were art history professors there, and some of Fabián's colleagues; few academics liked to crawl out of their hiding places to attend events in fields not strictly their own. I saw Ruth and said hello. She was surrounded by a group of doctoral students arguing that Ramírez shouldn't be qualified as a Mexican but as a Latino, a Hispanic, a Chicano, a Mexican-American (he had lived in the US for forty of his sixty-eight years).

I was in no mood for an academic discussion about identity, so I left Fabián with Ruth and moseyed my way through the exhibition. It was divided into subjects that represented the painter's obsessions: horses and riders, landscapes, women, trains, and tunnels. The drawings were massive and they captivated me, they were like a revelation. I was already aware of Ramírez's talent, but until then I had only appreciated it from a distance, the way one can value art without actually responding to it or feeling anything. I hadn't really grasped it, apprehended the work. I could have made the typical excuses—seeing reproductions in books and online is never the same as when you experience work live—but in this case it wasn't really true. Now I wished I had written the essay for the catalogue; I had missed a great opportunity.

I particularly admired the horses and riders section; it was the most crowded of the show, and the one with the lion's share of paintings. I homed in on the details of the drawings—the belts loaded down with bullets, the horses looking skyward, the parallel lines framing the compositions, the dominant colors of red and violet. I read the commentaries. Some three hundred drawings were attributed to Ramírez, eighty of which featured riders on horseback.

It was about creating symbols out of obsessions, mapping the great territory of the world in order for a few objects or individuals to become part of a personal mythology. Now I realized my problem: I had begun backwards. It takes years of painting and writing before a person can find what their specific recurring themes are. The process maps the principal coordinates of any work of the imagination. I hadn't even begun telling my story yet, hadn't given it a body, and I expected it to be full of symbols.

I came across one of Ramírez's painted *calaveras* in the section dedicated to landscapes. They're illustrations featuring skeletons. There was a skeleton playing a violin beside a couple dancing to the music, sketched completely out of perspective (the man's head was enormous). Undulating fields were drawn in wavy lines, houses in childlike strokes, cars motoring along a dirt road.

I was already familiar with José Guadalupe Posada's *calaveras* and with other artists who are now closely associated with the Day of the Dead and Mexican folk art. They were usually cheerful in their satire, dressed in festive clothes, ready for a party. Here, Ramírez's skeleton expressed a sort of grotesque grimace; it looked like a villain's mask for a Hollywood horror series. But I found the combination fascinating: a disfigured face, a festive violin.

So there's my novel. Instead of zombies and skulls with Freddy Krueger–style faces, they will be Mexican, but seen through the lens of North American horror films.

I went looking for Fabán to tell him what I had come up with, and found him causing a scene: there was a crowd around him and Ruth, who were locked in a heated argument. I walked over to see what was going on.

"Get out of my face, you fat piece of shit," Fabián shouted. "I'll kill you! Ramírez is Mexican, not Chicano, I couldn't care less how long he lived in California. People like you are destroying the university. Nobody can have an opinion because of your political correctness. And if someone dares, you gang up on him, like what you're doing to me."

I elbowed my way through the crowd and pulled hard at Fabián's arm. "Please, will you just shut up," I begged. I covered his mouth but it was useless: he was unbound. Ruth shouted back that he was going to be sorry for having threatened her. A couple of professors stepped in to calm her down; they escorted her out of the exhibition. The security guards mobilized around Fabián, warning him that if he didn't get hold of himself, they'd arrest him and take him away by force. I promised I'd take him home and look after him myself.

I had to shove him to get him out of the exhibition. We took a cab. "I want to sleep alone tonight," he said. Boy did I feel like answering back, but his face had that detached expression I knew so well.

When the cab stopped in front of his house, I asked him what had happened.

"I'll text you tomorrow when I wake up."

He stepped out of the cab, and I told the driver to take off.

I was furious when I walked into my studio, thinking how the two of us had been to completely different shows that evening. I had focused on Ramírez's work, looking for ways to apply his creativity to my own story; but for Fabián it had served as a means for provoking a messy situation and a concomitant dose of self-pity.

That was how our lives flowed those days: we did things together, but it didn't really matter. However much our lives brushed up against each other every now and again, our paths were leading us irreversibly away from each other.

The man who had aroused me so powerfully was now relentlessly turning into a ghost.

I would have liked to take pity on him, but I think I was just too exhausted.

6

Rodeo, 1999

Jesús showed up at home with a canvas bag stuffed with jewelry, perfumes and dresses. Renata hugged him and told him she had missed him. She was furious though: this time he'd gone too far, left her alone way too long. Jesús held his tongue so as not to call her puerca, crazy bitch, super puta and if she didn't shut her fucking mouth he'd dig her eyes out with a knife, smear her body with spit, and throw her over a fucking cliff.

The gifts shut her up. "What cute earrings, they're silver too, and this brooch must have cost an arm and a leg." Lila, the new neighbor who had become her best friend, was right when she said that maybe this was the price of being with Jesús. "It's his way of life, and you should respect it and not try to compete." She lived comfortably because he had papers and could cross the border whenever he wanted to for work. Lila wished she were married to someone like that. Who wouldn't want to be? It was stupid of her to complain.

Jesús went out and bought several sets of black curtains and hung them over the windows in the house. He told Renata to keep them closed at all times, even when the sun was shining. He had enemies and was afraid of being spied on. He even covered the kitchen windows with newspaper.

"It looks really weird," she said. "It's hot inside, and now we don't have natural light. How am I supposed to explain it to Lila when she asks?"

"You tell her that I have rosacea and the doctor ordered me to avoid being exposed to direct sunlight."

Renata looked puzzled but didn't say anything. Jesús's cheeks did have a slight blush to them, but she worked in a pharmacy and knew full well that you don't treat rosacea with curtains. Was Jesús going to shy away from sunlight forever? It seemed more likely that he was hiding from some enemy or other, but if that was the case, then what had he done? Who were the enemies?

She stewed over this for a few days, but quickly got used to the new order of things and forgot.

Jesús and Renata spent quiet days together. He tried to steer clear of sotol and coke. He had to stay alert, needed his reflexes wide awake. He was sure they were looking for him. He had to take precautions; he'd never give them the satisfaction of locking him away.

He tried to stick to a routine. He went back to teaching English in the mornings at the nuns' school. He got there early, avoiding busy streets. He'd stroll around town at dusk. When a cop ticketed him for rolling through a stop sign, he gave up driving and bought a bike. He got a dog, Tobías, who barked at anything that moved. He would take the dog out for a walk, swing by the pharmacy to say hello to Renata, and return home. That was when the images of the past few weeks across the line would overwhelm him, he'd see them as if he were caught in a nightmare: as if the events had never really happened, but the thought of them made his skin crawl.

He wrote it all down in one of his notebooks. Someday he'd take them to Father Joe. The first notebooks told a bunch of lies, but after a while they got interesting. Father Joe would understand.

At night he and Renata would visit the cantinas, chill out and listen to rancheras and corridos. He started drinking again. The sotol burned his throat, as if he were losing his tolerance to it.

One evening, when they got home past midnight, he was drunk and began struggling with the zipper of Renata's dress. She half shouted, half giggled, "Where are you going so fast?" They didn't make it to the bedroom; they did it right there on the living room rug. Jesús slapped her in the face, hard. She touched her mouth: her lip was bleeding. Jesús hit her again.

"Don't touch me," she shouted. "Don't touch me!"

He wanted to rip her apart. Make her cry for real.

"Don't you ever do that again, Jesús. Never. I saw enough of it at home. You hit me one more time and I'm outta here."

She scrambled to the bedroom and slammed the door. He heard her whimpering and hiccupping.

He got up, rammed the door open with a shoulder, took off his belt, and hit her with the metal buckle until her thighs, her back, her cheeks were covered with black-and-blue welts. "You fucking puta, who you think you are, bitch? Ordering me around like that. You think you can give me orders? Me? You lucky I let you live, puerca." He grabbed her by the throat and nearly strangled her. She gathered herself into a tight ball in a corner of the bedroom, wailing and begging his forgiveness, as he kicked her with the shiny steel tips of his boots.

After she blacked out, he pulled his pants down and penetrated her again. He cleaned the come off with her dress. He fell asleep right there on the floor.

The sound of his snoring was what roused Renata. Her legs were sore and her back ached so terribly she had a hard time getting to her feet. She could barely make her way to the bathroom, where she cleaned her wounds with alcohol and washed her body down with a towel soaked in cold water.

Should she go to Lila's and tell her what had happened? She couldn't stop trembling and sobbing. She was frightened.

She tried to lie down on the sofa for a while. She couldn't sleep.

The next morning she made breakfast as if nothing had happened. She didn't say a word to Jesús and kept her eyes lowered at all times. Her face was too swollen to go out, so she called in sick at La Indolora, saying that she'd taken a tumble and wouldn't be able to make it to work that day.

"yu think I don't now yu laf behin my back fukin hore bich now yu now whats coming KILL THEM ALL no rest no rest the lord is not with yu not with us holy be not thy name nobody free now they now time comes time comes time comes the minut the hour to lik my boots hore unnamedanimals got to eliminat like dogs like cows like pigs like david koresh was the profet and they killd can't do me no more waco KILL THEM ALL."

Lila's birthday was that weekend. Renata didn't want to go at first, she would stay home, there was a lot to do, but Jesús bought a video camera and said he wanted to film the party. Renata agreed: she would bandage her cheek, say she had fallen down.

Jesús had learned how to use the camera by filming Tobías. When he saw how he had caught the dog on the little screen, frolicking here and there with his tongue hanging out, he told himself that this was what he had been missing all along. Next time he crossed the line, he'd bring the camera with him. He'd film these puercas lying on the floor with a knife in their throats and their blood staining the rug.

Lila had decorated her house with wall-to-wall streamers and with garlands on the windows, giving a festive air more like New Year's than a birthday party. There were piñatas for the children, paper hats, colorful napkins and matching paper plates. Los Tigres del Norte and Los Tucanes de Tijuana were playing over the loudspeakers. There was a James Bond movie marathon on the television in the living room, with the volume on mute. Every once in a while one of the kids would come in and turn the volume up, and suddenly the room would reverberate with the racket of bullets and explosions over the music, making it seem as though it was all going down in real life. The first time it happened, Jesús was in the bathroom and it shook him up. He turned the volume down again when he got out.

He snorted a few lines on a card advertising a strip club in El Paso—*First Tuesday of every month is SuPEr TuEsDAy $5.00!!!*—then splashed cold water on his face. His cheeks were red and his face looked lopsided, as if one side didn't match the other. His hair was disheveled and in need of a cut. After having spent such a long time on the other side, he saw himself as darker than he really was, skinnier and dirtier.

He was this one, he was not that one.

He felt like punching the mirror but kept the urge in check.

The party lasted into the wee hours of Sunday. Once the children had been put to bed, Lila's brother, Tomás, sang himself hoarse, decked out in a fancy pair of tight-fitting mariachi pants. Renata helped fix the roast lamb, the fridge was stocked with cans of Tecate, and tequila, mescal, and sotol bottles were arranged in a row on the kitchen table.

Jesús drank some of everything and got trashed. He vomited on the patio and fell asleep on a bench. Renata needed Tomás's help to carry him home; they took off his boots, his jeans, his belt, and tucked him into bed.

When Jesús woke up around noon, Tobías was lying at his feet. His head throbbed and his stomach burned, so he immediately popped a few antacids. Renata tended to him in silence; she brought food to the bedroom—a fiery pozole to cure his hangover—and then went over to Lila's house to help clean up.

He finished the pozole and snoozed a little while longer. When he finally woke up again, he switched the radio on, and the first thing he heard was a name that sounded familiar to him. Was it even possible? The announcer barked out the news: US authorities had identified the criminal known as the Railroad Killer, he was an illegal Mexican.

He roused himself instantly: of course the name was familiar, it was one of the aliases he'd used to cross the border. A slight variation on his own name.

The US authorities believed the killer had fled into Mexico, and they were negotiating terms of his capture with Mexican officials. There was a chance that a group of FBI agents would be traveling to Mexico, though the Mexican authorities claimed that national sovereignty would be preserved at all times.

It was dusk. Shadows would soon engulf all of Rodeo.

He tried to remain calm as he got dressed and gathered his things. His jeans were hanging over a chair, but they had vomit stains on them; he rifled through the closet to find another pair. Tobías sniffed his crotch and Jesús shoved him away.

He put on a hat and shoved six bullets into the chamber of his gun. He'd better shake a leg. If they'd figured out the alias, it was only a matter of time before they identified him and established his whereabouts.

Running out of the bedroom, he bumped into Renata, who had just come back from Lila's house. Her shiny black hair was pulled back into two long braids that were threaded with colorful ribbons, and she was wearing a loose, ruffled red blouse and open-toed sandals that matched her newly painted crimson toenails. The bandage on her cheek was the only thing spoiling the nearly perfect picture.

"Are you feeling better? Why don't you rest, stay in bed?"

"I have to run an errand; I'll be right back."

He went into the bathroom and washed his face with cold water. His eyes were bloodshot and his hair was a wild mess. "My wrath shall come down upon all of them," he murmured. "The power of a million exploding suns, a rain of fire on their heads. KILL THEM ALL."

"What's up, Jesús? You're scaring me."

She had entered the bathroom and was now leaning against the door frame. Her eyes were open wide and she was biting her lips.

Jesús spun around and couldn't hold it back. "Hallowed be not thy fucking name," he said. He grabbed her, brought her close to him in an embrace, and sobbed. At first the tears came haltingly; then he broke down completely and there was no way Renata could calm him down.

Tobías came over again, but Jesús kicked him so hard the dog let out a plaintive yelp. He crumbled onto the bathroom floor at Renata's feet. She stayed quiet, staring down at him. Jesús looked at the earrings she had on, two silver teardrops he'd stolen from—where? From whom? He couldn't remember which of the victims they'd belonged to. Maybe it was better that way. All those bodies, all those faces, they should melt into a single one.

"I'm scared," Jesús said finally. "I'm scared, Renata."

"What's going on? You have to tell me. I can't help if I don't know what's happening."

"I've done something bad and there are men trying to find me."

"There's always a way out. What exactly do you mean by 'something bad'?"

"Something I have to deal with myself."

Jesús knew that once he left home and Rodeo, he'd never see Renata again. The years with her were over, same as the other relationships with women he'd ended years earlier. This was the life he'd been given and he shouldn't complain. He lost some but he won some too.

He thought back on the games he used to play with María Luisa in the patio and the empty field with the hollow tree, the nights they'd slept together on that mattress, on the sheltering bed. It had been easy to forget about that bitch Rocío. But Renata hadn't been so bad; he'd restrained himself with her. He hadn't killed her even though at times he really wanted to. Obviously there was something special about her to have tamed him that way.

He'd tried so desperately to grab on to something, set down some roots, but the itch to get back on the road was inexorable. Nothing else gave that same wild thrill as crossing the river, jumping a freight train, stretching out on the floor of an empty car or sticking his head out an open door, awash in the coolness of the breeze on his cheeks and the sweaty shirt that stuck to his body, and contemplating the passing desert landscape, the corn and tobacco fields, the towns and cities.

Jesús got back on his feet. "If anyone comes looking for me, please don't nark on me."

"What could I possibly say? I don't know anything!"

He put his hat back on, spun around and strode out of the house. She sat down on the sofa, not sure whether to feel happy or sad. Tobías came over wagging his tail so energetically that his whole rear end moved back and forth.

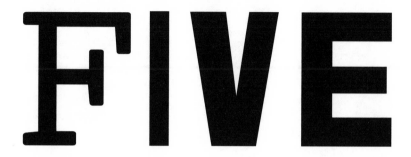

1

Auburn, 1959–1963

The professor came back to visit Martín one last time. They hugged each other when he walked into the room, and the professor noted how Martín's health had deteriorated since he'd seen him last, that he was completely toothless now. He had tried to secure a transfer for him to another hospital, since the quality of care at De Witt had been deteriorating over the years: the rooms were overcrowded, the walls and floors were filthy, the yard and gardens were overgrown, and the bathrooms stank. They lacked bandages and sterile needles, iodine and alcohol supplies weren't restocked responsibly, and the orderlies were trafficking the morphine and surgical instruments.

The professor felt he owed Martín an explanation for his absence. His Spanish was as nonexistent as ever, so all he managed to say, over and over again, was Helsinki. Martín nodded. He pulled out the years of drawings that had been accumulating in the meantime. The orderlies had respected the professor's instructions: the paintings were dated at the lower right-hand corner. The professor read them off; January 1957, April 1957, February 1958, May 1959 . . . The subject matter hadn't changed much. There were riders wearing bandoliers across their chests, undulating hills, trains and tunnels, landscapes and churches, animals and people dancing. The drawings had magazine cutouts pasted to them, collages that asserted Martín's range of obsessions: the flawless faces of women from advertisements, aerodynamic contraptions displaying the nifty, sleek, modern aesthetic.

Martín moved his hands in lines between himself and the professor, who understood that Martín wanted him to have the paintings. He thanked him.

One of the new orderlies showed up to tell the professor his visiting time was over. Seeing people caused Martín to become overstimulated; it wasn't good for his health. The professor was annoyed: he wasn't accustomed to being treated that way. But the orderly failed to heed his complaints.

The professor asked after Martín's health, and the orderly described his pulmonary difficulties. "Serious enough to be worrying?" "Very." He asked if there had been any changes in Martín over the years.

"As far as I can tell," the orderly responded, "he doesn't draw as much as he used to. He spends hours sitting in a chair outside, looking toward the garden. It's as if he were waiting for someone to show up. Whenever a car pulls up to the front door, he stands up and starts waving his arms as if he were greeting someone. The director came for a visit once, and he ran straight to his car to open the door for him. It was all we could do to restrain him. We needed a straitjacket, and even still he kept on crying and shrieking."

The professor took a long look at Martín, who was just beside him. He put his hand on his shoulder and squeezed, then gave him a pat on the back. "I missed you," he said. Martín smiled back. The professor noticed he had tears in his eyes.

"I won't leave you again."

"Oh seriously?" the orderly responded.

"In a manner of speaking. I'm going back to Helsinki. I don't know when I'll be back."

It was time to say their goodbyes. The professor told the orderly he would be taking Martín's drawings with him. The orderly nodded.

"So that's how it works, huh?"

"They aren't for me, it's to make people aware of Martín's art. I'm proud to say that the Guggenheim has accepted ten of his drawings. I sent his work to them years ago. They wanted to organize a show that contrasts the work of established artists and someone like Martín. They begged off in the end, probably thought the idea was too provocative. It's hard to get the big museums to pay attention. But I shouldn't complain, it's really amazing that they've accepted ten of his drawings now. Right, Martín?"

Martín nodded.

The professor left.

That night Martín didn't eat his dinner. He didn't want to take a bath, either. He just lay in bed, looked at the stains on the walls for hours and hours. His chest hurt; it was a deep ache, as if someone were branding his muscles with a hot iron. Like the blood wasn't circulating properly, had backed up and stopped its flow. Now it was squeezing up into his heart, trying to rip it out of his chest.

He finally fell asleep as dawn broke.

Martín spent the nights watching shadows fidget outside the pavilion window, the silhouettes of tree branches shivering in the wind. When the orderlies did their three a.m. rounds, he would close his eyes and pretend to be asleep, and then open them again as soon as they were gone. Random fragments of them lingered afterward, heads without bodies, long legs floating around the bed. The room echoed with sounds from elsewhere, laments of someone on the verge of death, a hacking fit, manic bursts of laughter.

He got along well with others but hadn't made any real friends. In pottery class people chatted at him, but he never answered them back. He worked outside on the grounds, happy to take in the fresh air, but ignored any efforts by other patients to communicate. They invited him to play games, watch television or a movie, but he was never interested. Every once in a while he'd watch some cartoons. The mouse and the duck and the squirrels. The drawings moved like they were magic.

He rubbed his face. He smoothed the thin mustache he would not allow them to shave off. He masturbated and tried not to make any noise, ashamed, knowing his soiled sheets and pajamas would give him away.

He thought about María Santa Ana and wondered if she was still riding with those other men, crossing the range of mountains by town, defending señor gobierno, the wind tickling her cheeks. He wondered how his children had managed being at home on their own. They were responsible girls; surely they'd got by just fine. Wasn't sure about Candelario, he'd never met the boy.

Even so, he was gripped with remorse. Should he have gone with his nephew? Why had he been so stubborn, why didn't he want to go home? What was he so afraid of? Discovering the truth about whether María Santa Ana had stopped loving him and run off with other men? So what if that's what really happened? Didn't he have the strength to get back on his feet? Had staying here been worth it?

The professor didn't visit anymore. And that boy in pottery class he'd been friendly with died. How had it happened?

His throat hurt when he inhaled. The doctors showed him pictures of his lungs. They said things in English, why did they insist on speaking that language? They wanted him to fret. Whenever he heard those weird sounds and words all strung together, he felt like stuffing cotton balls in his ears. What were they saying? He guessed right enough though: something wasn't good.

Uuuuuuuaaaaaa.

He had to get better so he could see the professor again.

Shadows stole across the windows. Was it a train? He closed his eyes. He tried to fall asleep.

One morning he complained of the pain in his chest and spat blood. They rushed him to the infirmary. A doctor checked his vitals, looking concerned, and said "Tests, tests." They wheeled him to another room. They came and went, buzzing all around, arguing with each other over what steps to take. One of them, a redheaded orderly who spoke a little Spanish, tried to explain and then said something that sounded like "emergency procedure." They gave him a paper to sign. Martín wrote an X and smiled at them. It was a fake smile, though: the ache in his chest was choking him.

He lay on the gurney for a long time before they finally made him undress and put on a gown. They wheeled him to yet another room. He wanted to ask about his drawings. If he could go and get one to keep him company. But he kept his mouth shut. They gave him an injection. He wished he could send a letter to his daughters. He'd draw them a picture of the building, the room with the windows where he spent most of his time, the patio and the garden.

His eyelids felt heavy. That wasn't a bad thing, because now everything would just disappear, all the machines and cables, the clamps and needles, the collection of scissors he glimpsed apprehensively on metal tables that the nurses and orderlies were carrying to and fro. This time was different, though, it wasn't him who was forcing his eyes shut. Now they wanted to close of their own accord.

He wanted to ask María Santa Ana if she still loved him. If so, he was willing to forgive her for having been with other men while he was away. She could even go on living in the mountains with her horse and her gun. But she'd have to accept that she belonged only to him, that's for sure. It wasn't going to be easy.

He felt like getting up and writing a few words in Spanish on the wall of the building. Oh, they wouldn't like that one little bit, nosiree. No they would not. He'd write: "Today it's going to rain. Today. It. Is. Going. To. Rain."

His strength was failing; he couldn't get up from the stretcher.

Where's the professor? Oh. He was his one true friend. But how could they be friends if they'd never actually been able to speak to each other? Well, no matter, he was his only company, that's for sure. And the boy who died too, but it wasn't the same thing. No, no, no. The professor was good. He'd be back someday, he'd try to take him out of the building and Martín would find a way to make him understand that this is his home and he can't imagine living anywhere else.

His muscles relaxed. His mouth felt thick and cottony, he

couldn't open it. His legs were tingling, now his hands. "Today it's going . . ."

It was a nice feeling, not moving. As if his whole body were swaddled in a tight blanket.

He closed his eyes.

He never opened them again.

2

Rodeo, 1999

Renata was on her way out of the pharmacy when Sergeant Fernandez approached her, accompanied by the FBI agent and two Mexican police officers. She knew what he wanted: that morning at La Indolora she had seen a photograph of Jesús on the first page of the local newspaper and read the article. She didn't believe a single line, it was all based on groundless speculation, and yet it shocked her to see Jesús associated with a series of crimes that were so heinous. Could that be why he was so panicked? What had him running scared? Her boss knew what was up—he may have recognized Jesús's photo—and had told her she should take the day off. She had gone home, but being in the house alone made her feel miserable: the photos of the football players reminded her of Jesús. The house was gloomy, so she removed the newspaper from the windows and opened the curtains. After he'd beat her up like that, she realized there was a lot about Jesús she didn't know, but she didn't want to judge him too harshly; all men make mistakes, and she had hoped that Jesús would eventually apologize to her. She'd returned to work after lunch.

One of the police officers flashed his credentials and asked if they could speak in private. They followed her home. Renata went to the patio and unleashed Tobías, who ran into the living room and piddled on the kitchen door. She gave him a plastic bone to keep him quiet while the sergeant admired how tidy the kitchen was, the dishes so neatly stacked, the scrubbed refrigerator, the bright light filtering through the windows. It wasn't the type of serial killer's home one is accustomed to seeing in the movies, psychopaths are generally single and not interested in building a plausible domestic life. The movies exaggerate real life, but there's an underlying truth: the only serial killer he had dealt with so far in his career—and his role had been merely that of a curious subordinate—was named Torrance and there wasn't a single piece of furniture in his entire house. He had slept on a mattress thrown on the floor and spent the whole day in the basement, where he had built a cell for his victims and kept a collection of home-crafted torture instruments.

Renata sat facing them on the couch in the living room, clutching a Kleenex and making an effort not to cry. Fernandez observed the decoration on the walls.

"Your husband's a little peculiar." He tried to get a conversation going. "Doesn't go in for football much now, does he?"

"A lot of people around here follow American football and baseball." Renata combed her hair with the fingers of one hand and held Fernandez's gaze. "Jesús even likes basketball. He says there aren't enough goals in soccer, and the gringos know that. Better to watch something that ends 40–23 than 0–0."

"Well, yes, I suppose you have a point. Sorry if I was being judgmental. Nobody likes that."

"I used to date a girl, a platinum blond who liked to dance salsa," Will Rosas, the FBI agent with Fernandez and the

Mexican officers, chimed in. "When I told her I couldn't dance, she said I was lousy representative of my culture."

"So what did you do? Did you break up?"

"I started taking salsa classes. Didn't do no good though."

Fernandez observed Rosas: his patent leather shoes, a freshly pressed shirt, that tie. Every iota the bureaucrat. He's awfully young to be doing this, he could be my son, but I guess if he likes it that way . . . He'll make himself a career, go far, but inside the office and not on the street.

"Jesús is innocent," Renata said. "He couldn't kill a fly, I know him, we been together for years. I read the things the newspaper says, and it's all pure lies."

The sergeant felt sorry for Renata; he noticed the black-and-blue mark on her cheek, and another cliché came to mind: the killer's neighbors, family, everyone saying who could ever have imagined such a thing, such a polite, good kid, so outgoing, so helpful. He would have loved to live in the nineteenth century, a time when sciences like phrenology and criminal anthropology were taking hold and they thought they could identify a murderer by the shape of his skull or jawline. We still use some of the characteristic expressions from that period—"he has a boxer's face"—but it's no longer considered a science. How many problems could be avoided if you could discern just by seeing a neighbor's face whether they were capable of murder, or could detect a partner's propensity for telling fibs or cheating on you.

"Ma'am, I hear you," the sergeant said. "The newspapers do tend to get ahead of their facts. Your husband is an innocent man until proven guilty. But we do have some evidence that indicates it might be a good idea to talk to him. If we bring him in, you can be sure he'll have a lawyer. He'll have the opportunity to defend his case."

"If you bring him in—where? Will he be tried here?"

"That will depend on the Mexican authorities," Rosas intervened. "We won't do anything that isn't in strict accordance with Mexican law."

"If we arrest him here," one of the officers said, "he'll be tried here. Mexican law will take care of your husband, as long as there's no extradition request."

"I need some kind of proof," she said. "Proof that Jesús is somehow involved in all of this."

The sergeant had come prepared. He opened a briefcase and flipped through a handful of photos until he found what he was looking for. He handed it to Renata. A couple was standing arm in arm in front of their home beside a new car. She was smiling at him.

"I don't see what this has to do with Jesús," Renata said.

"Look at her earrings," the sergeant answered. "They're the same ones you're wearing right now."

He handed her cropped and enlarged photos of the earrings. Renata took hers off and studied them closely. "Might be a coincidence," she said.

"And it might not," Rosas said.

Renata couldn't stand it any longer: she moaned and then broke into a sob.

The photo was a shock, Fernandez thought. He had better take it easy now, not take advantage of her.

"Jewelry went missing from the victims' homes," he said. "We have it all classified. Your husband has given you jewelry, right?"

Renata nodded, wiping her eyes with the Kleenex.

"I have nothing to do with this," she bawled. "I'm innocent. Jesús, Jesús . . . He hit me. Do you see this here?" She touched her bruised cheek.

Renata hesitated a moment but then got up and went into the bedroom.

The sergeant's words had fallen on fertile soil. They confirmed long-held suspicions she'd kept trying to avoid. Why did he disappear for months at a time? What job paid so well that he could buy her so much jewelry? She had been an idiot for not questioning him. Truth was she had simply preferred to look the other way. But he had beaten her viciously. She hadn't seen that coming.

One of the policemen followed her into the bedroom, where she retrieved two metal jewelry boxes. She emptied their contents on the living-room table. She should stay calm, she was doing the right thing: Jesús was no longer that man she had fallen in love with. It was hard to grasp.

The sergeant pulled a stack of papers from his briefcase.

"No need," Renata said. "I believe you. But how could it be true? He was so affectionate this weekend, so relaxed. We had a party at the neighbors' house and he filmed everything. He played with the kids, danced with everyone, drank too much, that's for sure, but he was in a really good mood."

"It's not uncommon," Fernandez said. He tried to put himself in her shoes and imagine what was going on inside her head. The sheer evidence was obliging her to construct a different Jesús in her mind, one who was at once strange and cruel, but also plausible—the signs were all there, all she had to do was fill in the blanks—but she'd want to cling to her old Jesús, the one she'd lived with all this time. She'll go through this back-and-forth for a while, this struggle between two different images, the new one being forced on her by reality and the old one that she had fashioned with patience and even love.

"You think? I mean, how could I have lived with a murderer for so long and not realize it?"

"You shouldn't feel guilty. It's perfectly normal. We all have secret worlds we keep hidden from other people."

Rafael felt bad before he had even finished his sentence. He should know better than to fall into the commonplace, the cheesy declarations. It wasn't his job to console her, but he felt compelled at least to empathize with her, try to see things through her eyes. It was easier to understand the victims than the killer.

"But not all of us are murderers!"

Renata burst into tears again. Rosas approached her and tried to comfort her quietly, using his broken Spanish. One of the Mexican officers got up, feeling awkward, and went over to scrutinize the posters on the wall. Fernandez insisted: "Will you help us, Renata?"

They waited a few minutes for her to regain composure. Rosas walked over to the sink and came back with a glass of water.

"I don't know where he is," she said, dabbing her eyes, a little more in control. "He never calls once he's taken off. I know he crosses the border, but that's all. I should have suspected something was wrong, but he told me he was working legally; he even showed me his green card."

"Does he have a relative that he's particularly close to? A mother or father, a sibling?"

"He talked about his mom and his sister. He lost touch with his dad when he was a little kid; I guess he took off and never came back . . . I know his mom lives in their hometown and his sister is somewhere up North. In Albuquerque, I think he said. He wanted to go see her, but I don't know if he ever did. I don't have her address. I never met her . . . One time I found the photo of a pretty young girl in his wallet. She was a young thing with black hair and green eyes. There was a very affectionate dedication on the back, I thought it must be some childhood sweetheart, like I said, she must have been around twelve or thirteen. 'I'll never forget you,' it read, and 'You'll always be in my heart.' I got jealous and called him on it. He told me not to worry, it was only his sister. I thought it was a little weird but didn't push it."

Albuquerque, the sergeant thought. That's a lead we'll have to follow up.

Walking out the door, Sergeant Fernandez thought about how sorry he was for the woman they were leaving behind. He gave Rosas a pat on the back and said "Good work" before getting into the Mexican officers' car. He breathed in deeply, as if his lungs wanted to take in all the air there was in the afternoon.

Air: that was exactly what he needed.

Back in Landslide, Fernandez got news that two more bodies had been discovered in a mobile home that was parked just a few meters from the train tracks in a town outside Albuquerque. Jim and Lynn Mercer, an elderly man and his daughter, had been stabbed to death, and the woman had been raped postmortem. The proximity to the train tracks and the fact that the killer had lingered at the scene for a good while, raiding the refrigerator and serving himself something to eat and drink, made Fernandez immediately suspect it was the work of the Railroad Killer. The fingerprints corroborated his fears.

He left his apartment without unpacking his suitcase and took a drive around the city streets. The killer had outsmarted them all yet again: he had crossed the border into his own country, and when everyone thought he would be hiding out in Mexico, he crossed back into the US. It was like the earth swallowed him whole every time, nobody ever saw him. Or was he simply invisible?

Fernandez pulled into a gas station, bought some beef jerky and the newspapers. The boy who served him was Mexican and could hardly speak a word of English. Dawn Haze would have loved that: there were so many of them now they no longer bothered to learn English. They got by just fine with Spanish and a few random phrases in English.

The INS, the Rangers, the FBI were pathetic as organizations. Bungling and ineffective, and powerless to secure the borders or capture the Railroad Killer. With all those fingerprints he had left behind, this dimwitted undocumented worker had checkmated the security officers of the Empire. Bunch of morons: they'd had him in custody how many times? And in their fervor to rid themselves of these pests who were hell bent on invading their country like an army of flipping zombies from enemy territory, they'd simply thrown him back across the line. "Mexicans are like the Chinese," Captain Smits had told him once; "they all look so much alike you lose them in a crowd." The comment had offended him, but he had preferred to keep it to himself.

He got back in his car thinking that he too was just another good-for-nothing *imbécil*: how many years had he been following the trail of this serial killer, always showing up just a little too late? So what if they caught him now? What did it matter? It might curtail a few imminent murders, but it gave no solace to the families the killer had already been allowed to tear apart.

But yes, it did matter. Of course it did. Preventing a single murder in the future would make up for all the errors of the past.

By day's end, Rafael Fernandez found out that the FBI had placed the Railroad Killer on its most wanted list with a twenty-five-thousand dollar reward for his capture. There he was, number one on the list, dethroning Osama bin Laden himself. Obviously their taste for hype hadn't changed an iota. So much hoopla with their Wild West posters, when they'd do better to concentrate on catching the asshole.

Suddenly it occurred to him: Albuquerque. Could the killer be trying to contact his sister?

He'd better get cracking.

The phone rang later that evening. It was Debbie. He hadn't called sooner, he explained, because there was a lot going on at work. He considered not seeing her but then changed his mind, thinking maybe a few hours with her would help him relax, so he asked her over. Debbie said that wasn't what she called for, and hung up.

3

Landslide, 2009

I started going out again, hitting the university parties, trying to get back the urge to hang out with my friends and lose myself in their problems, all of which were infinitely more frivolous than what I'd been dealing with recently. Being with Fabián was exhausting, and it made me think about everything I had sworn to myself that I'd avoid. I had left College Station because I'd seen how all my college girlfriends' lives were slowly but surely getting bogged down with *responsibilities*—children, careers— and they were turning into a troupe of the Living Dead. They were Corpse Brides. I'd already gotten my BA, but not because I thought of it as a means for gainful employment. I found a job in an advertising agency but left after a while and spent a full year not really knowing what to do, what direction to take, trying in vain to sell comic strips to the newspapers (they weren't very original, I owed practically all my ideas to the Hernández brothers), until a Guatemalan friend who knew my passion for reading convinced me to apply for a scholarship for a doctoral program in Latin American literature. At Landslide, though, I'd finally to own up to my romantic notions: I'd never find the creative stimulation I was searching for in class-mates and professors. I fully shared their passion for literature but not the clinical, scientific way they approached books. And Fabián? I relished the hours we spent in molten conversation and cannibal sex, but it was getting more and more difficult for me to dredge up the patience for his fitful five a.m. phone calls, feverish emails, and relapses, all of which proved that despite a slight change in behavior now and then, things remained pretty much the same. Neither was I the self-sacrificing type of woman the situation called for.

One night we went out for a walk in the rain after snorting a few lines (this time I gave in to the temptation). We were getting boisterous, laughing hysterically, when a van sped by and splashed us. Fabián threw a stone at it and shattered one of the windows. The driver lost control; the vehicle ended up stalled on the sidewalk with smoke coming out of the engine. Two guys jumped out and started arguing with Fabián. He antagonized them as if they were on equal terms, even though each one was at least a head taller than him. They shoved him around and he fell into a big puddle. He barked insults at them and tried to stand up but couldn't. I begged him to just drop it, let it go. It was nearly impossible to get him to pay attention to me.

Another night he took me to the ghetto looking for his dealer. He said Travis got him premium shit at a good price; he had contacts in the Mexican coke cartels operating in Landslide. I heard Travis threaten Fabián in a back alley, refusing to sell him another gram: he owed Travis money.

On our way out, Travis gestured to Fabián to come a little closer. When he did, Travis pulled out a gun and put it to his temple. In the semidarkness I could just make out the silhouette of a skinny man dressed in an overcoat. He was standing next to someone who came up to his neck.

"You wanna stay alive, bitch?" Travis asked Fabián. "Don't

act like no smartass then, and don't even think of coming back here without my money."

I heard Fabián's voice tremble, more out of humiliation than fear. He promised to pay him off at the end of the month when his paycheck was deposited. Travis sneered and punched him in the face. "Professor piece of shit. Your philosophy is fucked up, yo."

Fabián touched his jaw and grimaced. He turned around to leave, head hanging low.

Where was the arrogant man who used to make such categorical decisions where I was concerned? The haughty intellectual who crusaded against "politically correct" academics like Ruth? Who did whatever he damn well pleased with his students?

Now, as we stood on the corner trying to hail a cab, all I saw was a little, shrunken man.

One night I went out with Sam to see a movie about a serial killer in Milwaukee. Sam wanted to talk about the case on his radio show. In the university theater as I hooked my legs over the seat in front of me, I tried in vain to concentrate on the film. All I could do was wonder what Fabián might be up to.

Around fifteen minutes before the movie ended, Sam got up and told me he'd wait for me outside. I answered "Where's your stomach, man?" He left without responding. I reckoned the horror scene had upset him: the serial killer was trying to turn his victims into zombies, so he'd perforated the skull of a fifteen-year-old boy and mainlined hydrochloric acid into his brain.

I walked out and found him sitting down on the carpet with his back against the wall beneath a poster advertising a Will

Ferrell movie. In a flash I saw what he was going to look like in ten years: a solemn bald professor, incapable of joking around with his students.

"Sorry, can't take all that carnage."

"How's it go? In the shoemaker's house they walk around barefoot."

"Well, I think true crime is thought-provoking as a subject, but I don't enjoy watching extreme violence. That movie was pure pornography."

We walked to a bar a few blocks away called My House Is Your House. It was decorated with posters advertising wrestling matches, with photos of El Santo, the Blue Demon, and Huracán Ramírez. They had wrestling masks on sale, and the drinks were named after different wrestling moves. The screens were showing a video of El Santo.

"It's totally Mexican," I laughed, and ordered a Flying Scissors with lemon and salt.

"Actually no. You'd never find a bar like this in Mexico. Only the gringos could pull something like this off."

Sam asked for a round of tequila shots and kept them coming. I amused myself reading the signs hanging on the mirror behind the register. "You can't drink all day if you don't start in the morning." "Everyone's crazy except you and me, but I'm starting to worry about you." "If you never see me again, baptize him."

By the fourth shot, Sam said he had something to tell me.

"Does the name Railroad Killer ring any bells?"

"No. Should it?"

"Not necessarily. He struck the first time when I was a kid. Nobody knew it was him back then. There was this Swedish exchange student, I remember overhearing my parents talk about what had happened. For a long time her case remained unsolved. No suspects, no leads. But ten years later they were able to prove that the Swedish girl had been the serial killer's first victim. They call him the Railroad Killer. He was number-one on the FBI's most-wanted list."

"Serial killers are a dime a dozen in this country, it's hard to keep them straight."

"It tells you the dimension of our national tragedy. Dude slaughters ten people and a short while later nobody even remembers his name."

"What does the Railroad Killer have to do with you?

My cell phone rang. It was Fabián. I couldn't understand a word he was saying.

"Hold on a sec. I can't hear you, I'm going outside."

Once outside, I asked what was up.

"Babe, I need you here within the next few minutes." His voice sounded serious.

"What's going on? You're worrying me."

"I'm scared. I'm really scared. And I can't promise . . ."

Now I was seriously alarmed.

"I'm getting in a cab right now. I'll be there in ten minutes."

I took off without saying goodbye to Sam.

The house was quiet and the lights were out. I paid the cab and ran to the front door. I gave it a slight push: it wasn't locked. I switched the hall lights on and called up the stairs.

"Fabián?"

No answer. I ran up, trying to keep my wits. I turned the lights on in the main room of the second floor. My cell rang. It was Sam.

"Oh isn't that sweet. You really just took off?"

"I'll explain later, I promise," I said and hung up on him.

He was lying face down on the bed with his feet on a chair, eyes half-mast, staring at the floor. He wasn't wearing pants or shoes, and his white shirt was soiled. He was making guttural noises, as if his tongue were stuck in the back of his throat. I took a deep breath, kept my calm. I was so tired of his panic attacks.

I sat down on the unmade bed. There were photocopies of my most recent storyboard on the bedside stand. There was also an official letter from the deans notifying him that his contract had been terminated. They would pay him a year's salary, but he would no longer be associated with the university as of next semester.

He must have received the letter that afternoon. He had chosen not to let me know.

"So that's it. Fucking bastards. I told you this was coming, and you wouldn't believe me."

"I'm sorry about the letter but you really scared me, I thought you were going to . . ."

"For Christ's sake, it's dead serious. I'm leaving. Tomorrow if I can. I can't stand the thought of spending one more day in this fucking place."

"You'll find a good lawyer. You're tenured, supposedly that makes you unfirable."

"I want to be free of the university. It's been a long time since I've given a shit about teaching. It's time to make decisions now. Are you coming with me?"

I walked out of the room, sat down on the stairs.

"Michelle, are you coming or not? Answer me por favor!"

I just sat there for a while and didn't say a word.

4

Texas and New Mexico, 1999

This time he crossed near Ojinaga. He had to wait a while for the Migra's patrol car to drive by on the other side, till it was out of sight. He waded into the skinny part of the river and lost his balance. There was a point where he thought he was going to drown. It was a false alarm: when he stretched his legs, his feet touched the bottom and he realized the water wasn't deep. He stepped across from stone to stone and scrambled into the brush once he reached the other side.

Jesús's pants were soaked. He was carrying his shoes in a bag with some fruit and a few bottles of water. The sun scorched his back and shoulders. He knew to steer clear of El Paso, keep moving through the smaller towns where there weren't so many cops. He mapped out a route through Marfa, then Fort Stockton—his only option. There was a manhunt on now; he knew they'd be inspecting freight trains, patrolling the highways. He was ready if they caught him, though, equipped with fake IDs and social security cards.

He followed a trail through the desert scrub and acacia trees. He startled some deer that darted away as soon as he came into view. A rabbit lay dying beside a hollow tree trunk; there were bloodstains on its white fur and back legs.

A Migra helicopter materialized in the sky above him. He hid in the undergrowth and waited for the danger to pass. Had to get a move on. His coyote friend's instructions weren't hard to follow. But the sun made him woozy; it was hard to think straight. He drank some water, cooled his face with it. They weren't making his life easy. Some of his open roads now had dead ends.

In a sudden flash of lucidity he realized he might never be able to jump a freight train again, or nick a car and drive it back, and the ache of it overwhelmed him. Why was he being so reckless now, pushing his luck? He should never have risked coming back. He should have stayed in Mexico, lying low in one of the bigger cities.

"Holy be not thy name."

He knew perfectly well why he'd come back.

The van dropped him off at a gas station in Fort Stockton. He paid them more than he wanted to but didn't feel like wasting time negotiating. The contact was a rancher's boy, Mexican, and he made a business out of aiding the illegals who showed up in the area; the Migra had arrested him a few times, but his old man had connections and they always let him walk.

Jesús wandered over to the Antro and took a seat at the bar. A parrot pecking at an ear of corn eyeballed him from its perch on a shelf behind the counter. Selena's "Amor prohibido" was playing on the jukebox. Four men sat playing dominos at a table nearby, drinking beer.

He didn't bother concealing his face. He figured the best of all covers was not to cover up at all. He wasn't foolish though, he knew better than to expose himself gratuitously. So far nobody had recognized him; most likely things would keep running smoothly.

He scrutinized a Mr. T bobblehead on the counter. A beefy dude, no doubt he would be a tough rival for Mil Máscaras. But Mil Máscaras had that Mexican cunning going for him; he'd take the prize no doubt. He didn't give a shit about wrestlers anymore, bunch of fucking fakes. Though he'd root for them over a puto gringo any day.

What about the Niners versus a Mexican football team? Now that's a different story.

He flicked Mr. T's head and let it bob. There was a television suspended on a rack in the corner, and an Operation Stop Train announcement came on. They showed a rendering of the man nicknamed the Railroad Killer. Dark skin, curly hair, high cheekbones, and a long nose. He wore thick-framed glasses and a mustache. He'd seen that face somewhere.

The man behind the counter looked at him, but he hadn't been watching the television. He was as short as Jesús.

"Can I getcha something?"

"A beer please, any kind you got."

The bartender set down a plastic coaster with the Michelob label and served a bottle of beer with a glass. Jesús tossed a few bucks on the counter and got closer to the television. The journalist was in Texas, reporting on a massive roundup of undocumented Mexicans that was under way. It seemed like all men of Hispanic origin found walking alone in border states with Mexico were in danger of being detained. Panic and paranoia were running rampant among the population, and calls were flooding in to the FBI phone lines. In a partly outraged, partly waggish tone he mentioned that even a sheriff's son from a small town in New Mexico had been taken into custody. After the reporter finished, the station anchor threw in his two cents: Operation Stop Train was proving successful at engaging locals in the widespread Railroad Killer manhunt, but it was also creating deep rifts in communities that had sizable Hispanic populations, which would be difficult to reconcile. Nobody felt safe, not even the most upstanding members of the community, who were now afraid that their Anglo neighbors and coworkers viewed them as potential suspects.

Was Jesús responsible for all this? Of course not. The hush-hush mistrust and side-glancing had existed long before he came along. He had simply been a catalyst, a means to an end.

He thought back to his time in Starke, how deeply suspicious Randy had been of the state. The incident in Waco had given the government a perfect pretext for getting rid of white supremacist leaders like David Koresh. Now Jesús was just another government excuse, this time to cleanse the country of Mexicans like him.

He went to the bathroom and washed his hands. The face staring back at him in the mirror wasn't his. The cheeks began melting into bloody clumps, leaving spots of bare skull. His whole body shuddered.

He wanted to confess, to explain how difficult things had been, how hard it was to keep the faith. He wanted to go home.

He didn't, though. He couldn't fail Him now.

He'd been chosen specifically and had to embody the wrath of an avenging angel.

I ain't gonna die, right? 'Cause you promised. I can't die.

"Holy. Be not thy name. KILL THEM ALL."

He found a public telephone on his way out of the bathroom and dialed his sister's number.

When María Luisa answered, Jesús hung up.

He called back.

"Aló?"

"Hermanita . . . you recognize my voice?"

"Jesús. Of course I do. You OK?"

"A little nervous. *Tu sabes*, been awhile."

"I didn't mean that."

"What? What you think, I . . ."

"Jesús . . ."

"I want to see you. Lay low for a few days in your house. Till things settle down."

Do they know about her? Are they staking her out?

There was a long silence. Then:

"First I need you to promise me something."

"What."

"That you won't be bad anymore. It makes me so unhappy."

"I want to tell you about . . ."

"Don't tell me anything over the phone."

"Don't leave me alone. Please. This still your address?"

He read it to her. She said yes. Jesús felt like a kid again, hiding in the hollow tree with his sister, trying his best to figure out a story that would make her happy. But now she didn't want to listen to him. How could he make her laugh if she didn't give him a chance?

"Don't disappoint me again, Jesús. OK?"

He hung up, irritated. He gulped down the rest of his beer and went outside. The wind hit him in the face and blew dirt across his lips. He went to a park nearby and sat on a bench to write in his diary. He wrote: "The Unamed say I am the Angel of Jugment, I go to heven when I done wat I got to do." He'd do it, even if he had to tiptoe behind God's back.

Maybe he should try hitching at the truck stop, jump on the first truck leaving for Albuquerque. He'd shock her by showing up on her doorstep.

She'd always been his weak spot. It was high time he took care of it.

A police car drove by on one of the streets bordering the park. He tried not to look at it, to just keep writing.

He called María Luisa again from the truck stop.

"So you think I have something to do with . . ."

"Jesús, it's time to put an end to it."

Jesús closed his eyes and lowered his head. He felt as though he could almost touch her, as if she were right there beside him.

"Think about it. I could arrange it. I could make sure they respect your rights."

"I don't want them to kill me," Jesús said. His voice rose and fell following the rhythm of his breathing and heaving chest. "I hate jail, but I prefer it to being dead."

"Just calm down."

"I need to see you."

"You'll see me soon. Just think it over. And call me when you've made up your mind."

"It's so hard."

"I know."

María Luisa's voice had a soothing effect.

He longed for some kind of release, to be relieved of this burden in his chest that was suffocating him, weighing him down. He'd kept everything inside for so long, the despair, the agony.

"I'll call later."

"Do it soon."

Jesús put down the receiver.

5

Albuquerque, New Mexico, 1999

Sergeant Fernandez rang the doorbell and waited with his hands in his pockets. Thunder rumbled in the distance: rain was coming, and soon the streets of Albuquerque would be filled with puddles. The children playing in the ruins of the demolished movie theater on the corner lot would be forced to go indoors. The neighborhood was quiet, modest, punctuated by occasional sounds of shouting, Spanish phrases floating out through open windows. The shelves of local shops were stocked with Latino products—he had picked up some tamarind candies in one of them; homes were painted in assorted shades of yellowish-brown with imitation adobe walls made of stucco; the yards were chock-full of toys. Recent immigrants lived next to families who had been there for a few decades now, or descendants of people who had lived there long before the US flag had ever flown over the territory.

It was taking awhile. Fernandez wasn't alarmed, though: he knew they were expecting him, and obviously it was intimidating to be called on by a police officer. He knew the wife didn't have her papers. Best to keep the visit friendly.

The woman finally opened the door and invited him into the living room. A series of landscape paintings with volcanoes decorated the walls. He took a seat on the couch, which was covered in a plastic sheath. She asked in English if she could get him anything, and he said a glass of water would be nice. He watched her walk into the kitchen and out of his field of vision. María Luisa didn't look much like the one in the photos he'd seen, or the image he'd constructed of her from their phone conversations. Brown skin, check; long black hair, check; but there was no trace of the beauty that had unsettled her brother. Her glance was evasive, and her cheeks were mottled with dark spots.

María Luisa came back and took a seat in a green armchair opposite the couch. It was a new chair and didn't go with the rest of the furniture. Fernandez asked about her children. They must be at a neighbor's house until he leaves.

"I'm listening," she said.

The brassy tone in her voice made Fernandez think some men would find it easy to follow her lead. He imagined her in the restaurant where she worked weekends, and it struck him that she was the type of immigrant for whom coming here had been a bad decision. She could have gone far in Mexico, maybe studied to become a dentist or a veterinarian. She had probably thought that crossing the border would open up the world to her, but here she was just one more digit in a disposable labor force. She made more money, sure, but at the cost of living without dreams.

Anyway, who was he to invent other people's futures? He should be focusing on the here and now.

"I guess you know why I'm here," he said. "We have reason to believe your brother is closely tied to a series of crimes. We would like your help detaining him so we can talk to him, figure some things out."

The woman stared at the floor.

"We know you have some influence with him," the sergeant continued. "We're closing in on him, and it could all end real bad. You got it in your hands to save him. In exchange, we would legalize your situation."

She kept quiet.

"Has he been in touch over the years?"

"Yes." Thunder growled again in the distance. "He calls me sometimes but doesn't say nothing; when I talk, he hangs up. At first I didn't know it was him. But I got some notebooks in the mail a few months ago, and I know they're his even though he didn't sign them. So the next hang-up call, I figured it out."

"Can I see the notebooks?"

She went into another room and rummaged around. She came back carrying six notebooks, which she placed on the coffee table. Fernandez opened one and flipped through it, reading a few random sentences:

"Avenging angel has power to impoze justiss onearth . . . She don't disirve me but here the thunder of my voise . . . Juárez, Mexicali, Caléxico, Reinosa, El Paso, it all is mine, allmine."

"If you don't mind, I'd like to keep these."

She nodded. I'm proceeding correctly, Fernandez thought to himself, reviewing his own performance. The phone calls to gain her trust, the visit, everything was designed to make María Luisa understand that he wasn't against her but on her side, they were friends and could work together. He should avoid using the abstract term *the police* because that always frightens people. He had to turn it into a personal problem, make her feel that other people might be out to hurt her brother but he had his welfare in mind.

Before leaving, Fernandez told María Luisa to consider his offer seriously and to keep him posted if she received another call. She nodded. He gave her his cell phone number and took off.

Fernandez spent the next few days in business-as-usual mode, normal office hours, keeping up with the news. He observed the Railroad Killer phenomenon, how it was sweeping the popular imagination: there wasn't a single city or town along the Mexican border without a sighting or eyewitness account, or a possible suspect being held in custody. In Juárez alone, they identified eight cases of women who had been found murdered near the train tracks that could have been the work of the Railroad Killer. Fernandez knew in his gut these murder cases had no connection with his investigation: all Railroad Killer murders had taken place in homes and in the United States. The horror in Juárez was someone else's doing.

Small comfort, though. The sergeant spent late nights in his apartment eating pizza and drinking beer, reading police procedurals, drained by having to live in this constant state of uncertainty.

He called María Luisa and asked if she had any news. Nothing. He eyed photographs of happier days with Debbie and regretted having been so weak. He threw the photos away a few times, only to go back and salvage them from the trash.

One day she had showed up at his place to let him know she was leaving for Canada. He invited her in to the chaos and clutter that was his tiny living space—an old Domino's pizza box balanced on the table next to an ashtray made of green glass and his coffee-stained dossier on the Railroad Killer. She perched on the couch. He offered her a beer, but all she wanted was a glass of water, thanks. He put a Johnny Cash CD on the stereo and sat down beside her.

"So you meant it," he said.

"My cousin is there, and she really thinks I'll find something for me, there are opportunities."

Her lips were painted red, there was a sparkle of hope in her eyes, and her cheeks were glowing: the sergeant realized she hadn't really come to say goodbye. Everything hinged on how he responded. If he told her not to go. If he urged her to move in with him. He could be a shelter for her loneliness, some company. No need to make any kind of lifelong commitment. They could just give it a try, see what happened.

Fernandez picked up the ashtray. He hadn't smoked a cigarette in a long time, he only kept it there for visits from Debbie, who, try as she might, had never been able to kick her menthol Lucky Strike habit. The aroma of her cigarettes and the powdery sweetness of her perfume would mingle and linger in the air long after she'd gone.

He told her he understood her decision and knew how hard it was to live far away from one's family and customs. He told her about his childhood in Mexico, how his parents let him roam freely and he would spend whole days outside or in friends' houses in the neighborhood. How back then kids used to play outdoors, in the street. He used his hands when he talked, and the ashtray tipped from one to the other. Sometimes he regretted getting divorced, but he hadn't been given much of a choice in the matter. His kids had distanced themselves; their way of life seemed foreign to him and he didn't know who they were anymore.

"They'll come back," Debbie said. "Just give them a little time."

Fernandez put the ashtray down on the table and looked closely at the photo of Johnny Cash on the cover of the CD. Now there was a man to go on a bender, he thought.

Debbie stood up and said she had to be on her way. He asked if he could walk her to her car.

"Don't bother." They said their goodbyes, and she gave him a peck on the cheek on her way out the door.

For a few seconds, Fernandez thought he might still have time. He could run after her the way they do in the movies, tell her how much he needed her by his side.

He heard her car motor cough and turn over.

He spent the weekend fishing in a small Gulf town where he used to hang out with a group of rowdy, hard-drinking friends back in the day. He liked the fresh catfish and market shellfish, that chunky shrimp gumbo that gave him such oomph. Any fish he caught was thrown back into the sea: he was merciful to them so he didn't have to be soft with the hardened criminals.

The whole port area had been remodeled to attract tourists, and brand-new neon signs flashed over chain restaurants. Shops selling key chains and stuffed turtle dolls moonlighted as tattoo parlors. He missed the greasy spoons of his youth, where a person could eat and drink at a shabby wooden table and feel a slight menace in the air.

It was noon when his cell phone rang. He was seated at an outdoor table in one of those newfangled chain restaurants, basking in the sunlight. It was María Luisa, her brother was willing to turn himself in.

"But he will only surrender to you. He wants me to be there too. And you can't send him to prison."

"*Imposible*," Fernandez said, excited and exultant. "If we arrest him, he'll have to go to jail."

"But not for all of his life."

The sergeant thanked her and told her he'd be back in touch with the details, that she should keep the communication open with her brother. She agreed and hung up.

Fernandez headed back to Landslide immediately. He called his superiors from the road and alerted the FBI agent who was coordinating from Texas. He updated them all, and they expressed incredulity: What, you mean that's it? After a wild manhunt, the monster is just going to turn himself in? What were his motives?

"Maybe he knows he's surrounded now, he can't do anything or go anywhere," Fernandez speculated.

He pulled his car over to the side of the road. The desert landscape opened up before him; the sun, triumphant in a cloudless azure sky, beat down with violence on the brownish-purple plateaus in the distance, the thirsty, rock-strewn earth and dusty cacti. Two vultures hovered over a tree.

He took a breath and smiled. Then he got back on the road. He was happy.

6

Landslide, 2009

It was getting light out by the time I left. The street lamps were still on, though, and their radiance seemed strange and out of place in the dawn light.

Back in the studio, I cleaned the makeup off my face and made some coffee. As I walked by my laptop, my screensaver greeted me with a picture of Fabián cuddling me. Seeing his tango CDs, his books on my shelves, I asked myself what I should do with it all.

I fell asleep for a few hours. I dreamed that I was being chased around the neighborhood by the living dead, and the houses morphed into an endless city that covered the entire planet. The zombies never actually caught me, but they wouldn't leave me alone either. I hid out in an abandoned mansion and started aging in fast-forward, and when I looked out the window there they were, still waiting for me.

These were strange days, when time seemed to dissolve, to go haywire. Sometimes I would sleep all afternoon and stay awake all night. I tried to draw, but I couldn't. I wanted to write, but nothing came. I tried to read, I couldn't concentrate. Books I'd only skimmed piled up around the studio.

I talked to my mom, brought her up to date. She consoled me but also made sure to point out that it had been my own fault. Let it be a lesson. I asked her to change the subject: now wasn't the time for reproaches. "Whatever you say, hija," she said. "I have my problems too, you know. Your dad just bought two tickets for Santa Cruz, we're supposed to be leaving next month. It made me so mad because he didn't even consult me first. Now what am I supposed to do?" She didn't like the idea of having one-way tickets to Bolivia. No, she wouldn't go. But how was she going to leave him on his own? "*Dios mío*, that man is more stubborn than a mule." We hung up, each of us in her own world.

Fabián called me just once, to let me know I could go pick up my things. The following week he was leaving for Santo Domingo. I was surprised; I never actually thought he'd drum up the courage to leave. And although I'd promised myself that I would never see him again, I gave in yet again.

When I got there, he was packing his stuff into crates. The rooms were empty. He barely paused to greet me. It crossed my mind that he was still in love with Mayra, meaning I'd never really had a fighting chance.

I asked how he was doing.

"As well as can be expected, I suppose, given the circumstances."

He offered me a glass of water; he was sipping a bottle of Pacífico. We walked out into the yard.

I was tense and awash in memories of so many "mornings after" spent there in Fabián's house. Like when he tried to teach me how to tango, and I kept stepping on his toes and laughing, and he'd say "*Bolita*, you have two left feet!"

"Good luck," I said and hugged him. "Don't do anything crazy. It'll do you good to rest awhile."

"I'm not sure that I'll be getting much rest," he said, touching his forehead.

"Oh, well. I guess you'll be spending time with Mayra. I figured as much. Just didn't want to admit it."

"Yes, and no. I hate Mayra. I can't stand being around her. But what else can I do?"

I looked at him.

"I'm going to find my daughter. I told you that one day you'd understand me. You might not think my secret justifies my behavior, but you'd understand."

"Did you just say 'my daughter'?"

"Mayra had wanted to have a baby. I didn't. All I wanted to do was crawl out of the writer's block I'd fallen into after my first book. It would have been unthinkable with a child."

He coughed. There was a kind of twinkle in his eye that I'd never seen before, some sort of strength, or maybe it was determination.

"I don't follow you. What . . ."

"I told her I didn't want to have children, that the subject was moot. But we had a knock-down-drag-out over it. We were still brooding ten days later when she told me she was pregnant. That it had been a fluke. Of course I didn't believe her. She was happy; she said she thought this was going to bring us closer as a couple, but I was convinced it had been a big trick to keep me tied to her."

I was tongue-tied, floored; all I could do was stare over at the house where so much of what we had lived together had taken place, look up at the windows on the second floor.

"I dreamed one night I was prattling to a baby who suddenly turned green and then burst into a thousand pieces that scattered all through the house. I was terrified. I told her she couldn't have the baby. That if she went through with it, she was on her own. I wouldn't be there; I wanted no part of it. Not even my name. I would never acknowledge that I was the father, so she had better keep that information to herself."

"The same thing you told me."

"She insulted me, she threatened to lawyer-up, to sue me. I told her I would pay whatever I had to pay, that wasn't the issue. I tried so hard to convince her to stop, but I couldn't. And I hated her for that, for being so dead set on bringing a child into this fucking world. So his ashes could end up scattered all over the place, just like all the rest of us! And one day, when she had already started to show, she disappeared, just up and took off for Santo Domingo without saying a word. And I haven't seen her since."

So she had done what I never had the strength of will to do myself. She stood up to Fabián without letting him twist her arm, without giving in.

"The separation documents arrived three months before my daughter was born. So now I was free, I could return to my life. The irony is that I couldn't. I kept thinking about my daughter, about what I had done. If I was blocked before, now it was even worse. Someone who was exactly like me, someone who was me, came to visit one day and just stayed put. He sat down next to me on the couch with his long gravedigger's face, and scared the wits out of me."

"You could have tried to work things out with her."

"Things with Mayra are broken beyond repair. The problem is the baby girl. I'll never forgive Mayra for having had her without my consent, but it's not my daughter's fault. I'm no family man, but I admit to feeling curious about her, to know what she's like."

"I don't get it. Honestly, I don't. With everything you went through with Mayra, why did you allow the same thing to happen with me?"

"The paradox is that what happened with you was what made me finally hit rock bottom and decide it was time to climb out of the well."

I felt like punching him, spitting on him.

"If it's any comfort, I'm not proud of my behavior."

"Oh, so easy for you to say that, isn't it? You have your daughter. What about me?"

I had no stomach for self-pity anymore, but I was struggling to maintain my self-control, my sense of dignity.

"You have your writing," he said. "Your drawings. You'll go far, accomplish much, I'm sure of it."

"Yeah, you make it all sound so easy. You're such a cynic."

I turned around; I wanted to wish him the worst in life. This little road to redemption, this eagerness to meet his daughter, it wasn't going to last very long. Just another one of his pipe dreams; he'd needed rehab a long time ago, somebody should have told him that. All I'd done was enable his vices instead of helping him.

I stopped. I looked up and pictured myself arguing with him on the balcony. I looked around at the yard and expanse of property and imagined it during spring or summer, when the vegetation was lush and impossible to walk through: what a perfect place it would be to hide a body. He didn't really have a daughter. Mayra hadn't really left Landslide; in fact, her bones were rotting six feet under. Why should I believe

Fabián's story? There was no evidence to prove what he was saying. And just as he'd lied about his book for such a long time, he obviously had no qualms about keeping a con going with people for years and years.

An anonymous phone call to the police was all it would take. Report that I'd seen some strange man digging in the yard at night, burying something there. Fabían traveled light, like his friend from San Antonio. He dropped weight when he had to and kept moving on.

"Something wrong, Michelle?"

"No, nothing."

The vision of myself on the balcony evaporated. There was nothing to gain by imposing my imagination on reality.

I couldn't help asking him what he planned on doing when he got there.

"I don't know. Look for work that will allow me to continue writing."

There was nothing more to say. When he tried to hug me, I turned away.

Sam came around to the studio. He knew Fabián had taken off, and he complained that now he would be forced to restructure his committee, but then he said maybe it was for the better. I let him go on for a while and then told him to change the subject please, I don't want to talk about him anymore. He told me he'd been exchanging letters with a serial killer, and I was stunned.

"Yeah. They call him the Railroad Killer. Remember I was telling you his story?"

"Yeah, of course I do. The dude who killed the Swedish girl."

"He's being executed next week. He wants me to be there, in Huntsville. I don't want to go by myself. Wanna come with?"

"Are you out of your mind? What would I do in a place like that?"

"He wrote me a twelve-page letter because he listened to the special I did on him. He said that he listened to a voice inside that sent him to people where evil was nesting. All he did was what 'the Unnamed' told him to do. Then he went off on a tangent about the abuses of government, Waco, and how they murdered David Koresh, a whole bunch of stuff. I answered his letter, and then he wrote again. And again."

I didn't say anything.

He went on: "I read something once by an FBI profiler who said that serial killers are from the moon. What he meant was that their minds work like beings from another planet; it's impossible to understand all of what's inside of them. How they breathe, what they think, what brings them to kill this one or to pardon that one. What do they smell, hear, what do they see that excites them enough to actually commit a crime? Reading Jesús's letters made me think about that. His name is Jesús María José."

"Well, executing him is a very precise way of sending him back to the moon."

"So will you come with me?"

"Let me think about it."

His interest was so contagious I ended up completely gripped by the story of the Railroad Killer. A Latino serial killer like the Night Stalker, a Mexican. There's something there. A vast country where Latinos lose themselves and are found. It made me think about extreme forms of madness. I thought about

Fabián. Though there was no madness there, more like a surfeit of lucidity, of rationale, so much so that he did one idiotic thing after another. Unless, of course, we're really the stupid ones. Maybe we should be as paranoid as him, and suspicious of his paranoia. He took off and left the house as empty as his friend's house in San Antonio. Now he'll set up shop in Santo Domingo and open the doors wide for people to come in, when in fact the entrance is barred, he always lives shut away in an ivory tower.

Right after Sam left, I surfed around the Internet for the Railroad Killer. Something was stirring inside of me.

My idea for this graphic novel falls within the genre of fantastic literature, with elements of horror and superheroes. Like *The Sandman*, its success will rest on a combination of genres including fantasy/horror/ superheroes. It will lean more heavily toward fantasy than horror. It is set in the present with apocalyptic undertones.

It tells the story of a scientist who is married to a painter; they have a four-year-old daughter. They live in La Línea, a border city that belongs to the North by day and the South by night. One night when the scientist is away at a weekend conference, a serial killer enters their home. The killer slashes his daughter to pieces, then rapes his wife and leaves her for dead.

The scientist's name is Federico. The painter's is Samantha. The daughter is Aida.

Still in shock, the scientist buries his daughter. His wife is still in a deep coma and must remain in the hospital for a few more weeks. She comes out of the coma and ends up at home under the care of a full-time nurse; she is unable to speak and her stare is vacant. In an attempt to bring her back from this living death, the scientist hangs a few of her paintings around the house, filling her room with brushes, oil paints, water-colors, and easels. Maybe if she remembers that she had once been an artist, she'll return to the way she was.

Flashback to the woman's childhood and adolescence in the South, her trip by freight train to the North, the years during which she lived in a camp full of illegal aliens and discovered her talent for painting. Her obsessions: bridges, trains, and tunnels. The scientist visits the camp to run a few experiments there; they meet and fall in love. He helps get a special permit so they can marry and settle together in La Línea.

A second flashback tells the scientist's story. He was successful very early in his career, but for reasons that aren't entirely clear, he fell into a deep depression. He gets blocked; he loses his creative impulse. He starts experimenting with drugs that give him unusual strength. He fashions a black mask with silver lining around the eyes and begins living a double life. He prowls the city streets at night wearing his disguise. He says he's fighting crime in cities near La Línea, but the truth is more ambiguous. The scientist isn't able to distinguish between good and bad, and it isn't clear whether this is a result of the drugs or of some secret in his past. The only thing he really wants now is to find his daughter's killer and avenge her death.

I stopped writing at midnight. I finally had the groundwork for my story.

But now what? What was going to happen? Should I develop it using the kinds of plot twists that are so typical of B-movies: the woman discovers, clue by clue, that her daughter's killer was her husband? That the scientist is in fact a serial killer?

I called Sam to let him know the good news—that after struggling for such a long time, I had finally figured out how to articulate the story my own way; it was convincing and I could see my future in it. He'd see too. After ages of poking fun at my taste for zombie and vampire stories, for serial killers and superheroes, insisting on the idea that popular stuff can't have artistic merit, he'll now be forced to see how powerful the material is, that it can be touching and deeply moving.

He wasn't paying too much attention to what I was saying. He was using his self-righteous tone of voice, that hint of arrogant moral superiority. He was probably just feeling hurt.

"So nothing has changed. Instead of devoting time to things that matter, you're still drawing your little cartoons."

I took a deep breath, and for the first time in several weeks, I felt happy. No, I hadn't changed, and thank goodness for that. I had to keep doing my own thing.

I hung up without saying goodbye and went back to my drawings.

7

Landslide, 1999

Sergeant Fernandez waited in the Landslide train station next to María Luisa. They stood beside a bench in the vestibule per Jesús's instructions. The station was closed; undercover officers were on the lookout, and snipers were positioned in the rooms on the second floor with bird's-eye views of the entire hall.

María Luisa was wearing a black skirt and white ruffled blouse. She had high heels on, and makeup concealing the blotches on her cheeks. He'd been surprised to see her so done up for the occasion; her brother was a serial criminal, but she still wanted to look pretty.

Fernandez was having a hard time controlling his anxiety and kept looking at the huge clock between an Amtrak sign and a Citibank advertisement. It was eleven-thirty in the morning, and Jesús had said he'd show up at twelve o'clock sharp.

"What if he doesn't show?"

"He will."

"How are you so sure?"

"Because he promised me he would."

"Strange that he decided to surrender."

"Stranger that he killed so many people."

True. Who was he to fathom what drove a man to kill?

Fernandez allowed himself a moment's optimism. One should show compassion to all creatures scrabbling along their path in life, should be willing to throw a cloak of pity over the shoulders of even a man like Jesús.

But then he recalled some of the sentences and illustrations he'd read in the killer's notebooks—"my knife will soke the corupt in blood, that is everybody"—and he remembered vivid scenes of the crimes: the elderly woman stabbed to death in her bed, raped postmortem, the illustrator who had been hideously maimed in her home. And he thought, not this time. He just couldn't. This was a limit: there was no forgiveness for Jesús.

Still, he was happy to be an instrument of grace. Human grace, imperfect: the only kind they deserved.

María Luisa asked if she could smoke. He said yes, even though there was a sign in front of them proclaiming that it was prohibited in the station.

It was now twelve o'clock.

At five minutes past, the sergeant said, that's it: Jesús wasn't going to show up. It had all been a big bluff.

That's when he saw María Luisa stiffen and he followed her gaze.

There was a man walking toward them. He wore a dirty T-shirt and was carrying a blue Adidas bag. He was short, slight-framed, and wearing glasses. His hair was tousled.

It was him.

Fernandez palmed the pistol that was hidden in his shoulder holster and raised the thumb of his right hand just slightly, to gesture to the agents and snipers that the man had arrived.

Jesús stopped a few feet away from María Luisa and Fernandez.

"Hermanita," he said, his eyes wide open and afraid.

"Jesús."

"It's so nice to see you, *qué padre*," he spoke without looking at Fernandez, as if he hadn't even noticed his presence there. "I missed you. *Mucho*."

"I missed you too."

Jesús made a gesture as if to move in closer and embrace his sister. Without taking his eyes off him, Fernandez pulled out handcuffs. Jesús threw his bag down and lunged at María Luisa; Fernandez caught the glint of a blade in Jesús's right hand. He was drawing his pistol when he heard the shot. Jesús screamed and collapsed onto his sister; both of them fell to the ground. Fernandez grabbed Jesús and turned him over, pointing his gun at him, and shouted, "Don't move, don't you dare move." Jesús looked up at him with an expression of disbelief, as if the words being shouted weren't meant for him. Blood gushed from his right forearm.

Fernandez took a step backwards. María Luisa was sobbing. There wasn't time for anything else. The FBI had them surrounded.

EPILOGUE

Huntsville, Texas, 1999–2009

During the first few months, he counted every single hour of every single day obsessively, as if being imprisoned in Houston were just that, a matter of counting the days and hours. He checked the calendars during his frequent doctor's appointments for the pain in his knee, or for heart palpitations, migraines, insomnia, panic attacks. But eventually, he wasn't sure exactly when, he stopped noticing the slow passage of time.

He stared at the ceiling and walls, sprawled on a cot that hurt his back if he lay there too long, and scolded himself for having accepted his sister's arrangement. María Luisa came to visit regularly and told him that she forgave him, that he had done the right thing by turning himself in; he had prevented any further senseless deaths, above all his own. But obviously he didn't see it that way. He was convinced that his pact with the Unnamed meant that he would never die. They sure as hell hadn't been able to apprehend him. It would have been sweet and easy to continue outwitting the police. He'd still be out there running free if only he hadn't freaked out when he saw his face in the newspapers and on television, if he had exercised a little patience and waited for things to calm down.

When María Luisa convinced him to turn himself in peacefully, it had occurred to him that this would be the perfect way
to finally get at her. He was tired of being hunted, and now
he could kill two birds with one stone. Hand himself in and
make her see that she was high up on his list of undesirables.
He had grappled with confused feelings for such a long time,
and now he still struggled every day in his cell between the
desire to see her and be happy by her side and the desire to
hurt her, let her know how much she made him suffer. It had
been the kind of plan the brainless morons he knew in Starke
might have concocted.

María Luisa had reassured him that in return for turning
himself in, they had promised there would be no death sentence. But his lawyer explained in their first meeting that it
wasn't a binding promise. Some Ranger had made it without
consulting with the FBI or the state prosecutor.

"I don't get it," the public defender said. "You could have
turned yourself in anywhere in the whole country. Why would
you choose to do it in the state with the highest number of
executions in the nation?"

"Would you please calm down," María Luisa begged through
the Plexiglas when he told her what the lawyer said on her next
visit. He couldn't; he insulted her, told her he'd never forgive
her, he never wanted to see her again, she was a traitor, she
was on their side, she had betrayed her own blood. It upset her
so much that she let a few months pass by before returning. It
was better that way. How long had he been dreaming of her,
only to discover that she was another fake. She wasn't the
same person he had lived with in Villa Ahumada. She wasn't
even pretty. What were all those marks on her cheeks?

His lawyer, Brad Johnson, was the only person on his side. But how far could he trust him? He was young; he dressed in a suit and tie and used some sweet-smelling cologne that always made Jesús a little queasy. He could speak Spanish, but Jesús preferred to answer in English. Brad's mother was Guatemalan, and she told him it was his duty to support the Latino community. He accepted the case for humanitarian reasons, not because he believed he could achieve a not-guilty verdict.

"I don't believe in capital punishment, Jesús. It's contrary to what the good Lord wants for us. The old idea of eye for an eye, it's useless. We're supposed to turn the other cheek. That doesn't mean we're going to let you continue to do what you were doing. Absolutely not. Sooner or later you'll have to face the Lord yourself, whether you live out the rest of your life here or not."

"I hate this place, Mr. J. My problem ain't the Lord. I have his agent living right here in my heart. He always been there, you gotta believe me."

"It's not my place to argue about that, but maybe there's a, let's say, a cognitive dissonance between your faith and your actions."

"Yeah, fucking *disonancia cognitiva*!"

Jesús tried hard to clarify for him that that Lord didn't exist anymore. A minor God, a rebel, was who created the universe. The Unnamed. It was the only way to explain the Earth's state of imperfection. Brad nodded but looked at him sideways, unconvinced. Jesús went on to describe that night in Starke Prison when he was possessed by the Unnamed, how he had been transformed into an avenging angel and was given the mission to cleanse the earth of corruption. Brad interrupted him and asked:

"Whoa, hold on a second—what angel?"

"I'm half man, half angel."

"And how do you decide who the corrupt ones are that need to be eliminated?"

"A voice tells me when to stop in a town and go in a home and KILL THEM ALL."

"Kill anyone who crosses your path? The just pay for the sinners?"

"There no just and sinners. We all sinners."

"So that justifies killing anybody. Whoever it was, you were only fulfilling an assigned task."

Brad sat up.

"I think I have an idea, Jesús. A way out. The State of Texas wants the death penalty. My mission is to prove that you are mentally incompetent and can't be executed."

"But it isn't true."

"It's not?"

"I'm not crazy."

Brad didn't answer. Jesús continued: "It don't matter. I can't be executed 'cause I can't die, see? I don't believe in my death. I know the body rots. But I'm eternal. I am going to live forever."

Brad didn't argue. He came to see him again two days later. He gave him a black notebook like the ones Jesús had written in before and a supply of pencils.

"Write down everything that's on your mind. All your desires, your fears. You can exaggerate. The wilder the better."

Jesús thanked him for the notebooks. He got started writing and filled a fifty-page book in a single day. He explained his mission on earth and his dreams of traveling by train doling out justice, blazing sword in hand, trains that passed over rivers of blood and under steel-colored skies and a long, hard rain of ashes.

He avoided talking to fellow inmates as much as possible during mealtimes, in the bathroom, and in the yard. There was nobody there like Randy, who had somewhat alleviated his days in Starke. The Latinos, the blacks, and the whites were all equally corrupt here. He would make believe he had decapitated them, raped and impaled them, burned them with acid, bitten them in the neck and let them bleed to death.

He wrote it all down eagerly, leaving nothing out.

He wished the same for the prison guards, the doctors in the infirmary, the families who came to visit other inmates: a world of bodies waiting for the dagger that would bore a hole in them and deflate them, and once they were on the ground they'd be swept into the sewers. *Holy be not thy name.* The same thing for Brad: so close to him, and all he wanted was to twist his neck. The coward, always coming to visit him in the company of another agent. Not to mention María Luisa: he told her never to come back. The temptation was too great.

He felt like watching El Santo movies. They told him he had to follow the regular programming, they didn't take special requests. He asked Brad for El Santo magazines. "I'll see what I can do" was his response.

Brad showed up one morning with five El Santo magazines. The serial wasn't in sequential order, but it was better than nothing.

In *Lucha en el infierno*, El Santo went up against a group of kidnappers led by Rocke. Jesús enjoyed one of the strips where Rocke turned into a demon and fought against El Santo. It started when El Santo walked into a room. "On the other side of the doorway, he could feel his whole body start to freeze. Soon, the mirrors seemed to come alive. A bloodcurdling scream was heard, as if from beyond the grave. 'Our Father!' El Santo screamed. 'Ugh! Who art in heaven! Holy be thy name . . . Thy Kingdom come . . . Ugh! I can't breathe! Your will be done! Lord, don't let this demon take control of me . . .'"

The story ended with El Santo suspended in midair. Would the demon triumph? Jesús knew he wouldn't. El Santo always won in the magazines. It was so stupid.

In *Santo vs. el conjuro de la oscuridad*, Jesús enjoyed the story of El Santo confronting a giant snake. "I must be hallucinating." The serpent curled up against El Santo's body. "Agh! It hurts! You won't master me!" El Santo cut the serpent in two. "You may hurt me in body, but nobody will ever wound my soul."

Jesús threw the magazines in the trash.

Every so often, specialists came to evaluate him. They were bilingual and had the patience to listen to him and read through his notebooks. Brad was pleased: he told Jesús there was a unanimous consensus in favor of supporting the psychiatrist: "The patient's deliriums have completely taken over his thought process." Jesús was furious: he didn't ever want to see them again, the pigs, they were on the law's side and useless.

Sergeant Fernandez showed up regularly with other agents to ask for statements. Brad told him he didn't have to answer, but he wanted to talk. Fernandez told him reports had been coming in from other states as well as from Mexico and Canada, and he was suspected of having committed eight hundred unsolved crimes. Fernandez had thrown out several of them himself, all he needed was to ask about a few others. He described the cases and Jesús made an effort to remember.

He admitted to being the perpetrator of four other crimes, a few of them he wasn't entirely certain about, but they sounded familiar: A nineteen-year-old boy was found near the train tracks in Ocala, Florida. His girlfriend had been raped, strangled, and buried in a grave in Sumter County, Florida. An eighty-year-old woman had been found in her home near the train tracks in Carl, Georgia. A man had been killed in front of an empty home in San Antonio.

The state continued collecting evidence for his case. He would be brought to trial only for the murder of the doctor who was killed in the Houston suburb. The prosecutor believed there was enough hard evidence there to convict him.

Brad continued with the psychiatric evaluations, preparing the defense.

He learned about the attack on the Twin Towers and was sure that now the time for vengeance was at hand. Ashes were falling over buildings and people; the age of the superheroes was over. The giant would be chastised for years of abuse. After the cataclysm, the Unnamed would come and there would be a chance to start anew.

Renata never once visited him. He never heard from her again.

Sergeant Fernandez couldn't resist finally asking him *why* point blank before walking out the door. Jesús answered: "Why what?

"Why? Why did you do it?"

"I already said what I had to say."

"I see the facts and understand them," the sergeant said with a tired gesture. "But still the question remains, why? The Swedish girl, for example. What reason was there . . . Never mind, it doesn't matter. I guess you're just a glitch. An exception to the rule. But then comes the question, what if you're not?"

"Then you're fucked." Jesús said defiantly.

Fernandez got up and mumbled something that Jesús heard as "Unnamed my ass." And he left.

By the time the trial got under way, Jesús had already been incarcerated in Houston for four years. The trial lasted two weeks. The plaintiff's attorney described in exhaustive detail the murders Jesús was accused of committing. Brad spoke about mitigating factors, the defendant's mental disorders, that he believed he was half angel and half human. Jesús listened impatiently. When it was his turn to speak, he admitted his guilt and clarified the particulars, claiming to have done the right thing in each one of the cases.

Yes, he liked to hang around the house after committing his crimes, he didn't eat out of coldness but because anxiety provoked hunger. Yes, he sometimes took his victims' driver's licenses and studied them, because he wanted to know more about their lives before heading on his way. Yes, he took jewelry, because it was easy to hawk in pawnshops and because he could impress his wife; he never touched the money, though, he was afraid they would trace him through the serial numbers. Yes, sometimes he raped his victims after they were dead, because he hated the fucking gringas who never gave him the time of day and looked at him as if he were a piece of shit. There wasn't any reason to feel remorse, except at having trusted María Luisa.

The plaintiff's attorney said that Jesús was "evil in human form," and Brad defended him. Jesús was forced to keep his mouth shut the whole time, when what he really wanted was to contradict Brad; he didn't recognize himself in the *loco* his lawyer was describing. What was so crazy about being half human and half angel? They should spend a few hours inside his head, they'd see for themselves.

The jury quickly reached a guilty verdict. Brad's argument that he couldn't distinguish between good and bad was overruled. He had been lucid enough to use pseudonyms, elude the FBI and INS for years, and outmaneuver police from several different states and counties. He had the necessary perspicuity to select ideal homes to rob and vulnerable victims to kill.

The judge pronounced the verdict: Jesús would be executed by lethal injection. Brad embraced him, overwhelmed by emotion. Jesús broke down. Despite all the silliness of the mental incompetence defense, Brad had grown fond of him.

"Don't worry," Jesús whispered. "I'll never die."

"I'm going to appeal. In the end, justice will prevail."

"No need," Jesús responded. "Justice is me."

He was transferred to a maximum-security prison in Huntsville. When he got out of the van he saw the barbed wire fence, the sentry towers around the perimeter, the security post at the entrance, and realized how serious it was this time. They made him get undressed in a tiny space where a guard said, "Welcome to the death pit," and handed him a white uniform with the letters DR on the back for "Death Row."

He was shepherded to the prison wing where convicts condemned to death were kept. It was a separate annex, no inmate rehabilitation necessary, and they spent most of the day isolated in cells that measured sixty square feet. There were few perks; Jesús got them to allow a radio and permission to listen to it for half an hour a day. He could tune in to radio stations on the border. He'd get nostalgic over corridos and rancheras, music that he never liked before but that now reminded him of home.

He kept up with the news, the war in Afghanistan, and relished the fact that Bush couldn't find Bin Laden.

Women and autograph hunters wrote to him. His signature was worth fifty dollars. He sold locks of his hair. He even sold corns from his feet. Fucking gringos were batshit loco.

He got to know a few fellow death-row convicts. One of them, Cameron, had been wearing the DR on his uniform for nine years now; he was brawny and his forearms were covered with tattoos of skulls and snakes; they said he had torched his own home, killing his three daughters, who were all under five years old, though he claimed he was innocent and showed Jesús poems he'd written to the girls. He said the state had offered him life for a guilty plea, but he refused, he preferred to die. They'd never get him to declare he'd killed his own daughters.

Cliff had stabbed a man to death. Jeff kidnapped and murdered a woman. Wilkes robbed a jewelry store and killed one of the employees.

Later he realized it wasn't worth the effort getting to know them. They were there one day and gone the next. And that made him obsess about when his turn would come.

Cliff's last words were "I'm ready, I thank my father, who's in heaven, for the grace he's given me."

Jeff's were "I love you, Mom. Bye."

Wilkes asked Jesús to draw a rose a day before he went to the execution room. It didn't come out very well.

They were allowed out of their cells to mingle with other prisoners in the patio for an hour a day. He'd hang with Cameron and listen to him gab. Jesús wasn't into flapping his tongue, and he knew sure enough Cameron was guilty—fucking gringos didn't screw that kind of stuff up—but it was a good story. He put the pieces together slowly but surely as the days and months went by.

Cameron was born in Oklahoma in 1968. He never knew his mother. His father brought him up in a tiny, filthy house near the train tracks (couldn't sleep at night for the rattle of the freight trains). He got bad grades and by fourteen was addicted to sniffing paint. He dropped out of school, started shoplifting in the malls, and was arrested several times. In 1998 he met Stacy and they got married. They moved to Corsicana, Texas, where Stacy's brother lived. It was a depressing town some fifty miles from Waco, where jobs were scarce. They started fighting a lot because Cameron was getting plastered and whoring around. He'd hit her every once in a while. By 1991 they had three girls; Amber and the twins Kameron and Karmon. Stacy worked at her brother's bar, and Cameron was an unemployed mechanic. He would stay at home and watch the girls. The twins were a handful, he'd lose his patience and yell at them a lot, but along with Amber, they were the only things of any value in his life. He spoiled them with presents whenever he could scrape a few bucks together.

"Stacy took off early that day, it was December, so she went to Salvation Army to get Christmas gifts for the girls. I stayed home babysitting. The twins started crying, so I got up to get them some milk and they quieted down. Amber was still sleeping, so I went back to bed. Suddenly Amber's voice woke me up shouting 'Daddy, Daddy!' The place was full of smoke. I grabbed my pants and shirt and yelled for Amber to get out of the house. I ran into the twins' room, but by that time I couldn't see a thing. The burnt smell in the hallway was over-powering. My hair burst into flames. I smothered the fire on my head and fought to stay conscious, to get out of the house. I ran to my neighbor's and asked them to call the fire depart-ment. I wanted to go back in, but there wasn't no way. The fire-men took a while to get there, and I knew my kids were already gone. The police arrested me a week later, all I could hear was a voice in my head screaming 'Daddy. Daddy!' I thought it was some kind of a joke.

"They needed a motive. The girls' life insurance was only worth something like fifteen dollars and I wasn't the benefi-ciary, it went to Stacy's dad. But the district attorney in charge of the case, a real son of a bitch, said I was a sociopath and had killed the girls because they were interfering with my licentious lifestyle. As if going on benders and darts games with the guys were the world's most rotten sins. The 'expert' who testified for the prosecution said my violent posters—Iron Maiden and Led Zeppelin, the fallen angels and winged skulls and hatchets—revealed a death wish and possible interest in satanist deeds. Oh, I drank a lot, I admit it, and I got a little heavy-handed with Stacy every once in a while, but it wasn't all that bad. About the posters . . . how do you even respond to that? It was totally innocent, I just liked the music and all the paraphernalia, the look, I even got a skull tattoo. But the jury believed their story and turned me into a monster."

Jesús thought about the shack where Cameron had grown up near the train tracks, how he had sniffed paint, was a petty thief and mechanic, had posters of a fallen angel in his house.

Cameron was like his double, as if he had also been sent by the Unnamed. But why did he refuse to admit what he'd done? Was he really so afraid of death?

Jesús started hearing a voice at night that whispered, "Daddy, Daddy."

Cameron's turn came three years later. His last words were "The only statement I want to make is that I am an innocent man convicted of a crime I did not commit. I have been persecuted for twelve years for something I did not do. From God's dust I came and to dust I will return, so the Earth shall become my throne."

Tears welled up in Jesús's eyes when he heard about his execution. He was going to miss him. He was surprised to feel such grief.

After Cameron's death, appealing his case before the state became a matter of urgency, and he decided to look for a new lawyer. Brad had dropped the case, so, following the suggestion of another DR inmate, he took on Elizabeth Gillis. She was an energetic redhead who set about writing and sending appeals as if she really believed there was a chance for an acquittal.

Jesús sent handwritten letters to the journalists covering his case. He wrote to a reporter from Houston's channel KPRC that the prison food was disgusting and that he'd be voting for Steve Forbes or Gary "Beaur" in the upcoming Republican primaries because "this man do not want babies murdered."

A year later he wrote to the same reporter saying he was happy about the attack on the Twin Towers and that the country had better watch out because it had "deservingly" made enemies all over the world. He said the attack had been prophesied in the book of Revelation and the government wanted to kill all the prophets, including Koresh and Bin Laden. He said it didn't matter though because all prophets were one single voice and behind them was the Unnamed, and the Unnamed could not be touched by anyone.

He wrote another letter a year later saying that he admired George Bush but didn't agree with sending troops to Iraq and Afghanistan because it would make them hate him. He wrote about hearing his speech in El Paso on modernizing the border and understood the reasoning. People here were materialists and they only cared that commerce flowed freely. He wrote out one of Bush's sentences: "We want to use our technology to make sure that we weed out those who we don't want in our country—the terrorists, the coyotes, the smugglers, those who prey on innocent life." It made him laugh because the only ones they'd be getting rid of were the innocent ones, the honest workers and resourceful people like him who found ways to dodge the Empire "becose the empire is corupt and his end will be here pretty soon."

He made up with his sister, and when she visited he found her pretty again. He wished she would come alone, but her husband usually came with her. He was a threatening presence hovering over their visits and didn't let them talk in peace.

Whenever his mother visited, she ended up getting sick.

He never saw Sergeant Fernandez again.

Jesús was known in the DR wing of the prison for his conviviality. He ate very little, and his ribs poked out visibly when he was shirtless. He liked to visit the chapel first thing in the morning, and he tried to learn Hebrew but could never get past a few sentences. He wrote letters to anyone he could. He even sent one to Randy, though the letter never arrived. The convoluted script thanked him for illuminating his path and then cursed him for revealing that the God he believed in was an empty God.

He wrote Sergeant Fernandez saying, "The Unnamed look for you even in dreams and do revenge for abuse my sister she goodness to do the trap." He predicted unhappiness for the rest of his life and then a painful death. After a while Fernandez wrote back saying that he had spoken with his mother, who explained how "you were abused by an uncle when you were little, and at seven you fell into a ditch and broke your skull, which may never have healed properly." "There are reasons," Fernandez continued, "maybe everything can be explained by what happened in childhood, things you don't even remember. But I've decided that reasons aren't enough, that some things in life are unfathomable and that you are one of these unfathomable things and you have to accept the mystery of it." He went on to say that he didn't know and didn't care how painful his death would be, and as far as the rest was concerned, there was no need for prophecy: he wasn't happy.

One day his lawyer showed up with news, that following an internal investigation, the state of Texas had reached the conclusion that it had executed an innocent man. New evidence determined that the fire that had caused the deaths of Cameron Willingham's daughters had not been started intentionally.

"That's going to work in our favor," Elizabeth said, shifting her long red ponytail from one side to the other. "The state is going to be more cautious from now on. They don't want to make another mistake; it's bad publicity."

"But one tiny detail," Jesús said, "is I ain't innocent."

"Your mental state. You weren't aware of your actions."

But did she really believe that? Or was this all a big game and her way of showing him that she would stick with him to the end?

Jesús thought about Cameron after she left. Who'd have believed it? He had such a guilty face.

One of his last letters was twelve pages long, and it was addressed to a student who had a radio show at the university in Landslide. The program aired after midnight, but the broadcast that featured his story had been so popular that one of the prison guards recorded it and let him listen to it.

Jesús wrote to the kid, named Sam, that he would go "craisdy" if he didn't get this off his chest. He said that Janet Reno had betrayed him and the government wanted to kill him like they did David Koresh. He found out in prison that he was a Jew and that was why he was trying to study Hebrew. He said he forgave his sister María Luisa because they forced her to help capture him or she would "loose" her home, and they promised "residence and monetary help." He said that he'd turned himself in because he didn't want the bounty hunters to kill his wife and his mother. On the last page he wrote: "no tengo miedo sinse reality has not been good to me. I hear funy voises, like a person callingme, but no one callingme. I hear The Unnamed."

In his response, Sam asked Jesús to tell him more about the Unnamed. Jesús didn't respond to the question but wrote: "amá is die if I die but I don't die. three days I return. my body appear in Jerusalen and I fight enemies of israel. I am tempted by death more all the time and I may do it any time soon."

When Sam asked why he had committed the crimes, Jesús answered: "a evil forse come from the houses. the Unnamed send me to people need to die. I am avenging angel send by Unnamed folow hisorders."

His last written sentence was "I on a trip of no return on a train that go to ded and can't get down. but I come back after ded."

Though his lawyer appealed to the Fifth District Court, Jesús was scheduled for execution for the capital murder of Joanna Benson.

A week before the allotted date, he asked for a book of photos of the Mexican Revolution. One of the guards said he'd do his best.

Five days later the book arrived. It wasn't the same book he'd seen in one of the victims' houses, but he leafed through looking for the photograph that had made such an impression on him, of a man standing before a firing squad with a defiant expression and a cigarette hanging from his mouth, the gesture of someone who wasn't afraid of confronting death. He wanted to draw inspiration, confront death like that paisano.

The photo wasn't there.

The night of his execution María Luisa was there, along with Sam and his friend, his lawyer, Sergeant Fernandez, and Joanna Benson's husband.

Jesús started feeling anxious once he finished his last meal, pozole, bread, and a can of Corona. He put on the white uniform he was to be executed in.

When the police and orderlies escorted him to the gurney in the tiny green-walled chamber, he asked permission to read a few words. It was something his lawyer had suggested. Jesús had come to the conclusion that nobody ever listened to him and other people weren't interested in what he had to say, so he wasn't going to pronounce any last words. But Elizabeth persuaded him to read an admission of regret, of forgiveness, if only for María Luisa's sake.

"She betrayed me."

"Oh, drop it. Didn't you say we're all sinners? And that she's the only person you've ever loved? Think about the rest of her life. Let her live those years in peace."

Jesús accepted Elizabeth's reasoning. He read out: "I want to ask if it is in your heart to forgive me. You don't have to. I know I allowed the devil to rule my life. I just ask you to forgive me and ask the Lord to forgive me for allowing the devil to deceive me. I thank God for having patience with me. I don't deserve to cause you pain. You did not deserve this. I deserve what I am getting."

He spotted his sister in the group through the window and gave a half-smile. She didn't respond. The guards positioned him on the gurney and secured his chest with a leather strap. They secured his arms and legs with metal restraints. They covered him with a white sheet from the waist down. Two doctors inserted intravenous tubes in each arm. Fernandez could see Jesús's legs trembling. María Luisa's eyes welled up with tears.

Jesús said a prayer in Hebrew. He thought about the Unnamed and pleaded that He not fail him now. "I've done my part; it's your turn now." The person responsible for the execution pressed a remote control to deliver the sodium pentothal into Jesús's blood to put him to sleep. Next came the muscle relaxant pancuronium bromide to stop his breathing, and finally the lethal dose of potassium chloride.

Jesús felt a slight prick. A few moments later he was dead.

NOTES AND ACKNOWLEDGMENTS

More than ten years ago I saw a newscast on CNN that told of a serial killer in the United States, an illegal alien who had been on the FBI's ten most wanted list. The nickname—the Railroad Killer—caught my attention, along with the fact that he was Mexican. I had been living relatively near New York since 1977 and wanted to use the city's subway as a scene for a story; but after reading about Ángel Maturino Reséndiz, I thought the US railway system could be an interesting alternative. Years later, around 2006, when I was reading a San Francisco newspaper in a café in Berkeley, I came across the story of the painter Martín Ramírez. By that time I had been throwing around the idea of a novel that brought in stories of Latin Americans lost in the immensity of the United States. I remembered Maturino. My intuition told me that he, like Ramírez, belonged in the novel.

Jesús and Martín, the main characters of *Norte*, are freely rendered versions of Maturino and Ramírez. The books that most helped me imagine them are *The Railroad Killer* by Wensley Clarkson (St. Martin's, 1999) and *Martín Ramírez* by Brooke Davis Anderson (Marquand Books, 2007). The story of Cameron Willingham that appears in the epilogue is based on the story "Trial by Fire," written by the journalist David Grann (*New Yorker*, September 7, 2009).

I began writing *Norte* in July 2007 in Crescent City, California, and finished in Ithaca, New York, in January 2011. Over those three and a half years the manuscript went through many different incarnations. Many people read it and helped find the pathway, especially Liliana Colanzi, who was as demanding line by line as she was in her overall observations. Other important readings came from Maximiliano Barrientos, María Lynch, Valerie Miles, Mike Wilson, Raúl Paz Soldán, Marcelo Paz Soldán, Rafael Acosta, Yuri Herrera, and David Colmenares. Melissa Figueroa helped me revise La Jodida's dialogues. Willivaldo Delgadillo was my guide in Ciudad Juárez, together with Aileen El-Kadi and Socorro Tahuencas. I'm deeply thankful to all of them. And last but not least to Silvia Bastos and Pau Centelles, who gave me the unconditional support I needed.

TRANSLATOR'S NOTE

Valerie Miles

It was through an unexpected turn of events that I found myself entrusted with the translation of Edmundo Paz Soldán's novel *Norte*. I had been circling its creative process in one guise or another since its author and I first talked about it back in 2008, but, as happens in the publishing world's famous garden of forking paths, I ended up taking one route and Edmundo another. To quote Robert Frost, "as way leads on to way," I never imagined that serendipity would bring the novel back around to me in any other role than that of a gratified reader.

Edmundo had begun outlining the novel when we met during our respective sojourns in Madrid; I was the associate director of Alfaguara, the imprint where he was publishing his work, and he was on sabbatical from Cornell. Anyone who has spent time in Madrid can attest to the vibrant social and cultural scene there, which makes it famously difficult for a visiting writer to actually get any work done. But Edmundo's enviable discipline prevailed, and I had the chance to read an early version of *Norte* in 2009.

By then I had moved back to Barcelona, and he and Liliana Colanzi came to stay with us for a few scorching days in August. Poet Forrest Gander was also in Barcelona at the time, and with

Aurelio Major we all had a long, memorable Spanish lunch at the iconic Flash Flash and deliberated on some of the issues Edmundo was setting out in the novel, particularly the way in which the United States absorbs and domesticates the splendidly variegated Spanish-speaking cultures under blanket terms like "Hispanic" and "Latino." In the process, it invents a cliché on the undocumented worker, since society is often incapable of appreciating the singular in human experience, lumping personalities into sweeping typecasts for easy classification. The novel as form, luckily, being a work of the imagination, and by virtue a subversive one, counteracts this trend by exploring the space of individual experience, celebrating particularity and disputing the kind of intellectual indolence that turns a language spoken by people from over twenty-one different countries and their respective traditions into a shibboleth. As Azar Nafisi wrote in *The Republic of Imagination*, literature "enables us to tolerate complexity and nuance and to empathize with people whose lives and conditions are utterly different from our own." So as I translated *Norte*, one of my first concerns was finding a way to capture the diversity of these voices, to differentiate the characters clearly and not domesticate them or their language into an easy typecast. They hail from different countries despite the fact that they have the Spanish language in common, and the two who are Mexican, Jesús and Martín, are from very different backgrounds, social circumstances, and generations.

Some of the other concerns were how to capture the scenes of extreme violence without falling into the gratuitous, and how to strike the proper tone in depicting different forms of mental illness.

Edmundo is a Bolivian expat, a Spanish speaker in an English-speaking country; I'm an American expat, an English speaker in a Spanish-speaking country. We share an appreciation for how easy it is to get lost in a foreign environment, for the things you forfeit and the things you gain. But what happens to immigrants who are emotionally or mentally crippled? What happens to those forced to struggle against economic hardship and denigrating prejudices, especially when civic and governmental institutions, police forces and prisons, universities and health care systems all fail?

Edmundo was interested in mapping the lives of migrants who have gotten lost both physically and spiritually in the vast "North" as they scramble to find a better life for themselves. We kept the title of the novel in the original Spanish so as not to lose all the inherent cultural references that are immediately associated with the Spanish word. As it goes, if I tell you not to picture an elephant, you inevitably see a the pewter-haunched pachyderm; the image the word "North" conjures in an American reader's mind is not the same one as if you read the word "Norte." Meaning, it's not about Canada, no. North is a cardinal location on a compass, but it's also a space of the imagination.

In Spanish there's an expression, "perder el norte," which means to lose one's way, to lose sight of a goal, to lose control, to lose the sense of where is up and where is down on a compass. A few of the characters in the novel are based on real people who were uprooted, rendered anchorless, who lost their communities and their way in the vast, hostile territory that is the United States. Just as the border can be porous both physically and as a metaphor, identity too can be fluid; there is always a linguistic and cultural bleeding out in both directions, nothing is fixed, everything is in flux. Edmundo had been researching the life of Ángel Maturino Reséndiz, the real-life psychopath known as the "Railroad Killer," a train-hopping

Mexican drifter who served as inspiration for his character Jesús. Edmundo also became fascinated by the tragic life of self-taught outsider artist Martín Ramírez, the schizophrenic painter who had been swallowed into California's rickety mental health system for over thirty years. The third set of displaced protagonists, Michelle and Fabián, were still being drawn out of the ether at the time we first met, though it was clear that they would be of Bolivian and Argentine origins, he struggling with drugs and depression, possibly bipolar.

The novel was published in Spain in 2011 to wide critical acclaim and has since appeared in French under the imprint Gallimard and in Portuguese from the Brazilian house Companhia das Letras. In 2014, after I took on the task of translation, I traveled to the US for a conference on Roberto Bolaño, one of Edmundo's models for parts of the novel along with Elmer Mendoza, and we took advantage to spend a few days discussing some of these early concerns. I had already pinpointed a few of the language issues and formal decisions that would have to be made. He gave me some references and source materials, which were invaluable, especially in rendering Jesús's writing back into English, which was one of the trickiest parts of all.

The real-life Railroad Killer, Maturino Reséndiz, had written several letters from prison, some of which are still floating around in creepy online auctions. As I researched and found examples of them, I could see that his spelling was as dreadful as could be expected and stayed that way even though his vocabulary improved over time, as did his usage and sentence construction. Following Edmundo's lead, I tried to emulate that arc in Jesús's diary entries. It was a delicate job; I had to render effect more than translate, and try to re-create a

Mexican serial killer's broken English in a comparative process of linguistic reconstruction. Edmundo had in effect translated Ángel's broken English into Jesús's Spanish, so I had to take these back into the original language in a way that was as true to life as possible and invent a sort of proto-language. The challenge, I feel, is recasting the author's style while always keeping your own in check and subordinate to it, which is not always easy to do. It's a tip from none other than Javier Marías when referring to his own process, particularly with his translation of Lawrence Sterne's *Tristram Shandy* and Nabokov's poetry.

We met again at the Bogotá Book Fair and a few more times in Madrid and Barcelona. Edmundo wanted to approach the translation as if working on a manuscript. Many writers find it excruciatingly tedious to go back over a novel that has already been published, but Edmundo chose to use this as an opportunity for another revision of the original, to continue polishing the ideas, sharpening the dialogue, tightening structure and some of the psychology that moves the characters along. So the American translation is not always a direct translation; it evolved as a result of this ongoing exchange into a new version of the original novel.

Our conversations began tangentially at first, not directly on formal considerations such as the placement of dialogue but on the characters themselves, their emotional makeup, motivations, and how to strike the right tone for each voice. Are they based on real characters or not? If so, who and how closely? What materials did I have to work with that would help me gather a sense of their inner worlds, their outer surroundings? We talked about the American writers Edmundo read while preparing the novel: Faulkner, Cormac McCarthy, Bret Easton Ellis. We discussed how to balance the tenor in the

episodes of extreme violence, emphasize the suspense leading up to these scenes, and keep a smooth, tightly measured
timbre when describing the action, as he does in the Spanish.

I wanted to capture the slight linguistic estrangement of a
Bolivian writer using Mexicanisms, Americanisms, and Argen-
tinisms. He never falls into parody but is quite guarded against
overplaying linguistic tics or pitches, though he sprinkles
them in certain bits of dialogue to great effect. He writes in
understatement, allowing the action to move the narrative forward, prioritizing drive and sense of pace, following a style
predicated by Borges and Bioy Casares when writing as Bustos
Domecq: the invisible narrator. The prose is largely free of
adjectives, straightforward, close to the semantic tightness of
the noir novel but sans winks to the genre's parlance.

In *Norte*, Edmundo Paz Soldán uses a sort of backdrop sto-
rytelling technique that, like bas-relief, allows the voices of
the characters to rise up in contrast when he moves in and
out of their consciousness in free indirect speech. I've tried
to maintain that effect when possible, but in order to keep
the fluidity, and because it's difficult to render accents without
falling into caricature, some of the dialogue that was inside the
body of the text has been restructured into direct discourse
inside quotation marks.

This was a concern of Edmundo's, particularly that the narrative flow not be interrupted by footnotes or explanations or
lampooned accents, with the one exception being Jesús, and
again, mostly in the writing, not the dialogue. And I wanted to
preserve that feel of a novel that was narrated from the outside
of the US looking in, which meant devoid of couch-comfy jar-
gons or used-car border vernaculars that an English-speaking
writer might capture in prose but that is not really true to the

original tradition in which the novel was written, which pre-serves a certain narrative distance in that respect.

Edmundo once said that he can't imagine any family in Latin America that doesn't have some connection with the US, some family member who is here or has been here or wants to be here. Though *Norte* is written in Spanish, it is largely set in the United States, and much of the dialogue is in fact a Span-ish interpretation of what the English original might sound like to a Spanish speaker's ear. We never really know if Sam is speaking in Spanish or English to Michelle, only that from time to time his Argentine accent comes out. Or if Fabián and Michelle always speak in Spanish to each other, or if some of the other characters do, like Fernandez and his call-girl love interest, Debbie. We know Fernandez's English is bad enough that his daughters would tease him about it, yet that's the only reference we have. The author chose not to write Fernandez's voice in broken English, for example, when he talks to the fam-ilies of Jesús's victims or to FBI agents.

So how to recuperate the original English from the written Spanish, without falling into caricature? At first I tried pep-pering Spanglish terms here and there, slangy border English or Spanish, but the result was tiring, if not directly irritating, to read and felt like a cosmetic solution, a linguistic nip and tuck whose stitches were showing. Going down that slippery slope would have delivered a gum-chomping translation, dated before it was even in print. I also had to take into account the fact that the regions in which the stories take place are both real and fictionalized.

This novel represents a foreigner's view of the US. It's the case with Fabián's disgruntled opinions of American academia and with both Jesús and Martín's third-person storylines: Martín's story opens in the 1930s and largely takes place in California, Jesús's in the 1980s in the north of Mexico, in Juárez, El Paso, and other cities along the US border and Florida. Jesús speaks a lower-caste, urban, coarser type of Mexican Spanish, while Martín's speech is more naive and peasantlike, but in both cases their language is quick and flowing. Martín's sentences are peculiarly melodic, the result of a sensitive if disturbed mind.

The tension between these two stories is that they represent two different ways of being; Jesús is all motion and exploit, where Martín is stasis and introspection. The language has to reflect that. Jesús never stops wandering; he just acts out his compulsions, cravings, and desires. He restrains himself when he is able, and manipulates, but then explodes. In Spanish the pronoun is understood in the conjugation of the verb ("he jumped" becomes "saltó"), so in Jesús's sections I had to find creative solutions to avoid beginning every sentence with "he." At first I translated the sentences word for word; they are short and very easy to render. But the effect was almost like a litany, or some sort of a recitation with the repeating pronoun, which added an interesting and even eerie quality but wasn't in keeping with the spirit of the author's intention.

Martín can't communicate with the world outside himself in any language. There are some elements in Martín's story that I had to change completely, like the names he makes up for the orderlies in the hospital. Edmundo agreed that the original names, which play on Spanish categories of creole racial combinations, would have gotten lost in translation. We wanted to maintain Martín's candid sense of humor, however, and mimic the way he might hear people calling out to him.

The third storyline that braids through the novel is that of the young, very talented Michelle and her profligate professor and lover Fabián. It's the only story that's told in the first person. Here the conflict, the narrative tension, is found in the counterpoint between the creative act and destruction, authenticity and mendacity, truth and pure fiction versus imitation. It can be read as an analogy of the creative process, and it was important to clinch her voice as a renegade academic and budding artist and not just some star-struck ingenue. She is infatuated with strung-out professor Fabián, and though she seems to passively allow herself to be sucked into the vortex of his self-destruction, in fact she exerts a subtle resistance the whole time. She's observing something that fascinates her as a cat would observe a scorpion. And slowly but surely her voice grows stronger and more decided until she finally finds her way to the poetic act.

Here I incorporated George D. Schade's translation of Juan Rulfo's *Luvina*, one of the stories in his classic collection *The Burning Plain*. Michelle uses Rulfo's story as the base of her wobbly-kneed zombie mash-up novel, a genre that combines classic texts with another popular genre into a single narrative, often including zombies and vampires. Since Michelle is copying Juan Rulfo in a mash-up, I thought it was only fit to use the canonical translation of the classic story in a translation mash-up mirror. The effect is the same, especially since she hasn't yet made the jump to creating her own style, so at first the change in tone seems strange, creating a sort of translational *mise-en-abyme*.

A novel represents the very peculiar mechanisms of a single writer's imagination and how that has been shaped by his or her cultural context, tradition, language, and way of seeing and of hearing. So when it comes to translating a work of prose, and despite all the aforementioned reflections, I do believe the best a translator can do is to just sit down in a quiet place and get on with it. Approaches are as varied as the novels themselves, and usually as you move forward, either the problems grow to a point where you have to stop what you are doing and solve them with the author, or else they work themselves out as you get a feel for the novel's interior intelligence, its music, its structure. I think it's best not to throw a theoretical suitcase at a book but instead think of it as pulling a partner onto the dance floor and moving. At times you have to approximate, at other times you must stick tight as glue on to the original because the prose is measured down to the very last syllable, or because the signifiers are blinking at you from beneath their camouflage, like a figure in the carpet.

With *Norte*, given all the issues of being a Spanish-language novel written by a Bolivian author about Mexicans and Argentineans lost in the US, over several decades and with myriad characters speaking and writing in native or broken English, I needed this ongoing conversation with the author to capture the "spirit" of the words, thinking of Gregory Rabassa's ideas on technique. I have tried to remain faithful to its life-force, the voices of the characters, all the creatures real and invented that have come from Edmundo Paz Soldán's imagination. Some would say that being faithful means changing everything. Some wouldn't. As Lampedusa wrote in *The Leopard*, "Everything must change so that everything can stay the same."